RED ZAMBEZI

RED ZAMBEZI

By

Joe E. Hale

with
John Fremont

J&T PUBLISHING
Santa Paula, California

Copyright © 1989 by Joe E. Hale
with
John Fremont

All rights reserved. No part of this book may be reproduced or transmitted in any form or by any means, electronic or mechanical, including photocopying, recording or by any information storage and retrieval system, without permission in writing from the Publisher.

J&T PUBLISHING
Post Office Box 6520
Ventura, California 93006

Library of Congress Cataloging in Publication Data

Joe E. Hale

Congress Catalog Card Number 89-084419

ISBN 1-877781-07-X

TO ALL MEN OF HONOR

The only thing a man is born with
that no one can take from him
is his honor.
Only he can lose it.
Once lost, it can never be regained.

ACKNOWLEDGMENTS

To Jeff Cooper who spent time above and beyond—and wrote the Preface when only asked to read the manuscript for a possible review, an honor most appreciated. John Coleman (*Soldier of Fortune*) who responded with a very positive review from only the manuscript, a favor to the publisher most appreciated. John Hedlund the man who read and critiqued with a most jaundiced eye. Robbie Barrkman who corrected my Afrikaans. My mother who on reading the first draft simply said "not enough sex and blood", an oversight hopefully corrected. Kathy Taylor without her 'cue' cards to make the word processor at least manageable, this missive would still be locked within the guts of a unfathomable machine. Cyntha Frank who knows more about book publication than should be allowed and knows the 'good places to eat' in Fort Bragg. Chuck Hathaway whose talent created the magnificent cover after hours of debate with the much less talented author. Last but most certainly not least Tony Kirk whose constant nagging (for years) finally made me write the book, so blame him. Without all of the above none of this would have been recorded. The author alone, is responsible for any errors contained herein.

PREFACE

Red Zambezi is an account of Joe Hale's personal adventures in the fall of Rhodesia. He terms it a work of fiction, but each of the events he describes actually took place—only the names of the participants have been changed, except for those of senior public officials. I know Joe Hale personally, and I knew Rhodesia at the time of the debacle. I knew several of the actors in this story by their first names, and I am prepared to accept Joe's tale of their actions as truth, within the limits of accurate recollection.

Rhodesia was a splendid country—a place in which I would have chosen to live if I could not choose the American West. It offered space, wild land, social congeniality, excellent parks, libraries, restaurants and hotels. Its firearms policies were superior to those of other western nations, and the streets of Salisbury were clean, orderly, and safe. It contained multitudes of elephant, buffalo and lion, and its game management assured their increase. It was an altogether charming land, and it has been served up on a platter, by the chicanery of England the United States, to a tin-pot, Marxist dictator, who also happens to be one of the most rabid racists in Africa.

The story of Rhodesia's death agony is grim, and Joe Hale's anecdotes do not make happy reading. But the story must be told. We live in evil times, when the essential human values of honor, courage, truth, duty and courtesy are largely held to be obsolete. Those who discard these things in favor of dollars and sensual gratification cannot be expected to fret over obscure battles in far off places, but it remains nonetheless important to set forth the record of betrayal and infamy by which one of the last bright hopes of our culture was extinguished.

I cannot endorse the author's use of barrack room language, but in other respects I regard his book as a necessary contribution to our political, geographical and social awareness.

Jeff Cooper

TECHNICAL TERMS & FOREIGN WORDS

A/A	Anti-Aircraft, used primarily at terrorist camps outside the borders of Rhodesia. 12.7mm, 14.5mm and 23mm weapons. See Strella.
AK/AKM/AK-47	See Appendix.
ALPHA BOMB	Locally developed and produced bomb, weighing 1 kilo (2.2pds). Bomb was designed to bounce after hitting the ground and exploding 2 to 3 meters above the ground. This weapon was developed as Rhodesia didn't possess the ability to produce proximity fuses.
ANC	African National Congress, primary political party of the dissident blacks in the Republic of South Africa.
AP	Armour piercing bullet, used to destroy vehicles. Common loading in terrorist 12.7mm and 14.5mm machine guns.
BAOBAB TREE	Commonly called the upside down tree. The seeds of this tree was originally used to make cream of tarter.
BAZOOKA	See Appendix.
BILTONG	Dried meat, similar to beef jerky. Very popular as a source of protein in the bush.

I

BLACK IS BEAUTIFUL	Camouflage makeup used by the RDF to try and pass as an African.
BLUE JOB	Rhodesian Air Force, also called blues.
BRAAIVLEIS	Barbecue, a Saturday tradition in Rhodesia and South Africa.
BSAP	British South Africa Police, the national police force of Rhodesia. Rhodesia did not have separate police departments for each city or area as in the United States.
BUNDU	Slang word for the bush or outback. "Bash the bundu" meant going out into the country side.
BUNKER BOMB	Locally produced 1kg (2.2pd) explosive device using a regular grenade fuse, for destroying fortifications of any kind.
CALL SIGN	Each group of troops or operators had their own call sign. These call signs were used in all radio communications.
CAMO	Camouflage uniforms, worn by the RDF. Uniform regulations in the bush were rather lax.
CASEVAC	Casualty evacuation, usually by helicopter. The lack of helicopters in the RDF made Casevac's a chancy thing.
CHIMURENGA	Mashona word for "War of Liberation", was also used by the Matabele towards the end of the war.
CIO	Central Intelligence Organization, all intelligence matters were supposed to be cleared by the group.
CO	Commanding Officer.
COIN/COIN OPS	Counter Insurgency/Counter Insurgency Operations.
COMOPS	Political and military group responsible for co-ordinating all military action.

CORDTEX	Primer Cord, used for detonating cord, can be used as an explosive as well as tying main charges together.
DAK/DAKOTA	C-47 aircraft (DC-3). See Appendix.
DONGA	A ditch or gully.
DZ	Drop zone are selected for landing of parachutists.
FN	Fabrique Nationale Rifle. See Appendix.
FIREFORCE	The highly mobile units of the RLI, could be parachuted or use helicopters. During later stages of war, these RLI units made as many as three operational sorties per day.
FRELIMO	The Front for the Liberation of Mozambique, the political party that came in power after the withdrawal of the Portuguese. Also, the name used by the Rhodesians for the military in Mozambique.
FRONTLINE STATES	Those countries directly involved in the Rhodesian War - Zambia, Mozambique, Angola, Botswana and Tanzania.
G-3	Spanish Rifle. See Appendix.
G-CAR	Alouette helicopter. See Appendix.
GOMO	An African word for a mountain or hill.
GRAZE	Slang, meaning to eat. Can be used to describe food.
H-HOUR	Time attack is due to start.
HOT EXTRACTION	Removing troops while they are under fire.
HOT PURSUIT	International term used to legalize/justify crossing international borders to conduct military operations.
HULK	Locally produced explosive charge designed to blow man sized holes in walls and fences.

INDABA	Originally meant a meeting between African Chiefs. Became a slang word for any kind of meeting or get together.
JAMSTEALER	Rhodesian Army slang meaning a soldier that works in the rear or does not see combat. U.S. Army term is REMF.
JOC	Joint Operational Command. There were five JOC's in Rhodesia. This command structure was responsible for the joint operations of the Army, Air Force, BSAP and Special Branch.
KAFFIR	Derogatory term used to describe blacks.
K-CAR	Armed Alouette helicopter. See Appendix.
KNOCK-KNOCK	Locally made explosive charge designed to open doors.
KOPJE	Afrikaans word for hill.
KRAAL	Afrikaans word for native village.
LUP	Lay-up position, usually a spot undercover, used prior to taking a final ambush position.
LYNX	Cessna 337 aircraft. See Appendix.
LZ	Landing zone for helicopters.
MANIGI	African word, a derogatory phrase for white man.
MASHONA	The largest African Tribe in Rhodesia. See Shona, the tribe of Robert Mugabe.
MATABELE	The second largest tribe in Rhodesia. See Nabele, the tribe of Joshua Nkomo.
MNR	Mozambique National Resistance. Rhodesian sponsored group in Mozambique to overthrow FRELIMO after Rhodesia fell sponsorship was picked up by the South African Defense Force.
MUJIBAS	Young Africans used by the terrorists as runners and spies.
MUNT	A derogatory term for Africans. See Kaffir.

MURUNGU	African word for white man.
MUSHE	African word meaning good or nice. The expression Mushe-Mushe means as good as it gets.
NCO	Non-Commisioned Officer.
NDEBELE	African Tribe see Matabele.
NS	National Service. All able bodied men in Rhodesia between 18 and 50 had to register for National Service.
OAU	Organization of African Unity.
OC	Officer Commanding.
OP	Military Operation or Observation Post.
PE/PLASTIC	Military Explosive.
PF	Patriotic Front Alliance between ZANU (ZANLA) Mugabe and ZAPU (ZIPRA) Nkomo.
QM	Quartermaster.
RAR	Rhodesian African Rifles. Rhodesia's Black Regiment.
RATPACKS	Rhodesian Army field rations.
RDF	Rhodesian Defense Forces.
RECCE	Reconnaissance.
RF	Rhodesian Front Party. The party led by Ian Smith.
RLI	Rhodesian Light Infantry. This was the main fighting unit within the RDF, other than Special Forces units.
RPD	Russian light machine gun. See Appendix.
RPG	Russian Rocket Propelled Grenade. See Appendix.
R&R	Leave for rest and recreation. Also known as 'Rape & Rest'.

RV	Rendezvous.
SAS	Special Air Service. A special forces unit whose motto is "Who Dares Wins". This outstanding fighting unit's strength never exceeded 260 officers and men.
SB	Special Branch Intelligence unit of BSAP.
SHABEEN	African term for illegal liquor sales. Also the location where illegal liquor can be drunk.
SHONA	African tribe. The largest tribe in Rhodesia, to which Mugabe is a member.
SITREP	Situation Report.
SKS	Russian semi-automatic rifle. See Appendix.
STRELA/SAM-7	Surface to Air Missile. Russian copy of American Redeye SAM.
SWAPO	South West African People's Organization. A Russian backed terrorist group fighting in South West Africa.
TA/TF	Territorial Force. The non-regular RDF Army which made up the majority of the fighting forces in the RDF. All men in Rhodesia from 18 to 50 years of age had a military commitment of some kind.
TERR	Rhodesian slang word for terrorist. Also called a CT or Communist Terrorist.
TTL	Tribal Trust Land. Those lands set aside for African use only.
UDI	Unilateral Declaration of Independence. Rhodesia's Declaration of Independence, the Preamble of which reads very much like that of the United States.
UNAC	United African National Council. The party of Abel Muzorewa, the first black Prime Minister of Rhodesia. Also known as the ANC.
WO	Warrant Officer.

ZANLA	Zimbabwe African National Liberation Army, the military wing of ZANU. This group (currently in power) was backed by the Chinese Communists. Controlled by Robert Mugabe.
ZANU	Zimbabwe African National Union. The political wing of Robert Mugabe, the current ruling party in Zimbabwe.
ZAPU	Zimbabwe African People's Union of Joshua Nkomo. The political wing of this party backed by the Russians.
ZIPRA	Zimbabwe People's Revolutionary Army, ZAPU's Military wing, controlled by Nkomo and Russian backed.
2IC	Second-in-Command.

PROLOGUE

"The war is over, Colonel."

"Maybe it's over for you, Greg."

"That's for damn sure. My war ended when the Ambassador was recalled and Captain Wilson put me behind a desk. But none of us are going to be here much longer."

"Some of us have nowhere else to go."

"Like who?"

"My people."

"The Americans don't give a damn about you or your war!"

"And I don't give a damn about them! They're not my people."

They were drinking beer in a tiger bar in Bangkok and shouting above the amplified rock'n'roll. Girls with black hair and doll faces, wearing high heels and little else, danced on the runway behind the bar. Colored lights created the illusion of gaiety, but even the seabees looked bored. The owner, a balding roundfaced man, sat on a stool in front of the cash register and chewed on a toothpick and thought about lemongrass soup with succulent prawns, Remy Martin with Coca-Cola, eager girls and flush GI's. It was only February, but already the year felt old. It was 1975, and everything was seedy.

Sergeant Gregory Andrews was completing his second tour of duty. Although he'd never attended college, he was fluent in several languages, including Vietnamese and Swahili. Linguistics was one of his hobbies; killing people was the other. He'd served under Lieutenant Colonel Joseph Austin in the past as an interpreter and respected him for his marksmanship and courage, but he'd heard somewhere that Austin had assaulted a Brigadier General and almost been court-martialed. Andrews finished his drink and called the bartender. "Two beers, right here, right now," he shouted.

"No more for me. I've got work to do after the rain stops."

"You've been working with the Hill People, haven't you?"

Austin threw some money on the bar and rose to leave. The roundfaced Thai climbed down from his stool and ran over to scoop it up. "You're out of line, Greg," he said. "I don't talk about drink when I'm working." He motioned to the owner that the money was for both their drinks. "See you around, Sergeant."

"Wait, I'll walk out with you. Maybe it's let up." He took the bottle with him. "Where are you staying? Maybe we can share a cab." When they got outside it was raining so thickly they couldn't see across the street, but a taxi driver swooped down on them like a buzzard. "I've never hunted Cambodian gooks. Can you use a translator? They say it's not all that different from what the Hill People speak."

"I've got a crew. When do you report back to the embassy?"

"Monday, but you can get me out. They've got me typing reports now. I can hit a gook between the eyes at fifty meters, but I can't hit a key on that goddamned typewriter to save my ass."

"Get you out?" Austin's astonishment made the driver jam on his brakes. "No, not you." He waved the back of his hand. "Keep going, more, more! Greg, I used whatever was left of my credibility and still had to threaten a general with exposure just to get permission to fly into Cambodia. I couldn't get you transferred from the latrine to the kitchen."

"Maybe it won't be necessary. I've got some connections of my own. What's the job?"

"Not your kind of work, Greg. It's more a mission of mercy. I promised my people I'd protect them and, now that the Khmer Rouge are running things, I've got to make sure they're all right."

"And if they're not? If the rumors about what's going down in Cambodia are true, what then?"

"Then I've got to try and get some of them out."

"You're going to rescue gooks when there are American MIA's being tortured in jungle camps in Cambodia? I don't get it."

"Neither did the general." *Only those who have seen the elephant and heard the owl understand.* "The Hill People aren't gooks. They're my family!"

"Oh." Something turned off inside Greg. "Look, Colonel, I don't get involved in personal matters. I'd like to go, but—"

"Nobody invited you, Sergeant. I've already got a crew."

"When do you leave?"

"Soon as the weather breaks."

"Should clear up in a day or two."

They rode the rest of the way in silence.

The Huey was blacked out. Its markings and identification numbers had all been removed. They were flying as fast and as low as the helicopter could go without trimming the tops off the trees.

The six men were all dressed in tiger-striped camouflage and were carrying AK 47's with basic load. None of them carried identification or wore a badge indicating rank or unit. If compromised, they could not be linked to a military organization and would be treated as renegade American soldiers, freebooters or dope smugglers. They knew they could expect no help from Uncle Sam. Like Colonel Austin, they were there because they were family.

Austin looked at the spinach whipping below. Was he crazy to come back? His retirement papers had been approved; paperwork was all that remained. Twenty years and only a Lieutenant Colonel. That's what you get for not keeping your damn mouth shut! *That's what you get for reminding your superiors of their 'solemn' promises to the Hill People.*

The people of Cambodia had never liked the Montagnards. The Montagnards felt the same way about the Cambodians, but reserved their abiding hatred for the Vietnamese, their persecutors for hundreds of years. The Americans had been only too happy to exploit the situation.

The Khmer Leou, or Highland Khmer as they were known in Cambodia, were related to the Montagnards in Vietnam. When the United States decided to wage an invisible war on Cambodian soil, Lieutenant Colonel Joe Austin was sent in to forge a military alliance with the Hill People. As head of the Military Assistance Command (MAC V) program in Cambodia, Austin gave his word that the Americans would protect the Montagnards against attack from the Communists whose enemy they had become by assisting the Americans in the first place. After the Khmer Rouge captured Phnom Penh and seized power, Austin's superiors refused to allow him to keep that promise. It was only after he threatened to talk to the press about America's 'unofficial' presence in Cambodia that he received permission to put together a small team of volunteers to pull the village chief and his family out of the area *if* he found them, *if* they were still alive, and *if* they would come.

The sterile Huey settled down on the LZ like an angry hen. Austin climbed out and looked around. He knew these mountains well. He and his men had spent six years here, living and fighting alongside the bravest, most honorable people he'd ever known. He had trained them to use modern weapons in place of their ancient crossbows and poisoned arrows. Under his tutelage, they had become skilled soldiers. From primitive tribesmen who threatened no one, they had become armed adversaries, a danger to whoever was in power and a people to be feared, all courtesy of the United States Government.

In return for this dubious distinction, the Hill People helped the American military choke off the supply routes used by the North Vietnamese. Later, they helped pinpoint and mark target areas for the massive B-52 air strikes that Nixon said never took place.

When it came time to repay the debt, the Americans looked the other way. No one cared! A terrible crime against humanity was being committed in Cambodia: two million people out of a total population of seven million were being slaughtered; and the United Nations could not even pass a resolution censuring the Khmer Rouge! And yet, as horrible as the self-inflicted genocide was, even worse treatment was reserved for the Hill People.

As Austin led his unit down the path into the village, he was troubled by the awful silence. No dogs barked, no birds sang, no monkeys quarreled in the trees. As the sweep-line hit the edge of the village, the silence hummed like bees swarming. "What's the matter with the damn roosters?" he said to Corporal Evans. Something was very wrong in the village.

It was empty! He didn't see a single living thing in this, one of the largest villages in the entire highland, a village of over five thousand people who had lived here for over a thousand years. There was no sign of human life, hardly any life at all except for slowly moving flies.

Austin split his unit into two groups to facilitate a search. Time was running out; it would be dark before long and he didn't want his men to spend the night here; he didn't want to be anywhere near the Khmer Rouge after dark. It was a dumb idea to be anywhere near the village in the first place. Just then, a hushed call came over the radio from Corporal Evans. "I'm at the gardens. Come here. It's bad." Slowly, carefully, the men converged on a familiar spot, the plot where the village grew their sweet potatoes, the basic staple of their diet for six years.

There, like squash, all the women of the village were buried up to their necks. Row upon row, they had been planted. Row upon row they had been harvested, their throats cut by a scythe. These were the women who had fed them and cared for them, the women Austin had promised to protect as long as the sun rose. His word meant no more than the word of his predecessors when they promised the American Indian land and buffalo forever. When it came to politics, what was the word of an officer and a gentlemen worth?

Some hundred meters away was a deep gully that had been used as a garbage dump. Here was the final resting place for the remaining villagers. At one end, fifty bodies were tied together by a single rope. They had been mutilated by ax blows before being killed, as if the executioners had conducted experiments to see how many parts could be chopped off before the subjects died. The bodies were of boys under twelve years of age. The rest of the males had been shot. Their hands had been tied behind their backs, and they had been tossed into the garbage dump to rot in the sun. Plucked by carrion eaters, cleaned by insects, not enough flesh remained on the bones for Austin to identify father or grandmother.

During the trip back to Thailand, no one on board the Huey said a word. Back in Bangkok, Austin filed a report which no one bothered to read. They stamped his retirement papers and shook his hand and gave him some brochures from an insurance company and an investment firm. He was an officer with no military future, an American with little regard for his country, a man who had broken his promise, a man without his honor.

1

On a brilliant fall day in March of 1975, Joe Austin flew to Rhodesia to be interviewed for a job that not even the pukka English gentleman who recruited him knew much about. Austin had been moping about his home in Sydney, when he received the phone call from a Mr. Smythe-Jones.

"I've a proposition for you, old chap," a cheery British voice shouted at him, "I think I can be of some assistance to you."

"What is it?" Austin asked, immediately suspicious.

"I can't really discuss it on the phone, dear chap."

"Are you a lawyer?" Austin asked. *Who else would sound so friendly at 0700 except someone on retainer.*

"I beg your pardon?"

"Do you represent my wife?" He swallowed to check the anger rising in his throat.

"I'm not a solicitor, Colonel Austin, I can assure you of that. I do think you'll find what I have to say rather interesting."

"Do you know what time it is?"

The response was muffled, as if his caller had to lower the phone to check his watch. "Two minutes past seven. I trust I didn't wake you. I was told you're an early riser."

"By whom?"

"That will be made abundantly clear if you will be kind enough to meet me for coffee, shall we say in half an hour?"

Curiosity overcame suspicion. "You seem to know a lot about me. Do you know where the Harbour Restaurant is?"

"I'll find it."

Although he couldn't think of anyone with current reason to harm him, Austin tucked his model 39 Smith and Wesson into his waistband before leaving the house. "Better safe than regretful Grandpa Bass used to say, and that old codger had lived to ninety despite being on the kill list of half the outlaws in Oklahoma. *What kind of a goddamn name is Smythe-Jones, anyway?* he wondered as he pulled his Volvo into the parking lot across the street from the Harbour Restaurant and walked cautiously over.

The little man could have been a solicitor, though he looked more like a London banker in his three-piece suit, but he seemed happier to see him than Austin could have expected from a member of either of those professions. "Where did you say you're from?" he asked, for the little fellow was evidently not Australian, which made Austin happy for him.

"I didn't, actually, but now that you ask I'm at liberty to say that I represent an African country interested in your rather unique skills. You are unemployed at the moment, aren't you?" Smythe-Jones beamed at him and, without waiting for a reply, added, "If you'd like to learn more, I've a first-class airline ticket in my satchel." The dapper man unclasped his briefcase, and Austin noticed the faded, upside-down gold initials: S.L.C. *Seth. Saul. Sidney.* Instinctively, the soldier unbuttoned his jacket and felt the cold warmth of the weapon in his belt, but what Smythe-Jones was gingerly fishing from his worn leather case was in fact a blue BOAC folder.

Austin removed the ticket and examined it. Made out in his name, it was a first-class roundtrip ticket to Salisbury on a flight scheduled to depart in three days. "Where is Sal-is-bury?" he asked.

"It's pronounced 'Sawlz-bury' and it's in Rhodesia," the little fellow sniffed.

"I see. And is your named pronounced Sam, or is it Stewart?"

"How—" The involuntary word told Austin he'd guessed right. "Samuel is correct, but I prefer to be called John. I hope there's no need for you to know my last name."

"None at all," Austin laughed. "I'm just happy for you that it's not Smythe-Jones. Now, which of my 'rather unique skills' is your country interested in."

"It's not my country, actually. I'm an Englishman, Colonel Austin," he said nervously. "I find Rhodesia a bit too, uh, exciting for my taste, though it has all the amenities you would expect of a civilized country, I assure you. I'm just doing my bit for an old colony, as it were. As far as your skills are concerned, I'm sure I don't . . ."

Making the jolly Englishman nervous reassured Austin. "Beats me what they could want. All I know how to do is fight, fuck and drink. Does 'Sawlz-bury' have an over-abundance of women, Samuel old bean?"

"I really couldn't—" Samuel began, but whatever it was he couldn't was drowned out by Joe Austin's booming laughter.

The flight lasted twenty-six hours and by the time the 747 dropped out of the skies over South West Africa and started its descent over the bleak, vast Kalahari, Austin was exhausted and in ill-humor. Through the window he could see nothing but the scrub of the veld and baobab trees that looked as if they'd been planted root-end up.

The sky was high and blue over the mile-high capitol city, and the tarmac glared in the sun as the jet taxied to a stop fifty yards from the white concrete terminal. Austin waited for the other first-class passengers to debark before climbing down the stairs, by which time the line waiting to pass through immigration and customs was twenty people deep and spilling onto the airfield. He started in the same direction, but a tall, hatless man with a military bearing stopped him. "No need for you to go that way, Colonel Austin. Come with me, please."

"With pleasure," Austin said, searching for his sunglasses. "You must be—"

"Ted Sutton-Price," was the instant rejoinder. "Welcome to Rhodesia. I daresay you look like you could do with a drink."

"Or two," Austin said, meeting the man's eyes without having to look down, feeling the firm grip of the welcoming handshake. "Everyone here have two last names?"

They walked through a side door, a guard saluting as they passed, and into a modern terminal of polished brick walls and marble floors, immaculately clean. "Just call me Ted. I've been told you're a man who says precisely what's on his mind. I believe I'm going to enjoy having you here."

"Any man who can walk me past customs and immigration when I'm feeling like the bottom of a birdcage gets to be called whatever he'd like," Austin said. "I'm feeling better already."

Ted took his claim check and handed it to a black man who was smartly dressed in short khaki pants and a Sam Browne belt across a short-sleeved khaki shirt. Brown knee socks and highly polished brown oxfords completed the uniform. "Our driver is with the BSAP," Ted said. "That's British South Africa Police."

Austin didn't know if it was all right to shake hands with a black man in Rhodesia, so he just said, "Pleased to meet you."

The policeman stamped his foot and said, "At your service, sah!" Then he stamped his foot again, turned about, and trotted away. A minute later he returned with Austin's luggage and carried it out to an old, white, well-kept BMW 2000 with license number 4545. "Just my caliber," Austin remarked.

"That's jolly good," Ted laughed, "and it reminds me," he added when they'd settled themselves in the back of the sedan, "have you a toy or two you'd like to make legal?"

"Never leave home without one."

"You'll need this, then," Ted said, handing him a card that stated that Joe Austin was a guest of the Prime Minister and that any courtesies rendered would be much appreciated. "It can work wonders with sticky wickets."

Austin slipped the card into his shirt pocket. "I usually give my sticky wickets a dose of WD-40. Opens 'em right up."

"Beg pardon?"

"Never mind."

But Ted laughed anyway.

It was a fifteen minute drive on a good road through scrub bush, jacaranda and acacia, past an army barracks, past the well-tended lawns of suburban houses hidden behind wrought-iron gates, and into the heart of the modern European city. The driver pulled up in front of the Ambassador Hotel and the doorman, a tall black man resplendent in an ill-fitting uniform, ushered Austin and Sutton-Price into the small but well-appointed lobby of an old colonial hotel. Reservations had been made in the name of Mr. Joseph Austin, tourist. A bellboy in red jacket and cap led Austin onto the elevator as Ted took his leave by saying there'd be a tea at Mr. and Mrs. Smith's the following morning at 1000 hours, "if that's convenient for you."

Austin noticed the entrance to a dark mahogany bar beside the elevator cage and said he'd be ready "even if your 'Mr. Smith' has a mouthful of other last names all connected by a string of hyphens." Waving goodbye, he was jerked up three stories to the top floor where he was able to look out the window and sniff the fresh, clean air; ordered a bottle of Lion Beer from the bellboy and drank the lager (too sweet to his taste by half) down in one prolonged swallow; washed his face and kicked off his shoes before falling asleep in an easy chair while Lucille Ball cavorted on the small black and white screen to canned laughter and Austin's stentorian snores.

At exactly 1000 hours the following day, Austin stepped into the back seat of the same BMW that had picked him up at the airport, and driven, it appeared, by the same black British South Africa Police officer. "Whipping around in this is a lot more fun than pounding the beat, I'll bet."

"German automobiles respond better than vehicles from other countries, don't you think?"

"Where'd you learn to speak our language like that?" Austin made the mistake of asking as they left the city and entered the rolling hills to the north.

"English was bestowed upon all the colonies, sir. Isn't that how you came to speak a version of it?"

"A version?" Austin snorted, then laughed. "I guess you got me that time." At the end of a quiet street, they drove through an open gate flanked by two African guards armed with FN rifles. "This Smith fellow must be a muckety-muck in the military to warrant guards at his residence," Austin said.

"I would think so, sir, but he's not military; he's the Prime Minister."

"*Ian* Smith?" Austin groaned. "That's who lives here?"

"His family as well, sir."

"Jesus Christ, when am I going to learn to stop putting my foot in my mouth?"

"Excuse me, sir?"

"Never mind. I'm speaking in versions." But to Ted Sutton-Price who came around the corner as he climbed out of the car, Austin bellowed, "Is this what passes for security in your country? Hell, I could have had a gun at the driver's head and a trunk full of explosives! I could have blown up the white hope of Rhodesia. Instead of stopping the car and requesting some sort of identification, then confirming same, they came to attention and addressed me with a superb Present Arms."

"Trunk full?"

"Yeah, trunk." Austin pointed, then waved. "Explosives. Go boom! Get your driver to translate."

Ted found that hilarious. "Driver to translate? Good one, that. Elephants have trunks. Autos have boots."

"In America they have galoshes."

"You Americans, really!" He took Austin's elbow and led him around the unassuming residence that was home to the Prime Minister of Rhodesia. Ted was wearing a pair of casual slacks and an open-necked golfing shirt. Having assumed a "tea" was at least a semi-formal occasion, Austin had dressed with care in a dark blue suit, wing-tip shoes, white shirt and dark blue tie. They walked around to the back lawn where twenty to thirty guests were also casually attired. Austin felt ridiculous. To make matters worse, his shoes pinched. *This is not going to be fun*, he thought.

They went up to where a tall, middle-aged man with pale blue eyes and thinning gray hair stood talking to a moustached man in a safari jumpsuit and a smaller, heavyset man in a tweed golf cap. "Colonel Austin, it's a pleasure to introduce you to Ian Smith, General Peter Walls and Major General John Hickman."

The Prime Minister shook Austin's hand and said, "I must apologize for not having any hyphens in my name, but I'm sure you'll find punctuation sufficient to satisfy a schoolteacher here somewhere."

"I'm sorry," Austin stammered, "I didn't know—"

"No need, no need, gave us all a good laugh, it did."

"So this is the celebrated American Colonel," boomed a man with thick white hair and a deeply tanned, chiseled face as he joined their group. "I'm Ken Flowers," he said, extending his hand. "Someone get the Colonel a drink." Grateful not only for the suggestion but for the tie that Flowers also was wearing, Austin took an immediate liking to him.

"What do you recommend?"

"I'm a gin-and-tonic man, myself," Flowers said, "but General Walls here swears by Hansa Pilsener."

The man in the safari suit admitted he was partial to the brew "even though we import it from South West Africa. Call me a traitor, but the Germans are much better brewmasters than the English."

"I wouldn't trust it," General Hickman said.

"I tried your Lion Lager yesterday and found it somewhat sweeter than I'm used to," Austin said. "For my taste, the best beer comes from Australia."

"I'll drink Castle over Hansa any day of the week," General Hickman pronounced. Removing his cap, he fingered the brim before tugging it back on. "You a golfing man?"

"I enjoy a game now and then," Austin said as he observed the arrival of two new guests, a hawk-nosed man of about sixty accompanied by a beautiful blonde no more than half that age.

"Tennis is my game," Flowers was saying, watching Austin. "Do you play?"

The blonde tugged at her companion's arm, but he was busy lodging a complaint of some nature with anyone who would listen. "Some," Austin said, "but my sport is competetive shooting. I used to play football, but I'm not as fast as I used to be."

"None of us are as spry as we once were, Joe," Ian laughed. "You don't mind my calling you Joe, do you?"

"Not at all, sir," Austin said, wondering if other heads of state were as modest and friendly as this man. The only other world figures he knew were Vietnamese, and to a man they were all arrogant and hyper-sensitive. He wanted to express his gratitude for being invited to the party and made to feel welcome, but suddenly he wasn't sure that 'Mr. Smith' was an acceptable form of address. Was 'Mr Prime Minister' more appropriate? Unsure of himself, he cleared his throat and looked over to where the blonde woman's companion was in agitated conversation.

As if he knew what Austin was thinking, the head of state said, "That's settled, then. And, Joe, please call me Ian. Everyone else does."

"That might be a bit difficult, sir."

"Nonsense," came a voice from behind him. "And I won't be called anything but Janet myself." An attractive, prematurely white-haired woman walked briskly up to him and took his hand. She was a bit plump in her yellow sundress, and looked as if she'd not only just baked an apple pie but eaten it, too. She took his hand and, in the instant, Janet Smith made Austin feel as if they were next-door neighbors, and he returned her smile with a heartfelt one of his own.

"Have you ever been to a *braaivleis* before, Joe?" she asked.

"I beg your pardon, ma'am, I mean, Janet."

"*Braaivleis* is Afrikaans for barbecue. Americans, I'm told, invented the custom. At least I haven't heard the Russians lay claim to it. Have you, Ian?"

Just then Austin caught a whiff of sweet pungent smoke from the grill. "That strikes me deep in the heart of my salivary glands," he said and breathed deeply. A black waiter wearing black trousers, white shirt and black bow tie approached bearing a tray of frosty drinks and bottled beer. The tray was emptied before it reached them, and the waiter ran back for more.

"As you can see, we don't stand on ceremony here," said a tall, red-faced man. "I'm O'Brian of the Selous Scouts."

"If you'd attended a decent school, you'd feel differently," Flowers offered, and everyone but Austin laughed at O'Brian.

All eyes turned as the blonde woman in the blue sundress walked up, her hawkish companion not far behind. "The minister is dreadfully upset," she said in a European accent. "His driver had a terrible encounter with a taxi. The taxi driver was drinking, I'm afraid; the minister found a bottle of cane beneath his seat."

"I'll see his license is revoked," the minister was shouting at someone behind him. "*Hoch!* Let him think twice before he takes another drop." Uttering a string of swear words in what sounded like German, the minister brightened, smiled cheerfully at everyone and announced, "Halloo, I'm starving for some *boerewors!*"

"Were you hurt, Dieter?" Janet asked.

"It will take more than a Renault to put a dent in me," he said, "but ve need a law to punish rude taxi drivers."

"Cut their heads off," General Walls snorted.

"Wery funny, General. Make a note, Brigit: for government wehicles, never hire Matabele as drivers. Totally, absolutely unreliable!"

"Mashona have calmer temperaments. They make much better drivers," General Walls said.

"Matabele have quicker reflexes," General Hickman argued. "They are better drivers because they respond faster."

Austin waited for the argument to subside to be introduced to Brigit, whom he feared was Minister Dieter's wife. She looked at him, curious, looked away, then thrust out her hand. "I'm Brigit Wolfe. You are from Johannesburg, am I right?"

"Joe Austin, Los Angeles, California, by way of Sydney Australia, but you're close enough."

"Don't be silly; I'm completely wrong. How do you Americans say it? 'Off the base.' " He laughed and she smiled quickly before looking down.

"What kind of minister is, uh, your father? I couldn't make out what he was saying but I never heard a preacher swear like that."

"You're very amusing, Joe Austin, but I advise you not to go after detective work. Dieter von Neukirk is neither my father nor a priest but the Minister of Information." She said this smugly and glanced up at him and smiled again, sudden as the sun after a monsoon.

"I'm *very* glad to hear that," Austin said and would have shaken the old man's hand enthusiastically, but the minister had collared a waiter and was busily demanding a plate of *boerewors* be brought to him "charred just so and make it qvick." Brigit shrugged and flashed Austin a sunny smile but then, before he could think of something clever to say, she saw a friend playing lawn croquet, someone she hadn't seen "since forever," she said, and ran off, but not before giving him another smile and saying, "I'll see you again, no?"

Austin exchanged his empty bottle for a full one from a tray borne by a passing waiter and watched Brigit hug and kiss a dark-haired girl holding an orange croquet mallet. Behind him, Ian Smith was busy soothing the ruffled feathers of his Minister of Information.

Later, as Austin sampled the hearty food—thick steaks and the spicy coiled sausage known as *boerewors*, smoked ham, cole slaw, macaroni and potato salad—he asked Ted if the Prime Minister was always so accessible. Ted ran a finger across his thin moustache and said, "Ian is the only honest man I ever knew who became a politician and remained an honest man. What you see is what you get."

Austin whistled. "That says a lot. What do you get with Brigit?"

"I don't know. Dieter might be able to say. She is a looker, isn't she? But you're married, aren't you?"

"Last time I checked," Austin said. "Now about this job, what exactly—"

"There's plenty of time for business. Come see me tomorrow morning at 0900, if that suits you. My office is in the Milton Building. It's just across from your hotel. For now, chew on the air as well as the food. See if it suits your taste," he laughed, waving over an elderly gentleman whose drooping mustache lent him a wise but worried look. "Here's General Jamison, who is now retired, but full fills the post of Rhodesia's unofficial greeter. Anything you want to know about us, Jamison'll tell you."

"Fire away," Jamison said.

"You don't know what you're getting into," Austin laughed. "I'm a man of many questions."

"My favorite kind of student," Jamison said. "Have you plans for the evening? Be happy to show you the sights."

"You know a good place to drink?"

"Young man, I know them all. How long are you visiting with us?"

"I've a return flight to Sydney on Friday."

"Hah! It would take a fortnight to visit every saloon and tavern in Salisbury. We'll have to hit the best spots and leave the rest for next time. You are coming back, aren't you?"

"I don't know yet," Austin said he was unaware that Rhodesia would be his home for the next five years, a place where he could redeem the honor he'd left at a mass unmarked grave in the highlands of Cambodia.

He had scanned the phone book and taken note of the unusual number of shops specializing in guillotines, and now Austin was reading the casualty list in the back of the *Rhodesian Herald*, amused that the front page was reserved for news of bedsitting vacancies and other classified advertisements. He was chuckling to himself and observing the guests when General Jamison entered the hotel lobby. "What d'ye find so comical?" Jamison asked.

"I wouldn't know there was a war going on from the newspaper. It's all about cotton and pigs."

"Typical British understatement, my lad," the general explained, tugging at his moustache. You won't find much in the way of 'military presence,' as you chaps put it, in Salisbury, though I daresay you'll find us prepared for any exigency. No need to worry the ladies and frighten the natives. They're skittish enough as it is, what? Now then, will you require anything from your room? My driver is waiting outside."

"I'm ready. Where to?"

"A general perspective, I thought, unless there's something in particular you'd like to see."

"Where are the executions held? I'd like to see your guillotines." Austin said when they were settled in back of the general's Mercedes.

"We are not bloody wogs, sir!" Jamison said, affronted. "We hang the bastards!"

"Then what are the guillotines for?"

The old man cackled. "Typical British overstatement. We use guillotines to cut metal. Every machine shop in Rhodesia is a manufacturing plant. If other countries won't sell us their products, our entrepreneurial industrialists make copies."

"I get it. It's just semantics." *They're just words, Colonel. Promises are just words.* "They'll get you in trouble, though."

"Beg pardon?"

"Never mind. Where are we?"

"Charter Road. We're going to Salisbury Kopje. It's the highest point around and affords an absolutely marvelous prospect." They turned on Rotten Row and drove past native women in brilliant green and electric blue dresses, many bearing babies on their backs. "So, what d'ye think of our Prime Minister?"

"I'm impressed by his ordinariness."

"I know what you mean. I wondered about him when I first met him," Jamison admitted. "Ian's not one for protocol, but he knows what's going on, he does. He was a war hero, you know, an RAF fighter pilot. His Spitfire was blown out of the skies over Italy in '44; he fought for months behind the lines with Italian partisans. Walks with a limp when he's tired. His body has felt the surgeon's knife more than once."

They were stalled behind a donkey cart. Their driver, a dour black man with sunken cheeks, leaned on the horn. "We've had a few presidents who were war heroes. I prefer them to peanut farmers myself."

"Can't say that I blame ye. Now, Ian's the first Rhodesian Prime Minister born in Rhodesia. His father, Jock

Smith, was a butcher, a breeder and racer of horses, and a prodigious walker. Both he and Ian's mum were awarded the OBE. Although Ian hails from middle-class stock, service to crown and community were bred into him."

They inched past the donkey cart. "He never wanted to be a politician," Jamison continued without commenting on the acrimonious exchange between drivers. "Like your president, Ian's a farmer, but I assure you that's where the resemblance ends. His neighbors made him stand for Legislative Assembly and, before long, he was Welensky's Chief Whip and the die was cast. Except for the treachery of Britain, I don't think Ian would have supported UDI."

"What's that?"

"The Unilateral Declaration of Independence that makes us unbeholden to Britain or anyone else on God's green earth. Britain sold Rhodesia down the river after having promised us our independence, and we thank God that Ian had the balls to stand up to the bastards!" Jamison tugged at his moustache, a fierce old warrior ready at a moment's notice to charge into battle.

"I don't know much about politics," Austin said slowly. "Politicians have always struck me as ruthless cowards, men who are willing to slit their mothers' throats if it furthers their goals, providing they can blame it on someone else."

Jamison swallowed several times to regain his control. "Ian's not like that. He's very straightforward about politics, very level-headed. He's right-wing, to be sure, but he's not an extremist. 'People think you can't be a strong right-wing man unless you are an extremist,' he says, 'but extremists are weak men, the first to get up and run when somebody stands up in front of them.' If the British think he'll cut and run, they don't know Ian Smith like I know him, by God!"

The road wound up the hill past dusty brush and rock outcroppings. A fat native woman pushed her bicycle to the side of the road to let them pass. "Janet Smith strikes me as being salt-of-the-earth," Austin said. "Most politician's wives look like a good shit would do them a world of good."

"She was a widow when they met, you know. She was born in South Africa of Scottish parents and was a history teacher prior to marrying Ian. They were married long before Ian became involved in government and she didn't much like the idea. You wouldn't know that now, of course. A gracious woman, the Africans positively revere her, though one might say she's gone a bit too far in that direction. Not everyone needs to know how to read and write, if you ask my opinion."

"Tell me about the natives," Austin said. "I understand there are two main tribes."

"Quite so. Matabele and Mashona. Care to hear a bit of our past?"

"I'm all ears."

"Our history is rather ill-defined up to the middle of the nineteenth century, although the ruins of Great Zimbabwe point to a well-organized state in the early fifteenth century, and Portuguese explorers of the sixteenth century documented contacts with a paramount chief called Monomatapa."

"There's a hotel by that name."

"Quite right. Ivory hunters and adventurers in the mid-nineteenth century, men named Hartley and Selous, drew the attention of the modern world to the area north of the Limpopo river. Frederick Courtney Selous led Sir Cecil Rhodes' Pioneer Column in 1890, and that was the beginning of the first European settlement in Rhodesia."

"I met a man from the Selous Scouts this afternoon."

"O'Brian. A hot-tempered Irishman. His family has been here for generations. Most people don't realize that when Europeans settled in Rhodesia in the late 1890s, there were only 400,000 Africans here. The explosive increase in the native population has resulted from European health services, particularly preventive medicine in the Tribal Trust Lands. There's also been influx from neighboring countries, Africans seeking employment or protection from tribal warfare and such."

"Tribal warfare?"

"It's been going on for centuries. The Matabele were chased here from Natal by Shaka Zulu at the beginning of the 19th Century. They in turn subjugated the Mashona, a Bantu tribe that had migrated here from the north. They're all relative newcomers."

"Like the whites."

"The Pioneers who left Capetown in search of gold at the behest of Cecil Rhodes were not the first Europeans to visit. There were missionaries, Portuguese traders and, of course, Dr. David Livingstone. I presume you've heard of him?"

"You presume correctly," Austin said.

"Ah, here we are." They had reached the crest of Salisbury Kopje. In the distance, boulders were balanced precariously as if only the passing of some cartoon character was needed to bring everything tumbling down. Below, the city glistened. Jamison pointed out the Earl Gray building where sanction busters and intelligence agents plotted means to keep the minority government in power "despite opposition from most of the civilized and all of the uncivilized world," Jamison said.

"Why is that?"

"Communist propaganda, if you ask me. It's not because of our racial policies, I promise you. We're not like South Africa. Apartheid has never been practiced here. There's little fraternization, of course, but public places are open to all races."

"How big is Rhodesia?"

"Approximately the same size as your home state. You did say you were from California, did you not?"

"No, but that's all right. Your people seem to know a lot about me."

"There was a briefing, but I wasn't in attendance. None of my business, really." He muttered under his breath. "Where was I?"

"California."

Jamison brightened. "A wonderful place. I was there shortly after the war. Before Disneyland, more's the pity. . . . A Texan wouldn't be impressed, but Rhodesia is a large country by European standards, and within these 151,000 square miles are the wonders of Victoria Falls and Lake Kariba in the north, the mountains of the eastern border, the flat bushveld of the great game reserve at Wankie in the west, and the Zimbabwe Ruins—once thought to be King Solomon's mines." He followed Austin around the hill's perimeter but kept talking. "We are a landlocked country, bounded by Zambia (Northern Rhodesia prior to the treachery), Mozambique to the east, South West Africa to the west, and Botswana and South Africa below us. We're a high plateau between the Zambezi and Limpopo rivers, a tourist's delight that has become a battleground." Jamison fell silent, blinked a few times rather forcefully, then stared out over the *veld* as if mapping strategies. "I do tend to go on. Forgive an old man his love of country, won't you?"

He was no longer standing on a *kopje* overlooking Salisbury but on a hill above a Montagnard village. Children were laughing in the sunshine. In the garden . . . *In the garden* . . . He pulled himself back. The sun was setting and lights were beginning to twinkle on in the city below. A girl seated on a nearby rock drew her boyfriend beneath her shawl as if gathering the twilight around them, and Austin felt suddenly lonely. "Where do people go when they haven't a family to go home to?"

"I visit my daughter in Makaha. Oh, I see what you mean. You mentioned the Monomatapa Hotel before? There it is." Jamison pointed to a modern, multi-storied building. "First rate. The club on top is called the Ten Thousand Horsemen. Decent dance band, if you go in for that sort of thing. A bit too contemporary for my tastes. I prefer the Bagatelle in Miekles Hotel; it's clubbier. A young fellow like you would probably prefer Samantha's Disco. I've a grand-daughter named Samantha, did I mention that?"

"No, sir."

"Marvelous child, I adore her. Now, look, there's King George VI Army Headquarters. I'm frequently there making a bloody nuisance of myself. And there's Cecil Square Park. If you like the out-of-doors, Lake McLlwaine is thirty-five kilometers to our west, on the Bulawayo Road. I don't fancy watersports, myself; bilharzia is endemic, I'm told. I prefer birds; we've some marvelous aviaries, and there's a positively enormous botanical garden, Ewanrigg, about forty kilometers from here. What else, now? Borrowdale Racetrack is to the southeast; you're likely to find Sutton-Price there in season. There's Harare, the black township. It's safe enough, but I wouldn't venture there except on business and never unarmed."

"I rarely go anywhere unarmed."

"Quite. There's a decent shooting range, some five golf clubs, though for my money Royal Salisbury's the best, a lion park and snake pit that thrills the ladies. There's no scarcity of taverns, I daresay, but you can't see them from here."

"What say we get a bit closer to one of them."

"Splendid idea, lad. Would've thought of it myself in another minute."

On the way back, Austin asked Jamison to describe the opposition. "First thing you must understand is that there are two main African tribes in Rhodesia. The Mashona are in the majority, though that doesn't seem to faze the Matabele who have always been rather warlike. The word '*shona*' in Matabele means 'dog,' which sums up the attitude of your average Ndebele. As you might imagine, ZANLA's leader, a Mashona chap by the name of Mugabe, isn't on the best of terms with ZIPRA's leader, a fat Matabele named Nkomo. If we can exploit their differences, focus their attention on one another rather than the Europeans, we've a fighting chance."

Austin sought clarification. "Which ones are the communists?"

Jamison laughed. "Don't make the mistake of confusing tribalism with political parties. ZANLA and ZIPRA are in no way like the Democratic and Republican parties in your country or the Conservative and Labour parties in England. We are not dealing with the right to work versus free enterprise but with the right to live versus slavery. Political situations in Africa are based solely on tribal lines, and where the majority tribe—or the tribe with the most power—has assumed power in Africa it has never shared it with any other tribe. Democracy as we know it is completely foreign to the African mind. In fact, they think us crazy to allow a minority voice to be heard. Ah, but here's the Bagatelle. You will join me for dinner, won't you? They serve an excellent roast and the wines are relatively decent despite sanctions."

Austin found the food bland and the atmosphere stuffy, so he was not unhappy when Jamison pulled a watch from his waistcoat and discovered that time had escaped him. "Once I fall to talking about Rhodesia, there's no stopping me, but you must be getting tired, what?"

"I think I will call it a day," Austin said. "No need to drop me off, General. I feel like walking."

The feeling must have passed rather quickly, for no sooner was he outside than he hailed a taxi and directed the driver to Samantha's Disco. Jamison was right; the place was jumping. He elbowed his way to the bar and was trying to signal the bartender when he heard a familiar voice call, "Canadian and Coke, right now, right here!"

"Greg, is that you?" Austin pushed his way across the room, not much of a chore since people tended to melt out of his way when they saw the big man coming.

"Colonel Austin, Jesus Christ, is that you?"

"In the flesh. What are you doing in Rhodesia?"

"Killing gooks, same as ever," Greg smiled, the same thin smile that had made Charley shudder, a smile like a knife opening. "What're you drinking?"

"I've taken a liking to Hansa beer. I see you're still polluting good Canadian."

"Costs an arm and half a leg, too. Hey, bartender!"

"Hoch, mon! Can't you see I'm busy. My Kaffir he's drunk someplace, and two hands is all God gave me." The bartender extended his meaty tattooed arms and, before he could retract them, Greg took hold of his wrists and pinned them to the bar. The bartender tried to move but couldn't. A customer laughed and nudged his buddy. "Let me go, Gottverdamm!" the bartender swore, his fingers helpless as minnows in the maw of a shark.

"Canadian and Coke," Greg smiled. "And a Hansa. Right here, right now!"

"Okay, Yank, all right," the bartender said and Greg released him.

"I don't think you'd make a very good Peace Corps Volunteer," Austin said.

"I think you're right," Greg said. "What brings you to Salisbury? Last I heard, you were fighting the U.S. Army."

"Yeah. I lost."

"They kick you out, Colonel?"

"They intimated my services were no longer required."

"Bastards."

"Can't say I blame 'em. They could've court-martialed me."

"You ever see your friend, Pak Nol, again?"

"Yeah, I saw him." *Dead and unburied.*

"You'll like it here. No jungle, no leeches, and no confusing the gooks with allies."

"I'm thinking about it."

"You're gonna need a driver. Someone who can shoot."

"I haven't taken the job yet."

"With all due respect, sir, you'd be a fool to pass up this war. It's one of the few places left in the world where you can do some real soldiering. It's a great place to live, and not a bad place to die."

"Say something funny. I've already had a dose of Rhodesian patriotism."

Greg was eager to oblige. "I was just telling Karl, that sorry excuse for a bartender, about this Afrikaner who could have been his cousin. Let's get a table." They found one near the end of the bar, and Greg told Austin about a salesman from Johannesburg named Fritz. "Fritz flies into Zambia on business, rents a car at the airport and first thing he does is to run over a drunk who happens to stagger into the street in front of his car. Well, you know, someone calls the police and they arrest poor Fritz for reckless mayhem and haul his white ass to jail. The next day, the prosecutor, a black dude in a white wig, demands he be tried for manslaughter and the magistrate, who also looks like a negative that needs developing, asks him how he pleads. Old Fritz is real nervous and he says 'Ich bin not guilty, herr magistrate, the Kaffir was drunk and fell under the wheels of my car.'

"So the magistrate adjusts his wig and clears his throat and says, 'This is the free and independent state of Zambia, and the man you ran over was not a Kaffir but a citizen of Zambia, a Zambian.'

"So Fritz apologizes and says he didn't know and the magistrate accepts the apology and allows how the deceased was an alcoholic and all charges are dropped and the Afrikaner flies home. His friends are at the airport to meet him, and they all ask Fritz what happened, they read in the newspaper he'd been arrested, and so forth. And he says, 'It's the truth, my friends, with a rental car I drove over a Zambian.'

"And they say, 'A Zambian? What in the hell is a Zambian?'

"And Fritz says, 'I don't know, but he is the closest bloody thing to a Kaffir you have *ever* seen.' " Greg howled and looked for Karl, but the bartender was at the other end of the bar and did not look up.

"Your accent sucks," Austin said.

"I've only been here a couple of months," Greg said, still laughing. "Have you heard the one about—"

Precisely at 0900 the following morning, Austin presented himself at Ted's office in the Government Building across the street from the Ambassador Hotel. As yet unsure of the rules of the game, he'd left his sidearm in his room. An unarmed guard, well past retirement age, stopped him in the lobby to inquire, apologetically, as if sorry to intrude in what was no doubt none of his business, whom Austin wished to see. Upon learning he had an appointment with Mr. Sutton-Price, the guard looked at a sheet in front of him and said "Appears to be so," and directed him to the second floor, room 201.

This was intolerable to someone as security-conscious as Austin. He was not only unknown to the guard but intimidating in appearance, and yet he was being permitted to pursue his own way, unescorted and possibly armed to the teeth, into the heart of the building where the Prime Minister, his deputy and the rest of the country's leaders were carrying out affairs of state. *An English-speaking Russian could go bananas here!*

He entered room 201 without knocking and without disturbing the elderly woman who was happily typing away. "Stick 'em up!" Austin bellowed, and the little grandmother nearly fell out of her chair.

"My, you gave me a start!"

"In hopes of avoiding a most bitter end. I'm Colonel Austin. Mr. Sutton-Price is expecting me."

"I'll tell Mr. Sutton-Price you're here." She took two or three steps before returning to say, "Please have a seat, Colonel Austin. I won't be a minute."

When he was ushered into Ted's plush office he discovered Ian Smith was also there, and they both rose to greet him. *This is not the way things are done in Saigon*, he thought. After the customary greetings and ritual tea, they got down to business. The Prime Minister just sat there, allowing his deputy to do most of the talking.

"In case you've been wondering, your name was conveyed to us by Captain Wilson. Quite a few officers and enlisted men with experience in Vietnam have found their way to Salisbury, and if their records are good and their skills useful we manage to find something for them to do," Ted said. "Captain Wilson has spoken very highly of you and, though he never served under you, he was in a position to evaluate you for us."

"How's that?"

"He processed your after-action reports."

This told Austin that Captain Wilson must have had one hell of a security clearance and was probably associated in some way with the CIA. Austin had on more than one occasion run into Company operations in Cambodia. He hadn't cared much for their field operatives or for their abuse of the trust that he had worked hard to develop in the Montagnards. The information also told Austin that Rhodesia had a source in the Pentagon that allowed them access to U.S. military personnel records. He wondered who else knew about him. "And what do my reports tell you?"

"One facet of your experience that interests us was your ability to establish liaison between the Montagnards and the military hierarchy," Ted said.

"It didn't help the Montagnards much," Austin said softly.

"We're not only impressed with your ability to lead off-shore excursions," Ted said, brushing aside his response, "but your ability to separate political aspects from military ones and measure their effect. You see, world opinion has isolated us to some extent, and we require some assistance in evaluating the advisability of specific actions."

"To be blunt about it," Ian interrupted, "The world press has pilloried us."

"To be blunt about it," Austin said, "if you're thinking about fighting your war in the newspapers, you might as well lay down your arms and ask for terms, because you're already defeated."

"We have no intention of doing that," Ted bristled.

"Glad to hear it," Austin said. "I wish the U.S. had felt that way."

"I need someone I can count on to tell me or my representative the absolute truth concerning incursions into neighboring countries," Ian said. "We need someone who can evaluate intelligence prior to such raids and make recommendations not only about the advisability of the raids from a military point of view, but also the response we can expect from the world press. And if it is recommended that we pursue our objectives, we need timely liaison with the Ministry of Information so that our side of the story gets out in the most plausible terms. In other words, we must justify our need to violate international borders in the pursuit of an internationally unpopular war."

"Whew!"

"In exchange for your services, we offer you the rank of full Colonel and a salary commensurate with that rank. You will report directly to me or to my representative. Ted will for the time being serve in that capacity, won't you, Teddy?"

"It would be a pleasure."

"Ted will see to it that you have the office and staff you need to fulfill your duties, along with a Rhodesian diplomatic passport and whatever else you and your family might require to make transition into our society smooth and painless. How does it sound to you?"

It sounded, on the surface, like a sweetheart of an assignment, but the military moves in mysterious ways. As a uniformed officer reporting directly to a civilian as part of the chain of command, the assignment was absolutely guaranteed to piss off every officer in the Rhodesian Army above the grade of Colonel. In time, Lieutenant General Walls proved to be an ally, an absolute tower of strength even when he did not agree with Austin's methods. Major General Hickman, however, never got over the affront to protocol.

Had Austin known the lengths to which top brass was willing to go to thwart his efforts, perhaps he would not have accepted their offer so readily. Had he considered Sophie's reaction, perhaps he would have asked for some time to think about it. Instead, his mind already brimming with ideas he'd never been allowed to pursue in Southeast Asia, he smacked his lips and winked and said, "You've got yourselves a deal, gentlemen."

"This calls for a drink," Ian said. "Where's that French brandy you tipple on, Teddy?"

The Prime Minister's chief of staff removed a key from his pocket and unlocked a handsome mahogany cabinet. He carefully poured brandy into three shot glasses and offered a toast. "To the war, lads!"

"To the war!"

The stewardess on the long return flight to Sydney reminded Austin of Dream Harrington. He hadn't thought of the curvaceous, flirtatious daughter of Chief Warrant Officer Joseph Harrington in years. Harrington had sired four juicy daughters and coached the horniest high school football team in Southern California. Competition was fierce for a spot on the Riverside High team, fiercer still for a date with a Harrington girl, for rumor had it that Dream, Dawn, Debbie and Dido lusted for linemen. They were all cheerleaders, but Dream was Homecoming Queen and the star of Joe's hottest fantasies.

One way to make Harrington's team was to show an interest in the military, and before long every Riverside Wrangler was a member of the National Guard. Austin had to lie about his age to get in, but Dream proved harder to enter than the National Guard and the only time he scored was when he picked up a ball the fullback had fumbled and rumbled twenty yards for the only touchdown in a 7-3 win over Bakersfield.

It was 1950 and all was well with the world. The Wranglers won more games than they lost, and Austin finally lost his virginity to a teammate's sister after a victory party. He was so drunk he wasn't sure it had really happened, and he couldn't bring himself to ask anyone. He was going to accept a football scholarship to UCLA, but the North Koreans had other ideas. His unit was called up, the second National Guard division to go into action. Chief Warrant Officer Harrington's recruitment efforts had proven far more successful than the team's clumsy efforts at the virtue of Dream, Dawn, Debbie or Dido, though the subject was much discussed from Inchon to Seoul, and many lies were told. While it was a matter of honor to lay claim to a Harrington girl, it was something else to talk about screwing a buddy's sister, so Austin remained silent. The United Nations debated; the armies advanced and retreated; Austin was concerned with weightier things. One day he was certain he'd done it; the next he was equally convinced it was just a wet dream.

The tank unit that was attached to the headquarters company of their infantry battalion had suffered heavy casualties. Many of the replacements were West Virginians with little education, so young Austin, who knew how to read a map and was stupid enough to think he would *enjoy* combat, was put into a tank. When Chinese soldiers attacked the perimeter and engaged his unit, first it scared the shit out of Joe and then it thrilled him unforgettably. This is what copulating with a linebacker's sister *should* have been like.

Combat frightened him, but the alternative was unacceptable. He had become a warrior. Afterward, all he wanted to do was fuck, and he attracted pussy like a dead man attracts flies and never gave his buddy's sister another thought.

Joe didn't care much for army life, but the action beat any thing else he'd ever experienced, and he discovered he'd a knack for killing. He liked to ride up top with all the guns blazing: co-ax, bow gun, and canister rounds from the 76mm main tube. They wouldn't button up unless ordered to do so, and they'd shoot at anything that moved. He was a staff sergeant at 16, the youngest tank commander in Korea, although the Army wasn't aware of his tender years.

After two years, his unit was deactivated and what was left of the Riverside Wranglers went home. Grampa Bass was dead and Dream Harrington was married and Joe felt awkward and out of place. Then UCLA invited him to summer workouts. He was six feet tall by now and weighed 245 lbs. The coach must've needed a pulling guard who liked pain, because he gave Joe a full scholarship. The first class Joe signed up for was ROTC. He was ready to make a career choice, and Korea had also taught him that it was much more comfortable to be an officer than an NCO.

Austin's ROTC unit had a very active marksmanship program, and he joined the rifle and pistol teams. Competitive shooting soon became his chief hobby, surpassing even football. He was no longer having trouble getting laid, and he could see that shooting straight might one day prove more valuable than knocking linebackers on their asses. Eighteen years after accepting a Reserve Commission he was encouraged to retire from the U.S. Army. He was married, the father of two girls, and he possessed skills only the desperate could use.

No one met him at the airport in Sydney because no one knew he'd been gone. Sophie and the girls were not due back from Europe for another week. They were visiting the countess, Sophie's mother, a vituperative Polish noblewoman living in penury outside Paris. Austin firmly believed that the only good the communists had ever accomplished was to deny the countess power in Polish affairs. Sophie did not appreciate Austin's attitude toward her mother, though he tried to amuse her with a constant barrage of Polish jokes.

Sophie retaliated by attacking his competency as father and breadwinner. He, therefore, had reason to believe it might please her to learn that Rhodesia was willing to pay him quite well to evaluate military strategies. After he had listened patiently to a litany of the ills besetting the countess, after he learned what Paris designers were currently conspiring, and after he had kissed the girls goodnight and tucked them in, he fixed Sophie a cocktail and told her about the job he'd been offered.

"It's a two-year contract," he explained. "My rate of pay will be the same as any other regular officer, but there are some nice perks. Half my salary is payable in the currency of my choice and automatically deposited in the bank of my choice, anywhere in the world. A car, home and servants are provided at no cost, and they'll pay all our moving expenses to Rhodesia. After two years, if we want to leave, they'll pay all expenses to move us wherever we'd like to go."

"I don't want to move to Rhodesia," Sophie said.

"But you hate it here."

"Rhodesia is worse."

"How do you know? You've never been there."

"I know. It's full of blacks. You don't care how we feel. All you think about is yourself."

"It's a wonderful country. The girls will love it."

"They're not going. You want to go, go yourself."

"I will, by God!"

"Don't shout, you'll wake the girls."

"A marriage of ten years is on the ropes, and all you can say is 'Don't shout'? Well, if I want to shout, I'll fucking shout!"

"Don't curse!"

"Fuck you!"

"And twice to you!"

On April 3, 1975, Austin's thirty-eighth birthday, he said good-bye to his wife. He kissed the girls and promised he'd write. Australia paid no more attention to his departure than it had to his arrival after the war in Vietnam.

All his worldly possessions were in two suitcases, one of which contained enough hardware to trigger a shitfit in the pants of any customs official who dared to look inside. On the plane, Austin read a book about Rhodesia. He noted that the population was estimated to be 4,270,000 and was divided into four main ethnic groups: Africans, Europeans, Coloured and Asians. There were approximately 4,000,000 Africans, 250,000 Europeans, 13,000 people of mixed caste and 8,000 Asians. Greg had said he reckoned the odds at better than 15 to 1 in favor of the non-whites and figured he'd have to kill a whole mess of communists before there was any prospect of peace. This had pleased Greg and thinking about it amused Austin and made the long flight more tolerable.

According to his book, there were four main cities in Rhodesia: Salisbury, Bulawayo, Umtali and Fort Victoria. Salisbury was a modern capitol with tall buildings and clean streets lined with Jacaranda trees.

Bulawayo had been the capitol of the Matabele nation before Rhodesia declared independence and was still the industrial center and railroad hub. Its streets had been designed so that an ox cart pulled by a nine-span oxen team could turn around without backing up. 'Bulawayo' meant 'the place of the slaughter'.

Umtali was a beautiful city in the high veld where the mountains soared 2,500 meters (8,200 feet) above sea level. The Eastern Highlands were famous for their large tea and coffee estates. Some of the most vicious fighting of the Rhodesian War had taken place here on the Mozambique border.

Fort Victoria was Rhodesia's oldest city. Located in the low veld midway between Bulawayo and Umtali, Fort Vic was the mining center of the country.

Austin was soon caught up planning and analyzing various methods of neutralizing the enemy. The *modus operandi* of the terrorists operating under the banner of

ZANLA was to hit farms and kidnap villagers, then dash across the border to FRELIMO protected camps in Mozambique. O'Brian and the Selous Scouts wanted to wipe out these camps as well as ZIPRA camps in Zambia. General Walls endorsed the concept, but Major General Hickman cautioned against waging war on two fronts, "which is precisely what we'd be facing if we give our neighboring countries reason to declare war."

"Zambia and Mozambique are neighbors," Walls commented, "like lion and kudu are neighbors. It's time we faced facts, gentlemen!" he said, slamming his palm on the table and bringing Ted's secretary scurrying in to inquire if someone had fallen and required bandaging.

The ministers were divided and wanted assurances that whatever was done would be completely successful and cause no repercussions.

Because of the time required to plan and approve even the simplest off-shore excursion, it was a year before the first full-scale raid into Mozambique was ready for implementation. Austin had not been idle and neither had Greg, who was now his bodyguard and driver, but Rhodesian politicians were just as worried as their American counterparts about covering their asses, and Austin spent months preparing dozens of press releases to offset every imaginable occurence.

Major General Hickman foresaw far-fetched possibilities, Ken Flowers improvised the most unlikely scenarios, and Dieter von Neukirk demanded ramifications and justifications for every eventuality. Recognizing that most professional soldiers (MacArthur was a notable exception) disliked publicity, Austin plotted ways to divert press attention from the military to the politicians who, to a man, relished the spotlight. Still, the cerebral sparring and psychological testing exhausted him. He clamored for action and, when the last 't' had been crossed and the final 'i' dotted, he would have begged to go along with the raiding party had not Ted first suggested it.

Austin knew the idea of hitting the enemy where he lives was not new; it was as old as warfare. However, fighting a war with everyone looking over your shoulder, ready to condemn your efforts, no matter how well-meaning or brilliantly-conceived, made everyone nervous as postmen at a dog show.

Everyone agreed that FRELIMO, the *Front for the Liberation of Mozambique*, which was now Mozambique's ruling body and the chief supporters of ZANLA, the *Zimbabwe African National Liberation Army*, had to be taught a lesson. Rhodesia could no longer shy away from engaging targets just because they were readily identifiable as Mozambique Nationals.

Special Branch notified Ken of a large camp near Pungwe in Mozambique that was not only a training center but the supply base, recreation site and hospital for ZANLA's entire war effort. Some known terrorists were being treated there for wounds sustained in a recent attack on a Rhodesian farm. O'Brian had lost a man in a freak accident while pursuing some of these terrorists and he was hot for retribution.

In August of 1976, the Overall Co-ordination Committee gave its stamp of approval for a strike against the camp and related FRELIMO targets. There was just one catch: there would be no air support.

It was estimated there were more than five thousand ZANLA operatives at the training camp plus at least fifty FRELIMO officers and soldiers. The Rhodesians would have a total of eighty-four officers and men. In order to carry out the operation, armored vehicles were required. Since sanctions precluded their purchase from Europe or the United States, Rhodesia had to manufacture its own.

The little machine shops with their guillotines and smelters went to work. In most countries, it takes years for an idea to become a prototype. Rhodesia built the 'Pig' in 30 days! The vehicle might have infringed on a few patents, but that was for legal minds to debate. At core, the vehicles were Mercedes Unimogs, standard-issue West German Army trucks. After the addition of armor plate and a few FN 7.62 medium machine guns, plus a sprinkling of Hispano 20mm cannons scrapped from old Vampire fighters, the 'Pig' was ready to carry a contingent of Selous Scouts to Pungwe.

To twist a few minds, the 14 vehicles that comprised the flying column were painted in FRELIMO camo patterns. O'Brian chose an African beer-drinking holiday as the day to attack. Wearing 'Black is Beautiful' make-up and FRELIMO uniforms, Austin, Greg and the Selous Scouts set out to hit the camp. Their column consisted of only ten vehicles, two with 20mm cannons, one with a 12.7mm machine gun, and one with a .50 M2 machine gun as heavy weapons. There were also assorted .30 Browning and 7.62 FN machine guns.

The attack was planned to take place during roll call, the main morning formation when all camp personnel would be on the parade ground in the center of the camp.

At 0745, the convoy rolled up to the camp gates, and a Portuguese-speaking soldier in blackface ordered the gates thrown open so that their FRELIMO commander could speak to his Comrades-in-Arms. Snapping to attention, the ZANLA guards opened the gates, and the vehicles drove in and circled the parade grounds. Terrorists waved at them and ran to get closer.

The Portuguese-speaking soldier used a loudspeaker to get everyone's attention, conveying heartfelt greetings to the Zimbabwe National Liberation Army and asking the soldiers to maintain their proper formations until the treats they had brought were passed out. (This would make the job a little neater, a bit more thorough.) However, upon hearing the mellow tones of the translator, the troops broke ranks to admire the fine armored vehicles in which they would soon crush the Rhodesians. While milling about, they began singing ZANLA fight songs until the sound of machine guns drowned out their voices.

The commander's Unimog, with its twin 7.62 FN machine guns was in the center. The 'Pigs' with the 20mm cannon moved into position on each flank. The Unimogs with the 12.7mm and .50 caliber machine guns moved to the far right, and the two Unimogs with the infantry and dual 7.62mm machine guns moved to cover the far left flank of the main body.

Several thousand terrorists were milling around, singing songs of liberation and trying to touch their generous comrades. The salivating Selous Scouts were shouting, "Viva FRELIMO!" and waiting for the order to open fire. Greg was smiling from ear to ear, and Austin was worrying that there might not be enough ammo.

Meanwhile, the camp commanders had climbed down from their review stand and were trying to press their way through the ranks to see what had so disrupted the normal roll call and daily instructions. Officers were trying to get their people back into formation so they could welcome the visitors properly and according to protocol. Then a perceptive junior officer noticed that some of the visitors were not really black and wondered why this might be so.

Others also began to notice and wonder and then the cry of "*Murungu* . . . *Murungu* . . . *Murungu* . . ." could be heard. A few people started to back away but most weren't paying attention because the noise of the crowd was too loud and the occasion too festive. Soon there would be beer and food, *mealy* with *sadsa*, perhaps, and rousing songs.

The task force commander gave the order to open fire, and it was like mowing wheat. Two 20mm cannon and 13 assorted light, medium and heavy machine guns went off at point blank range. Hundreds of terrorists crumpled to the ground! They clawed at one another, trying to get away. They ran over and into one another, and they fell in heaps, blood splattering everywhere.

Without a pause, the guns hammered out the music of

war, and the terrorists danced frantically on the parade grounds. For 15 minutes, the guns continued to fire, until all movement had stopped except for the writhing of the maimed. The rate of fire was so heavy that Austin was not aware there was any incoming fire from the terrorists until he saw the Portuguese-speaking Rhodesian hit. After the cease-fire had been given, the source of incoming fire was determined and quickly obliterated.

While the scattered return fire was being suppressed, the camp hospital was set alight by tracer fire. This was unfortunate, for Austin had wanted to take some of the wounded back for debriefing by Special Branch. Austin ran into the burning building to search for a particular terrorist, but smoke forced him back outside.

All good things must come to an end, and though Greg and a few others tried to prolong the experience by scouring the banks of the river into which some terrorists had jumped in an effort to escape, soon all was quiet.

On the return trip, the main highway bridge over the Pungwe River was blown up. This prevented FRELIMO forces from following the column and closed the major highway link in that part of Mozambique for months.

The final tally saw the Rhodesians with five casualties: two whites and three blacks had been wounded, none critically. The terrorists reported 675 killed, 240 wounded and requiring continued hospitalization, 3610 slightly injured or unfit for immediate duty. Approximately 300 additional terrorists were drowned trying to swim the river. Unfortunately, not many Africans in a camp protected by water on two sides knew how to swim, a training oversight unlikely to be rectified.

Austin was able to report that the mission had been an unqualified success. Then Greg drove him over to Samantha's Disco on the off-chance he might find some strange stuff. Seated at the bar with Kitty Canty, a special reporter for the *New York Times*, was Brigit Wolfe. She looked good enough to eat and Austin had never felt hungrier. He bought them a drink, then bought one for the house. Kitty wanted to ask him some questions about the operation, but Brigit signalled him to be silent. "Kitty dear, the press release Minister Neukirk has just now issued is complete and correct. Enough work for one day. It's time to relax and enjoy life, isn't that so, Colonel Austin?"

"Call me Joe," he said. "Hey, Karl, let's have another round over here."

"Right here, right now!" Greg shouted.

"Joost now coming, boys," Karl said, "and kip yer dollars in yer pockets. Today the world knows we don't give Rhodesia up so easy."

Austin stormed into Dieter's office and slammed the *New York Times* and *Paris Match* on the Minister's desk. "Have you seen this crap!"

Headlines screamed: *African Refugee Camp Attacked! Hospital Destroyed!* The *Times* story, under Kitty Canty's byline, contained a detailed account of a raid by the Rhodesian Army and Air Force against a refugee camp inhabited by helpless women and starving children. The story began, "Hundreds of unarmed people were brutally slain in a savage attack by the armed forces of the white minority government of Rhodesia yesterday."

"Sons from bitches!" Dieter brushed the newspapers from his desk. "Ve had photographs from the Selous Scouts, your press releases in the fancy binder. Ve even give them ZANLA documents captured by the Special Branch vich list terrorist formations by rank and position inside the ZANLA organization. So, vat do they publish? A speech by FRELIMO and Samora Machel, the sons from bitches!"

Brigit came in with little pills and a glass of water on a painted tray. Still grumbling, the Minister of Information tossed the pills down, chasing them with water, and wiped his mouth with the back of his hand. "At least Kitty didn't mention Colonel Austin in her story," Brigit said.

"Maybe I should've answered her questions," he said grimly.

"Absolutely forbidden!" Dieter von Neukirk chopped at the palm of his left hand with his right. "They tvist, they slant, they make vat's right look wrong and vat's wrong smell like rotten *boerewors!* They are like jackals. They haf no respect for law or decency. I know them better than their own mothers. For forty years I haf vatched them. Am I wrong, Brigit?" He put the question to his secretary like a prosecutor demanding a guilty verdict.

The lissome blonde shrugged. "No one argues with you, Dieter. You were a professor at the university, head of the Journalism Department, isn't that correct?"

"Forty years," the minister said, then brushed aside his anger. "The *Rhodesian Herald*, the *Bulawayo Chronicle*, and the South African papers, they presented the facts, no tears and no embellishment. My students, of them I'm proud. What do ve care about the *London Times?* How many Rhodesians read the *Herald Tribune?*"

That evening, Austin dined with General Jamison at the Ten Thousand Horsemen atop the Monomatapa Hotel. "Why does the world hate Rhodesia?" the old warhorse asked rhetorically as he tucked his napkin into his collar. "To answer that question, we have to go back to November 11, 1965 when Rhodesia proclaimed itself free from the British Government. You should read our Proclamation of Independence some day; it will sound quite familiar to you. It starts: 'Whereas in the course of human affairs history has shown that it may become necessary for a people to resolve the political affiliations which have connected them with another people and to assume amongst other nations the separate and equal status to which they are entitled . . .' Does that remind you of anything, eh?"

"Porterhouse."

"How's that?"

"I'll have steak," Austin said to the waiter. "I like it rare; I want to see it bleed."

"Very good, sir."

"Steak and kidney pie for me." Then, to Austin, "The British know how to do some things right, by God. Too bad it's only in the kitchen. They straightaway knuckle under to colonials. Never did get over what that toothless little fellow in the loincloth did to 'em after the Second World War." Jamison slurped at his soup. "Where was I?"

"The Declaration of Independence."

"*Proclamation* of Independence. There's poetry if you like poetry. I don't care for it myself, with the exception of Kipling, of course. Listen to this." Jamison leaned back in his chair and declaimed: 'We, the Government of Rhodesia, in humble submission to Almighty God who controls the destinies of nations, conscious that the people of Rhodesia have always shown unswerving loyalty and devotion to her Majesty the Queen and earnestly praying that we and the people of Rhodesia will not be hindered in our determination to continue exercising our undoubted right to demonstrate the same loyalty and devotion, and seeking to promote the common good so that the dignity and freedom of all men may be assured, do, by this Proclamation, adopt, enact and give to the people of Rhodesia the Constitution annexed hereto. God Save The Queen.' "

"God save the Queen!" a couple at a nearby table echoed.

"For shame!" hissed someone else.

"Well," Jamison said after the soup had been cleared from the table, "the results of Rhodesia's quest for Independence were exactly the same as the United States: War! Not a war with England, but a war on two fronts, against two separate enemies backed by two separate governments with a common goal: that of depriving a new nation the right to survive.''

"When word reached the British Prime Minister that, after years of futile effort in trying to achieve her own destiny, Rhodesia had declared 'Unilateral Declaration of Independence,' Wilson had the gall to state that placating Black Africa was more important to England than supporting good government. Can't you just see the bloody floppies with their assegai and knobkerries parading before the press threatening bloody retribution and passing the hat.''

"Floppies?"

"That's what our lads call the terrorists, Joe. It's because of the way they flop around when you shoot them. They don't die like white people. They twitch and jerk like Mexican jumping beans." Laughing, General Jamison signalled the waiter to pour the wine. "And, don't make the mistake of thinking all Kaffirs are alike. The Mashona are Bantu. They were invaded at the beginning of the nineteenth century by a Nguni-speaking tribe from South Africa who were running away from Shaka, the all-powerful Zulu leader. The Kaffirs refer to this period as the *mfecane*, the troubles.

"Shaka, you see, had upset the applecart by changing the way wars were fought in South Africa. Previously, opposing tribes stood face to face and threw spears at one another. Then they'd pick up the spears hurled by their enemy and fling them back again. It was all good fun and very few people were hurt.

"Shaka changed all this when he invented the *assegai*, the stabbing spear. When an enemy tribe next came to fight, Saka waited for them to throw their spears and, instead of throwing them back, he charged and slaughtered the opposing tribe in hand-to-hand combat with these three-foot spears that were pointed at both ends. Shaka then killed the chief and took over his territory.

"Soon, Shaka's territory extended from the Indian Ocean to the Kalahari, from Tugela to the Limpopo and points north. After conquering a tribe and killing the chief, Shaka would spare those who swore allegiance to him. Nothing could then be done without his permission. He wouldn't let his men marry until they'd proven themselves in battle, the black man's answer to Lysistrata. After each battle, there'd be mass marriages. They'd all get drunk and rut in the mud."

The waiter served the steak and refilled their glasses. "Now, *there* was an army," Jamison said. "Discipline!" He leaned forward, raised his eyebrows and lowered his voice. "If our Kaffirs had half the discipline of that lot, we wouldn't be having 'incidents', we'd have a full-scale war on our hands.

"Let me give you just one example of Zulu discipline. All the cattle in Zulu Land belonged to Shaka, including the milk. One day, three herdsboys were caught drinking the milk of cattle they were supposed to be guarding. The headman sent them to Shaka's *kraal* to be punished, and they walked the whole way, over 100 kilometers, and presented themselves before Shaka. Because they didn't try to run away, Shaka granted them the honour of a warrior's death, which meant they were stabbed through the heart with an *assegai* rather than suffer the slow strangulation which their crime merited."

"How would Shaka punish a serious infraction?" Austin asked.

"When Shaka's brother was caught plotting against him, Shaka planted a fire-hardened, pointed stake in the ground. After binding his brother's arms and legs, Shaka sat him on the stake. For a short while, his lower back and rump muscles held him from slipping onto the stake, but eventually he tired and impaled himself. Slowly, first his bowels and then his stomach were pierced."

The waiter tried to refill his glass, but Jamison waved him away. The General collected African weapons, and he delighted in discussing implements of torture, particularly when ladies were present, though they never let him get very far. "At any rate, when things got sticky for Mzilikazi, one of Shaka's military leaders, the bugger didn't stop running until he'd crossed the Limpopo. The people he brought with him into Bulawayo were called *Ndebele*, or strangers, by the Mashona, and the two tribes fought at every opportunity."

Austin had finished eating, but Jamison had yet to taste his food. "The Ndebele," he went on, "were the forerunners of our Matabele, and they got along swimmingly with the early white settlers. Mzilikazi knew David Livingstone, and his son, Lobengula, granted mining concessions to Cecil Rhodes. I believe I've told you Rhodes' Pioneer Column built a fort near a village ruled by a Shona chief named Harare. On September 12, 1890, they named their post Salisbury in honor of Lord Salisbury who was prime minister of Great Britain at the time.

"In 1891, Britain and Portugal signed a treaty that allowed a railroad to connect Salisbury with the port of Beira in Portuguese East Africa, and that gave landlocked Rhodesia an easy route to the sea. While the whites were busily carving up southern Africa, the Shona and Matabele were attacking one another's villages. Leander Starr Jameson, an administrator for Rhodes' British South Africa Company, stepped into the fray, driving Lobengula north, where he died in 1894. In this manner, Britain took control of the country."

"Matabele and Mashona have been fighting ever since, although they managed to patch up their differences for a while when the OAU, the Organization for African Unity, threatened to cut off their funds if they didn't stop killing one another and start killing us."

"Surprisingly enough, UDI brought them together. Mugabe and Nkomo rejoiced because they believed that Great Britain would intercede militarily on their behalf, assisting them in taking over the country. The *kraal* chiefs and headmen in the tribal areas went on record in favour of Independence. They thought a united front with the white government would secure *their* positions and take the wind out of the terrorists' sails. History reveals that both groups were wrong."

"Is something wrong, sir?" A solicitous waiter bent over Jamison and watched him cut into his steak and kidney pie."

"Of course there's something wrong!" the General bellowed, then stopped to consider what it might be. "Chutney, where's the chutney. I always take chutney with my kidney pie!"

The waiter snapped his fingers and an African in a white housecoat ran off to get the condiment. "Very good, sir," the waiter said, filling their glasses with wine.

"That's enough for me," Austin said, putting his hand over the glass. "I would like some coffee, though."

"Very good, sir. Do you take cream?"

"No, I drink it black and bitter as my soul." Turning to Jamison, he asked, "What did the Rhodesians expect would happen after UDI?"

"We've never expected anything from anyone, but we hoped others would tend to their own affairs and leave us to tend to ours."

The busboy was returning with the chutney when Greg came running in. "There's been an incident at your son-in-law's farm, General. It's your granddaughter."

"Samantha?"

"Yes, sir."

Austin was out of his chair and throwing bills on the table to pay for dinner while the befuddled general was trying to elicit more information from Greg than he apparently had. "Dammit, tell me what's happened to Samantha."

"I don't know, General, but I think you'd better come with us. We can talk in the car." In the elevator, Austin noticed that the General was still wearing his napkin and, without saying a word, he removed it. The men left the hotel quickly, without attracting attention.

"There's a chopper waiting for us," Greg said as he gunned the BMW's engine.

Jamison leaned forward, gripping the back of the front seat. "Now, tell me everything you know."

"I was at Hurricane Joint Operational Command Headquarters when a call came in from a Special Branch operative after an Agri-Alert," Greg checked his watch, "at 1800 hours. A Territorial Sergeant named Barry Richards and his stick are meeting us at the farm."

"Casualty report?"

"Indications are that your granddaughter was alone at the time. It appears that a BSAP Constable is in pursuit of the terrorists. That's all I know." The words were clipped, Greg's tone was neutral, and he offered no analysis.

The helicopter was waiting for them and when they landed at the farm they were met by the police and Sergeant Barry Richards, a wiry third generation Rhodesian whose reputation as tracker and snake handler was well-known. He owned a dairy farm outside Que-Que and had once worked as elephant control officer for the Wildlife Department as part of the Rinderpest program to help control disease in cattle in Rhodesia.

"What the hell is going on?" General Jamison demanded after returning Richards' salute.

"I think you better come along with me, sir," he said and led the troubled group from the LZ through the torn-down security gate towards the farm house, a typical single-story brick home with a long veranda. Here Jamison would frequently sit when he visited. Here he would drink a sundowner and contemplate the beauty of the countryside. The veranda was the center of farm life in Rhodesia, for it was cool and protected from Mopani flies and mosquitoes and from other tiny insects that crawl into people's nostrils and torment them.

Tobacco and groundnuts were the chief crops, but it was rainy season and planting had not yet begun. They walked through the back door and out onto the veranda. Blood was everywhere. Austin could see no bodies. No one said anything. They could hear people crying inside the house, but they just stood there silently waiting for Jamison to say something. In one corner Austin saw a patch of red and white flowers that, on closer inspection appeared to be a bundle of bloody rags, as if someone had tried to clean up some of the blood that covered the veranda. Then Austin realized that it was not a bundle of rags at all but the body of a small child. Now they were all staring at it.

General Jamison went over and looked down at her for some time, saying nothing but making swallowing noises. Then he said, "Identity confirmed" and went inside. They heard more wailing.

BSAP officers were interviewing family members and servants. Greg and Austin stayed outside and Richards told them what was known so far. The body was that of a two-year old white girl, Samantha Jamison Blake. She had been left in the care of her nanny while her parents made a short trip to a neighboring farm. "The Blake farm has been under surveillance for some time, it seems, by an African Constable named Josiah Ncobe. Last year, a group of ZANLA terrorists broke into the compound when the Blakes were in Salisbury attending the General's 70th birthday. They stole some food and liquor and got clean away."

"So they thought they'd try again," Austin said.

"We think it was the same bunch. Mr. and Mrs. Blake were at a neighboring farm when it happened and returned home minutes after the terrorists left."

"They broke through the security gates and entered the house through the kitchen," a policeman told Richards. "We're dusting for prints now."

"There's another body inside," Richards said to Austin. "When the terrorists broke in, Samantha's nanny covered her head with a blanket and pretended the child was her own. That act of treachery cost them their lives, but they almost got away with it. At first all the terrorists were interested in was food and liquor. They made themselves at home, asked where the liquor was kept, and when the boss was due back. They had the cook prepare tea and a hot meal. All this time, the servants kept the nanny's secret. Meanwhile, Samantha had gone to sleep and her nanny took her to a back bedroom and tucked her in so she was completely covered.

"Apparently, Samantha woke up in the strange bed and started to cry. For some reason, one of the terrorists went to check on the child and saw that she was white and reported this to his leader who ordered her executed. He went back to get her and carried her out to the veranda where he stabbed her with his bayonet. Another terrorist went to the other end of the veranda and asked his associate to toss the girl to him. He caught Samantha on his extended bayonet and the two men played a macabre game of catch with Samantha's body while the nanny, held at bayonet point by the group leader, was forced to watch."

"Jesus!" Austin said.

Greg smiled savagely. "I'd like to get my hands on them," he hissed.

"Wouldn't we all," Richards said. "Anyway, Samantha soon stopped screaming and the game lost its edge. The terrorist leader then stabbed the nanny with his bayonet, pinning her through the chest to the back of the kitchen chair."

"There was something about a constable," Austin said.

"That's right. Corporal Ncobe was on duty in the area and was alerted by one of the servants. He was not carrying any weapons and had not time to summon help before the now frightened terrorists ran off. Samantha's parents saw him when they arrived home, but he had only time to direct them to the veranda before taking off in hot pursuit of the gang."

"Have you heard from him?"

"Not yet. Mr. Blake initiated the Agri-Alert system, then summoned a doctor to care for his wife who was overcome with grief and self-recrimination. I got here ten minutes after the police arrived, less than half an hour after the attack."

Just then the doctor arrived and was taken in to sedate Jamison's daughter who was being cared for by her husband. It was now too dark for Richards' stick to track the terrorists, but Corporal Ncobe was reputed to be a good tracker, and the police expected him to report in before dawn.

At daybreak, Richards sent a team out to cut the tracks of the terrorists and asked Austin if he would authorize setting up a blocking force using the helicopter. Several villages lay between the farm and the Mozambique border, which was where the terrorists were most likely headed. There was still no word from Corporal Ncobe, and it was feared he had fallen victim to the terrorists. While Richards' people got busy tracking, Austin, Greg and a BSAP officer named Joshua Tenneka flew over to a nearby village to question the *kraal* chief.

The chief emerged from his *rondaaval* as the chopper set down on the flat veld. He was a defiant old man of forty who saw nothing, heard nothing and insisted he knew nothing. Greg was sure he was lying. Spying a *maswikero*, the coldly grinning American asked the shaman if any strangers had come to the village the night before.

"Oh, no mastuh," the spirit medium said. "Is no stranger come near to this place."

"I think you're a lying son of a bitch," Greg said as he slowly pulled out his .45. "What do you think about that?"

"No, mastuh. I speak the truth."

"Then I guess you're gonna die for nothing," he said and shot the shaman in the face. The *maswikero* fell to the ground clutching the bloody mess that had once been his eyes and mouth, and gurgled until he died. All the while Greg watched the *kraal* chief. Then, slowly, he took a single step in the chief's direction and raised the .45 and asked, "You remember now?"

The dignity and nobility that the headman had worn like a talisman fled from his face and he showed them his teeth and smiled and cringed. "Das right, I forgot to remember the men who came for food but we gave to them no food and they run to the east," he said, pointing north, then correcting to northeast.

"He'll tell you anything he thinks you want to hear," Austin said in disgust. "Let's get out of here."

Meanwhile, Richards had picked up the terrorists' spoor and found they were no longer heading straight for the border but were trying to anti-track, or backtrack, to confuse their pursuers. They had cut through a Tribal Trust Land where the bush was thick and covered with acacia trees and tall grasses.

A local *kraal* chief who had a son in the RAR (the Rhodesian African Rifles) reported seeing three men in the company of a BSAP officer. Since no one had heard from Josiah Ncobe, it was now thought that he had deserted and joined the terrorists' stick. It was possible he was being held against his will, but this didn't make much sense. What would the terrs do with a prisoner?

On occasion, terrorists abducted students. In training camps near the border, the kids would be brainwashed and sent back across with a rifle in one hand and the quotations of Chairman Mao in the other. Recently, a missionary school at St. Mary's, some fifteen klicks from Wankie, had been attacked. A missionary and a sister had been killed, and fourteen students taken to Zambia for terrorist training.

But Constable Ncobe was too dangerous to be held prisoner. He was already trained and knew tricks that would make their heads spin. And what good was he to them? He was no repository of military secrets. They couldn't ransom him: a Kaffir wasn't worth anything. No, if the *kraal* chief was telling the truth, Ncobe had turned, and his training made him very dangerous. He would have to be hunted and killed before he trained others. Austin called in to report they were in hot pursuit of a renegade Constable. Major General Hickman came on the horn, furious at not having been notified earlier. "Who authorized your helicopter, Colonel?"

"We are in hot pursuit," Austin repeated, ignoring the question, "and request permission to continue east of Makaha towards Guro."

Outraged that Austin was outside his chain of command and could not be officially reprimanded, Hickman fairly spat into the microphone. "Permission to pursue denied!" he radioed. "Return the chopper to base immediately!"

"We'll do it on the ground," Austin said through clenched teeth. He instructed the pilot to take the chopper in and arranged to rendezvous with Richards in thick terrain near the Tribal Trust Land.

Since the average contact distance in Rhodesia during the rainy season was 25 to 50 meters, Austin packed an automatic shotgun. With this as his primary weapon, he carried a Smith & Wesson .44 Magnum as back-up, because anything over 50 meters could be handled by the .44. In loading the shotgun, he used a special mix: first a AAA round up the spout, then another, then four rounds of Special SG, and finally a rifled slug. (AAA is almost the equivalent of number 4 buck and Special SG is very close to OO buck in the U.S.) The .44 carried handloads, with bullets cast from a Keith type-240 grain mold. The bullets were cast from pure Linotype, ahead of 22 grains of 2400 powder.

Joshua Tenneka, who was familiar with the terrain, went on point, so Richards could attend to the Americans.

Greg and the men in Richards stick carried standard issue FNs along with whatever else they felt comfortable with.

The terrs were no longer trying to backtrack or anti-track in any way. They had their heads down, asses up, and were flat-out moving! Austin was starting to breathe a bit heavier than the others, though he was still keeping up with the younger men, when there was a sudden halt to the proceedings.

A large herd of elephants had cut the terrorists' spoor and the terrs had started following the elephants' tracks to conceal their own. An elephant is the biggest land animal in the world, but in heavy bush it is almost impossible to see at seven to eight meters. Elephants in the bush are not nice and clean like circus elephants but develop a mottled coloring from rolling in the mud. They do this to protect themselves from the sun and flies, and the mud dries the same color as the bush. Hunters have reported being unaware that elephants were nearby until they suddenly heard the disconcerting rumble of enormous stomachs.

When feeding, elephants travel at a pace akin to that of a man jogging. They cover ground quickly and don't make much noise in open veld. Tenneka was finding it easier following the elephants' spoor than picking flyshit out of pepper, and they were all moving briskly along when a very angry tuskless female discovered she was being followed and all hell broke loose! She broke from the bush right into Austin's path. His shotgun was worthless; any attempt to use it would have made one angry elephant completely unreasonable. He threw the shotgun away, drew his revolver and aimed for the elephant's eye, hoping this would turn her head and give someone else the opportunity to join the party, preferably Richards, who had killed more elephants than any man alive.

Austin's first shot hit the elephant about two inches below the eye, and it did turn her head. Had he been smart, he would have stopped there and then, but Austin wasn't prepared to cease fire until whatever he was shooting at fell down. As the elephant turned, he fired a heart-lung shot, which turned her back in his direction. He fired a third and fourth shot, trying for the brain locker, aware that an elephant's brain is about the size of a breadbox in a head the size of a Volkswagen. It was not all that obvious where to aim, particularly since by this time he was shooting almost straight up. There was elephant everywhere.

Then it was quiet, very quiet, and all he could hear was his own unsteady breath. The elephant had fallen exactly seven paces from where he had taken root and fired. Greg, meanwhile, had shot an 800 pound baby elephant that in following its mama had threatened to pound Greg six feet deep in muddy veld.

Fear caught up with them as they stood around the mottled mounds. "The tuskless female is the most dangerous elephant in the clan," Richards said. "They're the aunties' who take care of the young. Messing with their charges is an affront to their reputations as baby sitters. It pisses the hell out of them."

It took Austin an hour to find his shotgun. He'd thrown it about thirty meters, three times the distance that he'd shot the elephant. Greg suggested Austin had first tried to poke the elephant's eye out with his shotgun. "Colonel, before I go elephant hunting with you again, I think you should practice throwing the javelin. You missed that sumbitch by a country mile."

Richards cut the tail and one ear off the elephant. "I know someone can make you a fly-whisk of the tail and a briefcase of the ear," he said. "Give the fly-whisk to a lady. It impresses the hell out of 'em."

"There is someone I'd like to impress," Austin said. By the time they'd cut the elephant up and sorted it all out, it was getting dark and they'd lost the spoor on the group they were following. Ncobe had lucked out, but the BSAP were later able to identify the terrorists in his stick.

The BSAP special weapons group boasted an identification section as good as any in the world. They could trace a weapon to a particular terrorist and to specific contacts. During the war, terrorists' crimes were treated as crimes against the people of Rhodesia. Terrs were tried in civilian court by prosecutors who used the expert testimony of the Police Identification Unit to gain convictions just as a district attorney might use a police lab in the U.S. By taking samples of fired rounds from every contact, and by sampling every captured weapon and cataloging this information for future use, the BSAP were able to tie individual weapons to particular terrorists.

The leader of the terrorist stick that killed Samantha had bayonetted the nanny while she was sitting in a chair. It is not easy to stick a bayonet in someone. It's not only hard to stick it in, it can be even harder to pull it back out. The terrorist leader evidently had trouble getting enough leverage to pull his bayonet out, so he fired a round, which is the customary way of retrieving a bayonet. This releases the bayonet by opening up a larger wound channel.

When he fired the round, the AK ejected a spent cartridge casing. This was the only round that had been fired at the Blake farm. The spent casing was sent to police headquarters where it was cataloged. "One of these days," Austin said to General Jamison the next time they got together, "we're going to pick up the terr whose rifle shot that bullet."

"When we do," Greg said, wetting his thin lips, "there are some games I'm going to teach him to play."

There was little consolation in these words for General Jamison. Overnight, the old warrior had become an old man.

As long as Matabele and Mashona were busy killing each other, they did little damage to the Rhodesian establishment. The isolated raids on farms and missions, the minor border skirmishes at Victoria Falls and Lake Kariba, the occasional train derailment and mined road were all routinely handled by the British South Africa Police.

The BSAP was formed under a charter given to Sir Cecil Rhodes by the British Government. Since there was no standing army, they were responsible for police work as well as military operations. When Rhodesia became a true colony, Parliament mandated it field a separate army. Prior to 1963, the BSAP argued that its resources were adequate to the problem, that it was not necessary to increase funding for the army, and that the BSAP could handle any internal 'incidents' without assistance from the armed forces.

In time, the military's role increased in scope and function. Sanctions made it somewhat difficult to acquire weapons and aircraft, but South Africa's air force guarded the southern border against infiltration by ANC guerrillas. Until 1974, the only border that had to be carefully patrolled was Zambia's. After Mozambique won independence from Portugal, however, FRELIMO cut off Rhodesia's supply route from Beira and provided a haven for terrorists. The sinuous, artificial border stretched Rhodesia's security forces.

In 1975, foolhardy Mashona gunmen attacked a Matabele gathering in Zambia, killing Zambians along with Matabele speakers on the platform. In reprisal, Zambia's President, Kenneth Kaunda, made the Mashona *persona non grata*, and Mugabe's forces were forced to relocate to Mozambique.

Who should now appear on the scene but the great egoist, Henry Kissinger, hawking shuttle diplomacy to a part of the world that wanted no part of it or of him. By pressuring South African Prime Minister Voerster to withhold Rhodesia's war supplies, Kissinger was able to force Ian Smith to the conference table. To rub salt in the wound, he also forced Smith to guarantee the safety of Mugabe and Nkomo, which was like guaranteeing the virtue of hookers at a Shriner's convention. Smith bit the bullet, and the first meeting was held in late 1975 at Victoria Falls in a railroad car on the Rhodesia-Zambian border. O'Brian suggested dumping the car off the bridge but General Walls couldn't come up with a plan to extricate Ian before the car hit the water, so Austin and Greg patrolled the area instead, keeping an eye on the train where Smith was meeting with Voerster, Mugabe and Nkomo just in case someone else thought of attacking it.

Before the follow-up meeting in Geneva in 1976, Ken Flowers learned that Robert Mugabe was planning to kill Joshua Nkomo, the man many Africans considered the father of the revolutionary movement in Rhodesia. Mugabe had once been publicity secretary of ZAPU, the Zimbabwe African People's Union, under Nkomo. ZAPU was outlawed in 1962, and Mugabe and Nkomo went their separate ways. Mugabe now thought Nkomo had sold out. The Fat Man, as he was tagged, had certainly slowed down, and Mugabe didn't want Smith to negotiate with him. Pernicious tribal animosity also played a role in Mugabe's decision to assassinate Nkomo.

Everyone in the Rhodesian government except Ian Smith thought assassination was a terrific idea. Smith, however, had guaranteed Nkomo's safety. A high-level meeting was called to discuss the situation.

Ken Flowers, the head of intelligence, met with Major General Hickman, General Walls, Colonel Austin and Lieutenant Colonel O'Brian in Ted Sutton-Price's office to examine options. Ken was afraid that the assassination would be blamed on Rhodesia. Hickman, so far as Austin could determine, thought they should all walk around with their fingers up their noses so the world could see they weren't hiding anything.

"Let's take him out ourselves," Austin suggested. "We'll make it look like ZANLA did it, which shouldn't be too difficult since Ken has proof they plan to try."

"It's pretty risky," O'Brian thought. "Why not just let ZANLA do it? Matabele and Mashona have been fighting for over a century. It's not our affair if they kill one another."

"Nkomo has rented a chateau in Geneva," Austin said. "If what I saw in Pungwe was any indication, Mugabe's men won't get within a block of it before the Fat Man's guards blow them out of the water."

"Then we've nothing to worry about," Hickman said. "Our hands are clean." He held his hands up. Walls looked at him with disgust.

"What if they get just close enough to botch it and we get blamed for it?" Flowers asked.

"That's precisely what I think will happen," General Walls said. "Mugabe's hitmen will be carrying papers identifying them as RAR or BSAP. Hit or miss, we get blamed."

"If we do it, at least we'll hit, so let's do it," Austin said cheerfully.

"No!" Flowers said, and Hickman echoed, "No."

Walls and O'Brian thought it was worth a go. Sutton-Price suggested they ask Smith.

"I don't think he should be involved," Austin said.

"Deniability is an American concept," Flowers sneered. "We don't go in for that sort of thing here, you know."

Austin wanted to share another American concept with him, namely a punch in the mouth, but he restrained himself. "I used to like you, Ken."

"That's neither here nor there!"

"Gentlemen, gentlemen!"

"Let's have some tea!"

"Now there's an idea!"

Ted had Mrs. Barrington prepare tea while he sought Ian Smith's opinion. When he returned, he said to Austin, "The Prime Minister wants you to accompany him to Switzerland."

"All right!" Austin boomed, clapping Flowers on the shoulder just to show there were no hard feelings.

"It's not what you think. He wants you to ensure that nothing happens to Mr. Nkomo," Ted continued.

"Say again."

"Ian has guaranteed Nkomo's safety. He is honour-bound to do whatever he can to see that Mugabe fails in his attempt to kill him, and he believes you are the very man for the job."

Flowers lifted an eyebrow, murmured, "Poetic justice," and left the room before Austin could think of a retort.

And so, for the next three weeks, Austin and two lieutenants seconded from Walls' staff kept Nkomo under surveillance in Geneva. Sixteen hours sitting in a Mercedes, eight hours of fitful sleep at a pension across the street from Nkomo's chateau, Austin and his crew watched bodyguards watching bodyguards and played spy and counter-spy in a house of mirrors. When negotiations were underway, everyone hung out in the lobby of the hotel and practiced looking inconspicuous and made note of their inconspicuous counterparts. Had Peter Lorre and Sidney Greenstreet suddenly appeared, they would have fit right in.

The only noteworthy incident during the three week's stay was when the kitchen in Nkomo's villa caught fire. The lieutenant on the early morning shift discovered it and summoned the fire department which quickly put it out. "Funny way to assassinate somebody," he said to Austin.

"Just a coincidence," Austin replied. Whatever it was, the incident made Nkomo's bodyguards nervous and they maintained constant vigil over the Fat Man. Nothing else remotely suspicious occurred. Perhaps Mugabe knew the Rhodesians were watching and called off his killers, Austin figured.

Nothing noteworthy came of the negotiations either. Nkomo demanded unconditional surrender; Smith told him where to shove it; and Austin returned to Rhodesia where isolated incidents had begun sparking ominous guerrilla activity. By year's end it was civil war.

However, Austin had something more immediate to deal with. In his absence, Greg Andrews had gotten himself arrested for killing three generations of females: baby, mother and grandmother.

The Superintendent where Greg was being held refused to release him on Austin's say-so. "The locals are rather distressed by the incident." he said.

"The *locals* are distressed?" Austin shouted into the receiver. "You son of a bitch, do you know who I am?"

"Yes, sir, but without written authorization I cannot—"

"If my man isn't released immediately, and transport to Salisbury arranged forthwith, I'll have you digging latrines in Bulawayo tomorrow. Do you understand?"

"Yes, sir."

Greg sauntered in several hours later. "Thanks, Colonel," he said.

"What in hell happened, Sergeant? Better make it good."

"I was hunting, Colonel, down near the Sabi. It was after curfew in a 'no go' area and I saw these floppies coming out of the bush and it looked like they were wearing backpacks. All I could see were their silhouettes. I figured them for CTs and blew them away. On closer inspection I saw that one was carrying a child on her back and the other was hauling firewood. It was an honest mistake."

"Did you explain that to the Superintendent?"

"Yeah, I explained it to him, but the fucker doesn't like Americans or something. I think the Peace Corps is giving us a bad name."

The next day everyone in the Earl Gray Building was talking about how Greg was fighting the enemy by doing away with their breeding stock.

Greg had committed no crime since any African caught after curfew in a 'no-go' area was assumed to be a terrorist and could be shot, no questions asked, but Austin decided to rein in his handsome young aide before his exploits were front page news. Greg made light of the incident. "Do you know what Afrikaners get away with in Johannesburg?"

They were having drinks at the bar in the Ambassador Hotel one slow night and no one was within earshot. "This is not South Africa, Greg," Austin said sternly, but the crew-cut Sergeant was irrepressible. "Stop me if you've heard this one. These two Kaffirs are walking along the road outside Que-Que when an Afrikaner farmer spots them, levels his rifle and blasts both of 'em to kingdom come. His friend Fritz says, 'Ach, Hans, why did you shoot them Kaffirs? It's half an hour yet before curfew.'

"Fritz says, 'Yah, Hans, but I know them Kaffirs and they'd've never made it home in time.' "

Austin was trying to maintain his stern expression

when Kitty Canty walked into the bar on the arm of a well-dressed black man. "Jesus H. Christ," Austin said.

Greg looked up and the smile froze on his face. "Hey, you!" Greg shouted at the black man. "Come here, Kaffir!"

"Up yours!" Kitty shouted back.

"A white man would cut it off before he put anything up yours, bitch!" Greg said slowly, the grin still etched on his face. He looked the black man up and down, daring him to make a move. Kitty said something to her companion. He laughed and whispered something back. Greg crooked his finger at the bartender. "You serve them a drink, you'll never see me in this place again," he said, "you hear me?"

The bartender looked helplessly at Austin, who put his hand on the younger man's arm. "Cool it, Greg," he said. "It's not worth it."

"Let's get out of here, sir." Greg said.

"It's all right. They're going."

The reporter and her companion were talking about the lack of suitable ambiance and discussing alternate venues. Kitty took the black man's arm and, as she left the bar, she looked back at Greg and hissed, "When I finish with you, you're going to wish Kitty Canty had never heard of Colonel Austin or Corporal Andrews."

"Corporal!" This time Austin had to wrap his arms around Greg to prevent him from running after the laughing couple.

"She can't bust you, Greg, but keep it up and I just might."

"Can that bitch do anything?" Greg asked when he'd regained his control.

"Not much. One of the better ideas the English gave Rhodesia is the "D" notice, which is censorship at its best. Nothing that woman writes will ever be printed in this country. The *New York Times* is another matter."

"Nobody I know reads that commie paper."

"Then let her write whatever she wants and be damned," Austin said without conviction, for neither he nor his bosses needed any more bad press.

In late 1976, stung by Mugabe's accusations that ZIPRA was dogging it and not participating in the war effort, Nkomo authorized a series of violent attacks by the same gang responsible for the murder of the Blake baby. Mission schools, hospitals and clinics were targeted to intimidate the locals so that they would not use the mission's services. Nkomo did not realize, or did not consider it important, that many of the clinics and hospitals treated wounded terrorists and protected them from the Defense Forces. The Special Branch knew about it but had no hard proof.

Ted told Austin about one mission clinic in particular where a white doctor was suspected of treating wounded terrorists. "Without proof, we couldn't arrest her, so we tried to trap her. We sent in a wounded RAR man dressed as a terrorist, but she twigged and asked him who'd sent him. Since African soldiers are taught not to lie to a white, he had to admit he was with the RAR. She then refused to treat him despite the Hippocratic oath because, as she told him, he was a member of the 'Smith regime.' The African's wounds were real, mind you. The poor bugger had really been shot, but she absolutely refused to help him." Ted pushed a sheet of paper across his desk for Austin to examine. "She got hers, though."

"What do you mean?" Austin asked, speed-reading through the report.

"That stick of terrorists you've been looking for raped her and killed her day before yesterday. We just got a ballistics report from BSAP."

"That's the second clinic Ncobe's hit this week," Austin said, worn out after a week of being one step behind the renegade Constable. He removed a file from his elephant's ear briefcase and said, "At St Paul's Mission hospital near Lupane, a Dr. Decker and Sister Ploner were taken out of the hospital in full view of their patients, raped, and then murdered. Only a short time later, his group stopped a car near the Mission and forced the occupants out onto the road. Sister Frances was raped and mutilated while Bishop Schmitt and Father Weggarten were forced to watch. After Sister Frances was no longer able to respond to their demands, all three were shot and left on the road as a lesson to the local tribesmen."

"It would be funny if it weren't so damned tragic," Ted said. "St Paul's was noted for its care of African maternity patients and, ironically enough, Dr. Decker had also treated several wounded terrorists and had aided them in escaping follow-up operations of the Defense Forces. The bastards are killing off the only whites stupid enough to treat them."

A few weeks later, Ted called Austin on the phone. "It's not your boy, but I thought I'd let you know that Mugabe, not to be outdone by your Constable, ordered one of his groups to beat Nkomo at his bestial game. I just got a report from Musami."

"Christ, what happened this time?"

"Some brave ZANLA terrorists walked into the Musami Mission in Mashonaland and raped and murdered five nuns, while forcing five priests to watch at bayonet point before killing them. The BSAP killed two of 'em. We've got eye witnesses. Neukirk's holding a press conference. Want to have a look?"

"Yeah." *Planted in rows and harvested like wheat.*

"I'll call for a chopper and meet you at the airstrip in ten minutes."

The Musami Mission stank of death. Drunk on blood, the flies reeled and dropped and landed on their backs and couldn't right themselves. When Austin entered, Kitty was asking a black Sergeant Major how he could possibly kill his own people on the orders of his white superiors. Swearing, Greg started to push his way up front so he could confront her, but Austin was able to drag him outside. "You stay there, Sergeant, or I'll have you tied up. You hear me?"

"Yes, sir. I was just—"

Austin went back inside where all eyes were riveted on the Sergeant Major who, stamping to attention, replied in a great, booming voice, "Madam, what do you think my people have been doing for thousands of years, long before the white man came to Africa?"

"What do you mean?"

"You did not teach us to kill. If the white man leaves Africa tomorrow, we will continue to kill one another as we have always done."

"I bet she won't print *that*," he said to Greg after the press conference. "Let's go over to the station and see if they've identified the perpetrators."

The officer on duty reported they hadn't anything new, although they were holding a houseboy for lying.

"About what?" Austin asked.

"I'll make him talk," Greg said.

"I've had just about enough out of you," Austin admonished him before turning back to the constable. "Does it have anything to do with the attack on the mission."

"No, sir. It's really nothing," the officer said. "It's just a joke."

"Tell us about it. After what I've just seen, I can use a good laugh," Austin said.

"Yes, sir. You see, before the attack on the mission there'd been no activity at all. Our Section Officer had been around to check the station and all we had was this houseboy the Sergeant Major had arrested. Our Section Officer is quite a card, Colonel, so when he saw the houseboy shaking like a dog shitting peach seeds, he says, 'This Kaffir looks like a hardened criminal. What's he done?'

" 'Sah,' the Sergeant Major says, stamping his feet and coming to attention, 'we caught this chap riding his bicycle without a light.'

" 'Without a light, eh?' he says and shakes his head as if the world is coming to an end. 'That's a very serious offense,' the Section Officer says to the houseboy, 'd'you know that?'

"The houseboy figures it's all over for him and he throws himself on the mercy of the court. 'This boy not a bad boy, mastuh. This boy, he just a foolish boy.'

"The Section Officer proceeds to lecture the Kaffir at great length. 'It is very dangerous to ride a bicycle at night without a light.'

" 'Yassuh, mastuh,' the boy says. 'This boy nevuh do this thing again.'

" 'That's right,' says the Section Officer, 'because the penalty for riding a bicycle without a light is death by hanging. Sergeant Major, get a rope.'

" 'Sah?'

" 'You heard me. Get a rope.'

" 'Yes, sah!' and the Sergeant Major stomps his boots and goes to get a rope. The Section Officer grabs a chair, takes the houseboy by the scruff of his coat, and drags him outside. 'Do you know why it is such a terrible thing that you have done?'

" 'No mastuh. If I knowed, I'd nevuh, I swear—'

" 'Stop sniveling! Don't you know you could cause a white person to hurt himself? He could be driving and not see you and wreck his car running over your bicycle. Did you think of that when you went out for your joyride?'

" 'Mastuh, this bicycle was not my bicycle. I nevuh have such a bicycle—'

" 'It's too late for tears. Justice must be served,' the Section Officer says. 'Stand up on this chair and take your medicine like a man.' Sniffling and protesting, the houseboy stands on the chair which has been placed under a tree. The Section Officer tosses one end of the rope over a branch and puts the other end around the boy's neck. The African is trying to plead his case, it wasn't his bicycle, he works for a white master who lives just down the road, please call him and check, but no one is listening to him and the Kaffir doesn't see that the rope isn't really tied around the branch but looped over it with the other end in the Section Officer's hand. When he kicks the chair away and lets go of the rope, the African houseboy falls on his ass and the rope burns his neck. 'Now you walk your bicycle home, you hear?' the Section Officer tells him 'and don't let us catch you riding your bike without a light on again, 'cause next time we'll hang your black ass, you hear?'

" 'Yes, mastuh,' he says and bugs on out of there as fast as his feet will carry him."

"That's funny!" Greg howled.

"I thought you said you arrested the houseboy for lying," Austin said.

"I'm coming to that part. You see, the next day he's at work and the master of the house notices the rope burn on his neck and asks him what happened. The houseboy tells him what happened and, bam, the master knocks him right on his ass for lying to him, bounces his butt off the floor and fires him, so the African gets up and comes here hoping I'll confirm what happened and he'll get his job back."

"Now, I'm only here during the day shift, but I couldn't believe the gall of this Kaffir bastard trying to make trouble for a Section Officer and a Sergeant Major, so I tossed him in jail. I plan on keeping him locked up until he confesses that he made the whole thing up."

"That's funnier'n shit," Greg laughed. "I got one for you. This really happened. I heard it from Sergeant Richards. These two floppies are walking down Whiddecombe Road and they're a little drunk. A police car comes by and accidentally brushes one of them, and the other says, 'Lie down like you're hurt and we'll get some money from the man for sure.'

"The other one thinks it's too risky. 'Thass the po-lice; they gonna throw us in jail they find out we're lying.'

" 'How they gonna fine out? They's got assurance. It don't never mine to the govimint. We's gonna get money from thems.'

"So they're arguing and calculating and one floppy is lying on the ground and the other is watching the police car and giving the one on the ground last-minute instructions. The police car slows down; it turns around; now it's heading back. The floppy on the ground has his face scrunched up like he's in great pain. The other one is watching and talking and not looking the other way and a bus comes and runs over the guy lying on the ground, thump-thump, thump-thump. Kills the fucker."

"Road kill," The officer laughed. "A Kaffir'll eat road kill if it's fresh."

They all had a good laugh about that, and Austin and Greg went home in high spirits. Later that week, Austin bought a copy of the *Times* and was amused but not surprised to see that Kitty had not seen fit to print the Sergeant Major's words. What really astonished him, however, was reading that the World Council of Churches had suggested that possibly the Musami atrocities were the work of Government troops dressed as terrorists.

"What in hell is this world coming to?" he asked himself as he made his way out to the firing range. There were three gun clubs in Salisbury, two of which used the same range. Austin enjoyed competitive shooting and when he wasn't on ops could be frequently found practicing alongside other members of Rhodesia's military and diplomatic community.

There was a good deal of talk but not much shooting going on when Austin arrived. Brigit Wolfe was looking for someone to teach her how to shoot, and the competition was fierce to help her steady her aim. Second Lieutenant Philip Thornberry, a handsome and gallant man who bore a marked resemblance to Erroll Flynn and was an excellent marksman as well, had the upper hand but wisely bowed out when Austin showed interest. Since he was not only a better shot but outranked Thornberry and all the other would-be instructors, Austin tucked the shapely blonde away and taught her the difference between squeezing and jerking. It was only natural they continue discussing firing mechanisms over dinner.

Brigit's accent was as sweet as the trigger on her Smith & Wesson Model 19 .357 magnum. The gun had never been fired and, since new guns in Rhodesia were rare as rocking horse shit, what with sanctions and all, he asked her how she'd come to possess it.

"By post," she said. "My brother sent it from Germany. It is a good one, is it not?"

"It'll keep the wolf from your door all right."

She laughed. "You are very clever to make a joke on my name."

"I can do a few things," Austin smiled suggestively.

"I want to hear all about it," Brigit said, peering at him over her glass of champagne.

"Most of it can't be described. It must be demonstrated to be appreciated."

"You will find me an apt student." She wrinkled her nose. "Is it correct to say 'apt'?"

"It's music in my ears."

"No, I speak funny. I know I do."

He took her home and kissed her good night, but she wouldn't let him inside for a nightcap. Next day, he checked her out and found nothing to contradict what she'd told him. Her father was retired and living in the wine country in France. He'd been a Panzer Colonel in the German Army. Her brother was a successful West German merchant living in Berlin. Brigit had attended university in South Africa and had recently moved to Salisbury. She was single, twenty-six, and round in all the right places.

She lived in a small apartment house owned by a BSAP widow not far from the Milton Building where she worked. She played a furious game of tennis and loved

Indian food. They started dating. He didn't discuss his marital status with her, and she didn't ask. He gave her the elephant flywhisk for her birthday and they both had a bit too much to drink and made love in the back seat of the BMW in the parking lot of the Monomatapa Hotel while Greg drank Canadian and Coke at the bar and waited for them to finish.

6

Africa's fourth longest river, the Zambezi flows through the second largest man-made lake in the world, Lake Kariba. In 1976, the scenic river marked the border between Rhodesia and Zambia and was a hostile and defended war zone.

Reports from Special Branch kept coming in about a bunker on the Zambian side of the river, a machine-gun emplacement that was blasting Rhodesian fishing boats. Fish from the Zambezi provided the main source of protein for natives living on the river's edge, but the fishermen had become sitting ducks for the terrorist hunters.

There'd even been complaints from honeymooners at Victoria Falls, and Ted Sutton-Price wanted General Walls to do something about it. "It's not reasonable to expect tourists to dodge bullets," he said at a meeting called to discuss options. "It's just not *on*, old boy."

Colonel O'Brian offered a solution as effective as it was inelegant: "The SAS will use the area as a remedial training ground and a couple of their chaps will drop a bomb in the aperture of the bunker one dark night."

"What about world opinion?" Flowers demanded. "We're not in a state of war with Zambia; we can't just *bomb* them, now can we?" As usual, Major General Hickman agreed with Flowers while Walls sided with O'Brian.

"What other options have we, chaps?" Ted asked, eager to settle the matter so he could make it over to Borrowdale by post time.

"We could take an Eland armored car to the river's edge and put one well placed 90mm HEAT round in the bunker," Austin suggested.

"Good show!" General Walls shouted. "Save on petrol as well."

"Rather messy, wouldn't you say?" Flowers commented archly.

"And if the press found out," Hickman said, horrified at the thought, "they'd make it look like a full-scale attack against Zambia."

"If Kaunda were half as concerned about the press as you are," Walls said, "he wouldn't be taking pot shots at innocent fishermen."

"Gentlemen, gentlemen," Ted said, checking his watch.

"If you want the job done quickly and cleanly," Austin said, "I'd like to suggest we take out the gunner surgically with a sniper."

"We can't do that," Flowers said. "We'd have to put our man on their side of the border. Why if he were captured—"

"The press would have our scalps," Hickman said, nervously fingering his sideburns."

"What if it could be done from our side?" Austin asked.

"If it could," Ted said, "I think it would be a go, don't you, gentlemen?"

"What do you have in mind, Colonel?" O'Brian asked.

"General Jamison showed me a state-of-the-art device at King George VI: a World War II German artillery rangefinder."

"Hardly state of the art," was Hickman's opinion.

"Don't underestimate German optics," Ted said. "Carry on, Colonel."

"It's really a fine instrument, split-focus, about nine feet between optics, a very accurate range finder. If I can borrow it, General, I'll take it to the border and see if I can pinpoint the bunker."

"By all means!" Walls said.

Turning to Hickman, Austin said, "I've watched Lieutenant Thornberry perform on the range, General. He's an excellent shot. Would you mind if he came along with me?"

"I most certainly would," Hickman bristled. "My people are much too valuable to go swanning around the countryside doing little funnies."

"Now, General," Sutton-Price said, but Austin stopped him.

"That's all right, Ted. I'll do it myself."

"Waste of time, if you ask my opinion," Hickman said.

"Then it's settled, gentlemen," Sutton-Price said, rising. The meeting was over and he was off to the races.

After picking up the range finder at King George VI, Greg drove over to Austin's suburban house. He was staying there, too, in a furnished apartment beside the main house. It was certainly big enough—ten rooms on an acre of land—and barracks life at King George's had grown old.

They drove south to Bulawayo, then west to Wankie where they spent the night. Early the next morning they drove to Livingstone on the Zambezi and before noon had located the bunker on the opposite shore. It was 645 meters from the best vantage point on the Rhodesian side to the gun-port in the bunker. The 12.7mm machine gun controlled the river, and the Zambians were not the least bit shy about laying down a barrage at any boat that came within their considerable range.

The machine gun was a crew-served weapon. "It'd be nice if we could take out the gunner and loader at the same time," Austin said.

"That's tougher than hippo hide, Colonel. We'd both have to fire simultaneously at targets 650 meters away, precisely when the upper torso of both soldiers are visible at the same time. It might take a week for conditions to be right."

"Piece of cake, old boy," Austin said, sorry now he hadn't allowed Ted to pressure Hickman. Lieutenant Thornberry was a much better rifle shot than Greg.

"My sentiments exactly, Colonel. When we do start?"

"Day after tomorrow. Let's drive back to Salisbury tonight, pick up our weapons and supplies, and treat ourselves to a good dinner. How's that sound to you?"

"Sounds good to me," Greg said.

The next day, Austin selected his favorite long range rifle, a Ruger Number 1 in 7mm Magnum with a 4X12 Redfield scope. His handloads would consistently produce sub-minute of angle groups at 100 meters. Greg chose a .338 Magnum built on a Winchester pre-64 action with a Douglas Premium Match Barrel and a Leupold 12X target scope.

Since they knew the exact range involved, they set about zeroing their weapons at the rifle range for the exact distance. It was a windless day and, using the same sandbag dead rests they'd be using for the operation, they were able to keep all their shots in the head and upper-shoulder region of their standard L type target.

Early the following morning, they drove back to the Zambezi River, and that evening they constructed a hide of branches and mud. They worked in the dark so as not to alert their friends on the other side of the river. Their handiwork was crude, although pre-teens would have applauded their efforts, and they stumbled and cursed and laughed and fell and had as good a time as any pair of eight year old boys would have building a fort in the woods at night. Then they went into town for a shower and a beer and a few hours sleep.

They returned well before dawn with provisions and weapons, insect repellent and settled in for what turned out to be a three-day wait with minimal creature comforts.

Since the gunner presented less of a target, Austin decided that he would take the gunner, while Greg concentrated on the loader/observer, firing on Austin's shot. This meant that both targets would have to present themselves at the same time, and the duo across the river positively refused to cooperate. First one, then the other, played lookout: they were taking turns sleeping at the bottom of their bunker, Austin concluded. After three days cramped inside a filthy hide, sweating, cursing and telling the same Afrikaner jokes over and over, Austin was determined to find a better way. Not a single boat had sailed by. "Look, Greg, even the fish are nervous. They keep jumping out of the water to see what's going on."

"We could calm them down by throwing some worms at them."

"The worms would drown."

"Not if we hooked them to a line and checked on them every now and then."

"I've got a better idea. Let's go into town for a beer and consultation with Special Branch."

That night, Austin talked with a Special Branch officer named Fitzgerald in the JOC pub. Over a couple of pints, Austin outlined the problem. "There's no traffic on that bloody river."

"Right as rain, mate," Fitzgerald said. "Bloody Kaffirs may be ignorant, but they're not dumb. Every time they go out fishing, the bloody terrs strafe their arses. Now, none of 'em 'll go out. Can't say I bloody well blame 'em.''

"Well, we're tired of waiting around. Find us a few fisherfolk who'll go fishing tomorrow at, say, 1000 hours. That'll put the sun just right for us."

"How in hell am I going to do that, Colonel?"

"I don't give a damn how you do it, just do it! Try *bonsella*, you've got money you don't have to account for. Try intimidation. How long've you lived in this bloody country?"

"I'm from Salisbury," Fitzgerald said. "I've just been posted here temporarily."

"Do you like it?"

"Hell, no! There's nothing to do here."

"Find us some bait or I guarantee you'll retire here. You'll never get back to Salisbury."

"I'll do my best, Colonel."

By daybreak the next morning, Austin and Greg were settled in their hide and looking forward to a more fruitful day than the previous three. "Do you smell something, Colonel?"

"Just us."

"It's pretty bad, sir."

"What's that?"

"What, sir?"

"Listen! Do you hear an outboard motor?"

"Couldn't be, sir. None of the fishermen have outboards."

Austin almost jumped out of the hide. "Jesus, I bet it's a tourist!" He raised himself on one elbow and peeked out. "It will not look good in the international press to lose a couple of West German tourists. If they get caught in a crossfire, they will not appreciate that we've been stinking up this place for three days just so that they might enjoy their vacation."

"You sound just like General Hickman."

"General Hickman would insist we hold our fire. I have absolutely no compunction about wasting a couple of German tourists if it means not having to spend another day in this hole with you."

"How about two tourists from Dubuque and a nun from Kilkenny?"

"That's not funny. Tourists from Dubuque are not like trading stamps. If they are shot at, they will write nasty letters to the *Rhodesian Herald* and *Bulawayo Chronicle*. They will not just laugh it off the way German tourists might or the way a nun from Kilkenny would. General Hickman will not laugh it off, and neither will Ken Flowers. No, they will demand explanations in triplicate. They will demand someone to throw to the wolves. I will give them you. Kitty Canty will thank me for it."

"That bitch! You keep her . . . Colonel, look, our friends are stirring." They could see the boat now, a 16-foot police boat with a small cabin midship, and the opposition was tracking it and making ready to fire.

"Can you see who's in the boat?"

"Yeah, wait, hey, it's that Special Branch guy. He's all scrunched up behind the wheel, but he still makes a pretty good target. I guess he couldn't find a fisherman dumb enough to troll for bullets."

"They make mighty tough eating," Austin chuckled as he took careful aim.

"Look at that bastard move! I didn't think a police boat could move that fast," Greg said, also taking aim. "Hey, now he's steering on his bloody knees. Are you ready?"

"Just wait for me." Austin took a deep breath, let it half out, and squeezed the trigger. In less than a heartbeat, he heard the .338 echo the 7mm.

The police boat almost crashed into the bank, but Fitzgerald looked up just in time and corrected his course. Then he waved and gave them the thumbs-up sign.

"We got 'em!" Greg shouted. "We got 'em both!"

And so they had. General Walls and Special Branch were overjoyed. Even General Hickman was pleased and went so far as to suggest that Austin use Lieutenant Thornberry next time a funny needed doing. Happiest of all was Section Officer Marvin Fitzgerald. For his uncommon valor, he was promoted to Superintendent and transferred to Special Branch Headquarters in Salisbury.

One evening while Austin and Greg were swapping lies with members of the Police Anti-Terrorist Unit (PATU) for Salisbury, a call came in from Special Branch reporting that a pair of ZANLA terrorists were holed up in a house in Harare, the black township outside Salisbury.

"Would PATU be kind enough to come sort them out," the Special Branch officer inquired.

"Just now, mate," the police officer responded. "Colonel Austin would you care to come along to see how professionals handle this sort of thing?"

"I wouldn't miss it for the world."

Greg followed the PATU unit through the narrow streets of the black township. They could feel hundreds of eyes on them but saw no one. Most of the homes were of brick construction with the living area, kitchen and dining room open to the front yard. Most were two bedroom homes with one bathroom, solidly constructed but not ornate. Some were overcrowded, some were defaced, but most were in good repair.

On each side of the front doors were windows facing the street, and all the windows were equipped with burglar bars, which made getting in or out through them quite difficult. The back doors looked out over empty lots. There were no alleys or streets behind these homes.

In addition to the team leader, the PATU team consisted of four Section Officers. The weapons available to the police were the same as those available to the army, so Austin was interested in seeing which weapons the police chose for the operation. The team leader carried an FN rifle. Two of his men carried Uzi submachine guns and two carried Browning automatic shotguns. Not a grenade was in sight.

Austin carried two fragmentation grenades and two white phosphorus grenades in his car, as well as his normal compliment of weapons. He offered the grenades to the PATU unit but was told rather huffily that had they wanted grenades, they would have brought grenades!

"I can take a hint," he said.

"Then would you two mind standing back, old chaps?"

"Not at all." Greg and Austin stood behind a Land Rover with the team leader and watched the action unfold like a bad dream.

Two men were sent to the rear of the house to cover the back door and windows. One was armed with an Uzi and the other with a shotgun. This left two men to cover the front of the house, with the team leader giving overall coverage and direction. The front-door man opened festivities by knocking on the door, while his partner stood aside so that any rounds fired through the door would probably miss him.

"Are they going after terrorists or jay-walkers?" Greg whispered to Austin.

"Ssshh!" Austin cautioned.

"You in there, this is the police," the officer called out, "come out with your hands in the air." No one appeared, but the lights went out in the house.

"Did you notice," Greg said, "he didn't say 'Simon says'?"

"I noticed," Austin said, feeling edgy.

At that moment they heard the sound of breaking glass and the officer on the left side of the door cried out, "Grenade!" and threw himself flat on the ground. A heartbeat later, his associate on the other side of the door lunged for the ground. The explosion followed almost immediately. The officer closest to the blast was peppered with grenade fragments from feet to shoulder, while the other officer suffered only a slight concussion from the explosion. Fortunately, the terrorists were using Chinese fragmentation grenades, which were much less lethal than the grenades used by the RDF.

A burst of gunfire sounded from the rear of the house immediately after the grenade had exploded in front. The cadence of an AK on full auto, which was the only way the terrs knew how to use the AK, was followed by the deep-throated roar of the 12 bore and the distinct ripping sound of the Uzi. Everyone was in on the action, and it sounded like Chinese New Years. Then, in less than a minute, all was quiet.

After the grenade had gone off, effectively silencing half the force, Greg headed for the left corner of the house and Austin headed for the right, so they could offer covering fire down both sides of the house while watching the front.

Suddenly, one of the terrorists kicked the back door open and ran straight out, firing at random and hitting nothing, for the officers covering the back of the house were hidden from view. The gunman took ten or twelve steps and cut sharply to his left. Another terrorist came out on his heels, took half a dozen steps and turned right.

The first guerrilla's burst had sprayed in the general direction of the officer carrying the Uzi. Being a prudent chap, he dropped flat to the ground and didn't see the terr cut and run toward him until he had already run past, but when he finally saw the African he hit him with a twenty round burst. The second terrorist through the door cut directly towards the officer carrying the Browning 12-bore, and that stalwart fired two rounds of buckshot directly into the chest of the terrorist, ruining his whole day.

Now, the team leader asked Greg if he would help his men clear the house, and Greg, always anxious to get a lick in, jumped into the fray and pulled out a very frightened man and woman.

An ambulance was summoned for the officers injured in the explosion, and the regular police took over site operations. Greg and Austin rejoined their hosts back at headquarters for a couple of cool ones.

"Well, mate, what'd you think of the manner in which we handled the situation?" the team leader asked Austin, which was fortunate because Greg lacked tact at times like this.

"In that Sergeant Andrews and I are outnumbered better than ten to one," Austin smiled, "I will only say that I would have handled it in a slightly different manner."

"Is that so?" a Section Officer said icily. "Perhaps you might do us the honour of sharing some of your military expertise next time a similar situation arises."

"A professional soldier knows better than to volunteer," Austin said, in an effort to let the team leader off the hook.

Like Greg, the leader lacked tact. "You wouldn't be afraid, now would you?"

Greg was out of his chair like a shot, but Austin held him back. "Well, now that you're asking so nicely," he smiled, "how can I refuse? Don't hesitate to call when you'd like a lesson in the army way of handling urban guerrillas."

"That's a noble gesture, Colonel," the team leader said, "and I can assure you that you will be given the opportunity to demonstrate your superiority in the near future, if you are still so inclined."

The challenge could not go unanswered. "I gladly accept, with one condition."

"And what might that be?"

"If you call, I'm in command, and the operation will be undertaken the army way."

There was much hooting and hollering and, after finishing their beer, Greg and Austin left the premises.

The next day Austin told Lieutenant Thornberry what had transpired. "I'd really appreciate your assistance, if and when we're called upon to demonstrate our superior techniques," Austin said.

"If it's all right with General Hickman, you can count me in," the swashbuckling Second Lieutenant said. "And for a fourth, may I suggest Sergeant Major Halverson?"

"If he's willing," Austin said.

"You can count on that."

Since honor was involved, Major General Hickman offered no objection to Austin's seconding Thornberry and Halverson, although he did allow that it was all highly unusual and rather common. "Bloody Americans!" he muttered when he thought Austin was out of earshot.

Greg was responsible for gathering the equipment that would be required, if and when they were called. Thornberry and Halverson shared Greg's enthusiasm, but Austin felt that the chances of actually being asked to participate in a police operation were rather slim. However, he was not aware how seriously he'd wounded police pride. They were as eager to test army mettle as Austin's stick was to demonstrate their superiority.

A few weeks went by and then one day he received a call from Harold Brookings, a Chief Superintendent of Police, the man in overall command of the PATU units in the Salisbury operational area. "Special Branch has informed us that a group of terrs is coming into Harare to meet with a political officer. I'm told you have agreed to share your expertise with us. We don't require assistance, of course, but if you're interested in demonstrating the army's superior training and tactics I, for one, would be most interested in observing."

"Delighted to be of service, old chap" Austin said, calling him "old chap" out of sheer malice. "What's the purpose of the meeting?"

"From what Special Branch tells me," Brookings said, "it's a ZANLA recruiting party. We gather that one of the terrorists is supposed to be rather high ranking. We wouldn't want to let him slip out of our grasp, you know."

"Don't worry about a thing," Austin said, and put his people on alert. Two days later the call came.

The normal army stick, which is the basic fighting unit in Rhodesia, consists of four men including the stick commander. Austin decided to use a four-man stick for the operation, even though the police had used five men, which would have been safer. The house warming party consisted of Sergeant Major Halverson, a battle-hardened leather-skinned man of thirty; Second Lieutenant Philip Thornberry, the debonair marksman; Sergeant Greg Andrews, cold and blue-eyed; and sharp-shooting Colonel Joe Austin.

Taking personal command of this type of operation demonstrated Colonel Austin's complete lack of command responsibility, but army pride and honor were at stake and he knew he'd have an audience as large as security and secrecy would allow.

Austin's team met Chief Superintendent Brookings and his people at the Police Mess, where the gauntlet had been thrown and accepted. He was briefed by Superintendent Fitzgerald of Special Branch, who confirmed that there were at least four terrorists, plus locals, present in the house. "Is this information one-hundred percent confirmed?" Austin asked. "I don't want innocent people hurt."

Now it was Special Branch pride that was wounded. "I can assure you, Colonel, the terrorists' presence is confirmed."

They drove to Harare in three cars, two Land Rovers and Austin's BMW. The police had surreptitiously sealed off the area in case their presence was discovered before there was time to neutralize the house and its occupants.

Austin sent Greg to the back of the house. The young American was carrying his favorite close-range weapon, a Browning 12-bore automatic shotgun with magazine extension, loaded with eight rounds of Special SG buckshot. Lieutenant Thornberry was carrying a Beretta submachine gun, and Austin carried a Jumbo automatic 12-bore shotgun. The Sergeant Major was armed with a standard FN rifle, but one slightly different from that carried by the team leader during the police raid in Harare in that on the end of his FN was an Energa rifle grenade originally designed to take out tanks and armored personnel carriers.

The wooden front door presented little challenge. Austin gave the signal and the Sergeant Major fired the grenade at the front door. Wham! The entire door disappeared. A few seconds later, a second grenade was fired through the opening made by the first. This grenade was white phosphorus, and it burst against the back wall, scattering thousands of flakes of burning phosphorus over every inch of the open area in the house.

After the white phosphorus grenade went off, Austin started to count. "One, two, three, four, let's go!" On the run, Austin led Thornberry through the blasted door. Then he went left and Thornberry took the right side of the room and came face-to-face with three stunned terrorists.

The Energa rifle grenade had shocked everyone in the open area, and white phosphorus was burning everywhere. Thornberry opened fire immediately and promptly dispatched all three terrorists with bursts from his Beretta. Facing Austin was the biggest African he'd ever seen. Time stopped. Austin looked at the man with amazement. Every terrorist he'd previously encountered was quite slim. Smoke was swirling around and through it Austin watched the terrorist slowly raise his AK. Their eyes met, time returned, and Austin blew the African against the livingroom wall.

As the big terr fell, Austin saw three of his associates scuttling along the floor, trying to recover from the concussion of the blast so they could level their AKs at the two white apparitions that had abruptly and rudely entered their lives. A double-tap on the shotgun saved two of them the trouble. The third was now crouched in the far left corner of the room with his mouth open. He was trying to scream, but no sound was coming out. Phosphorus covered much of his upper body; he was glowing with it. Austin put an end to his pain with another shotgun blast. Alert for movement, he stepped quickly through the house behind the shotgun. Nothing moved.

The entire operation had taken less than a minute. From the moment Austin had given the word to fire the first rifle grenade, until they were all back in front of the house, fifty seconds had elapsed. Greg had not fired a round and was royally pissed off.

Expecting a hearty round of congratulations, if not a rousing cheer, Austin turned to acknowledge the police officers' admiration. He had accomplished no less than what his comrades in arms had accomplished, but without casualties and in less time. But there were no congratulations, no "Jolly well done, old chap." Instead there were glares that would freeze fire, angry grimaces, approbation and disgust.

As the smoke settled and sirens grew louder, the army and the police almost came to blows. Fitzgerald had to keep them apart. "It's all right! It's all over! Stand back!"

Later, at a grim victory celebration, Austin said, "If they wanted prisoners, why didn't they say so?"

"I guess they do things differently in the police," Greg said.

"I bet they don't ask us to demonstrate the army's 'door-opening' techniques again," Halverson said.

"I think they learned the first time," Austin agreed. "After all, a good teacher should only have to explain things once."

"Did you get a make on that big floppy?" Austin asked Superintendent Fitzgerald of Special Branch.

"We did. Washobe was his name. Trained in China, he was one of Mugabe's political officers."

"What does a political officer do?"

"Recites quotations from Chairman Mao. He's the communist equivalent of a witch doctor."

"Maybe that's what the BSAP needs," Austin laughed, "a police witch doctor. He'll put a big pot of boiling water in front of a CT hooch, knock on the door and all the terrs will run out and dive in."

"Don't let them get to you," Fitzgerald said.

If the police found Austin's methods impolite, less direct methods of solving Rhodesia's complex problems met with little success. Some of the means were so subtle and so clever that they backfired immediately. Other ploys were deceptively simple, but only the Government fell for them.

Hickman and Flower's proposed one such plan, which Sutton-Price endorsed and Group Captain Walsh of the Air Force implemented, whereby, as Austin sarcastically explained, "A clever Kaffir can win freedom and try for even bigger prizes before a live studio audience, or the bugger can stay where he is and eat shit."

"I bet he stays where he is and eats shit," Greg said, reaching for his wallet.

"That's my bet," Austin said.

The plan called for leaflets to be dropped on suspected guerrilla encampments on the Zambian side of the Zambezi urging the terrorists to "Surrender or die" and directing those who could read English or Matabele to come out of the bush with their hands raised, chanting, "We do not want to die. Save us. We are here."

Unfortunately, the terrorists were shy or did not believe they could achieve instant stardom, for no one popped out uttering the magic words, even though Major General Hickman himself was on hand to shake the hand of the lucky contestants. All that resulted from the ill-fated operation was to supply toilet paper to the terrorists.

An alternative solution was proposed by the Americans, possibly to offset the embarrassing image left by Henry Kissinger when he shuffled off to Buffalo, having declared the Rhodesian problem solved at Victoria Falls. The new solution was revealed to a confused *kraal* chieftain by a Peace Corps volunteer after sampling the local *dagga*.

Having made an intensive month-long study of African ritual and taboo, the volunteer, a recent graduate of Farleigh Dickinson University in New Jersey, decided to devote the rest of his entire two-year tour of duty to improving the lot of the Mashona through assertiveness training and Native American dry irrigation techniques.

The PCV, Lester Dorfman, a southpaw who in deference to what he thought were African values, had learned to eat with his right hand, appreciated the African's respect for his spirit mediums. Upon arriving in a Mashona village just outside the township of Norton, Lester made a moving speech in formal Swahili on the importance of folk medicine in front of the *kraal* chieftain and the assembled village.

Joe Austin and Greg Andrews were present because Norton had recently become a center for terrorist activities, and they suspected the support had less to do with political preferences than predictions of success promulgated by the village witch doctor. A local family arrested for feeding and hiding terrorist groups as they passed through Norton had informed the Special Branch interrogation officer that the *djuna* had predicted victory for ZANLA. The villagers were hedging their bets so ZANLA would not punish them after they took over. "She tell the future. She very powerful witch doctor, never make mistake."

Into this delicate situation danced pale and scrawny Lester Dorfman to dispense the knowledge he'd acquired during four years at Farleigh Dickinson U. and a weekend of EST. The Africans gathered around Lester to watch his skin go bright pink in the afternoon sun. "I have come," Lester said, "because I have heard of the power of your *djuna,* who can cure malaria with her wisdom." He tossed a bottle of pills on the ground. "I believe in her power."

"This guy's an idiot," Greg said after a rough translation for Austin.

"It could be worse," Austin said as a naked boy darted out to claim the bottle of Lester's pills.

"Her power," Dorfman continued, "reminds me of the Indian medicine man in my country who once cured my poison ivy with aloe vera. I had a terrible case and yet two weeks after using the aloe I was whole again." Dorfman cleared his throat and waited for the murmur to abate. When it did not, he continued, raising his voice assertively. "And yet this is as nothing compared to what the Peace Corps can do for you," Dorfman said, extending his red arms.

"A complete idiot," Greg said, continuing to translate.

"Could be worse," Austin repeated.

"I am an agronomist," Dorfman said, using the English term, for the word for agronomist in Swahili means 'spreader of manure' and is not dignified.

"Gromist," the *kraal* chief repeated, nodding sagely.

"I have come with knowledge to help you grow bigger and better zucchini and rutabaga than you have ever grown before."

"They can't tell rutabaga from rugby," Greg said, "and the kid's Swahili is terrible."

"It could be worse," Austin said.

"How?"

"They could *understand* Swahili."

Having worked himself into a sweat, Dorfman decided to go for a swim in the Hunyani River. The African girls washing laundry on the bank of the river pleaded with him not to go. "I'll be right back," Dorfman promised. "I am a very good swimmer," he said in English, making swimming motions with his arms so the English-speaking Mashona would understand. "I will teach you how to swim."

"Oh, no, mastuh," they wailed. "No good swim."

"Soon you will all swim like Mark Spitz," Dorfman assured them and, baffled by the simile, they stopped trying to tell the *Maningi* that swimming was not the thing to do in the Hunyani. Surely he knew more than they, for he was from America, home of Mohammad Ali, and he was a *djuna* and had magical powers and it was also possible that the guardian of the river did not like sunburned white flesh.

"See?" Dorfman shouted. "That was the Australian crawl. Now watch this!" Diving gracefully, Dorfman swam a good twenty meters underwater before encountering a Hunyani crocodile who, forgiving Lester his scrawny white body, ate him anyway.

Although there are many venomous snakes in Africa,

many more people are killed by crocodiles. The Nile crocodile is at home throughout Africa and grazes, without prejudice, in streams and rivers.

Greg, meanwhile, had run to the river's edge and was trying to shoot the croc without doing further damage to Dorfman who was thrashing about in the churning water. The Sergeant either felt an affinity for his compatriot that the Colonel had apparently outgrown or he wanted an excuse to shoot at something. Greg got the croc through the eye, but not in time to save Dorfman, and both bodies soon washed up on shore half a kilometer downstream. The villagers were much more interested in the croc because there's only so much one can do with white flesh and thin skin, even if the authorities were to permit it, which they most assuredly would not. It would take many Peace Corps Volunteers to approach the value of one Hunyani crocodile.

Austin paid little attention to the tumult surrounding Dorfman's demise. Something more important had caught his eye.

On the Hunyani River Bridge high above the bloody water, the witch doctor stood on the main highway between Salisbury and Bulawayo and appeared to be counting the number of military trucks and units traveling between the two largest cities in Rhodesia. She had friends willing to pay for this information, Austin speculated, although she might pass along today's information at no cost, for not only was she rid of the American, but the Peace Corps had already paid for his room and board in advance.

Of course, she would deny she was keeping track of troop movements, and Austin didn't have the proof that the police, still smarting from the Harare showdown, would demand. "Keep an eye on her," he told the local BSAP officer-in-charge, "and bring her in for questioning now and again to keep her nervous."

"Terrible way to die," Greg said on the way back.

"Couldn't be better," Austin said. "I should've pinned a medal on him."

"The Peace Corps Volunteer?"

"No, the croc. Lester Dorfman was potentially a real pain in the ass. Like a document shredder for humans, that croc solved a problem before it became a problem. The Peace Corps should consider training all its personnel in the Hunyani River."

The terrorists had methods of solving problems that were much less imaginative. ZANLA petitioned China for weapons; ZIPRA sought theirs from the Soviet Union. Both countries were happy to oblige needy acronyms, and it might as well have been Christmas for all the toys the terrorists discovered beneath the baobab tree that year.

It was, in fact, a glorious morning of a type that can only be found in the low veld in springtime. Austin rang up Brigit and said, "Let's play hookey and go for a ride in the country."

"Can Oso come, too?" He'd recently purchased a fine young Rottweiler and was training him to guard the house, though Brigit seemed intent on treating him like a poodle. There'd been a recent series of burglaries in his suburban neighborhood, and, not only would Austin's gun collection command a high price, his weapons might easily find their way into terrorist hands.

"No, Brigit. Oso can't come, and neither can Minister Neukirk, your maid or the milkman."

"But I don't want *them* to come with us."

"Good. Then I'll have Greg pick you up in half an hour."

"I don't want *him* to come, either."

"We'll need someone to watch the car when we go dancing."

"I thought you said a ride in the country."

"I did. If we leave right away we can reach Kariba before dark and take in a show." The town of Kariba was a lakeside resort and tourist mecca that boasted game-viewing, fishing and water sports. In the evenings there was fine dining, dancing and roulette at the casino hotel. "Lieutenant Thornberry will be there. He's on his honeymoon."

"That would be so much fun," Brigit said, "but can't we take Oso and leave Greg?"

"Next time," Austin said. "Just as soon as I teach Oso to drive."

"Oh, all right, but don't send Greg. I'll drive to your house." She was half an hour late, but she looked lovely in a blue cotton sunsuit. Austin welcomed her warmly and showed her the picnic basket he'd prepared. "You should have told me. I would have brought my bratwurst. Ask Dr. von Neukirk how good is my bratwurst."

They drove north by way of Trelawney and stopped for lunch in a field where impala were grazing. In deference to her, Austin did not ask Greg to join them but left plenty for his bodyguard to eat and drink when he took Brigit for a walk through a meadow of wildflowers. "It's a beautiful country," he said.

"Whom did Philip marry?"

"Philip?"

"Philip Thornberry, you know."

"Oh. Her name is Carol. After you meet her, I'd appreciate learning your impression of her."

"Why is that?" She stooped to pluck a flower, then twirled it by the stem.

"I might ask him to join my staff."

"I'd like that," she said, and Austin felt a sudden pang of jealousy. He was glad that the dashing Second Lieutenant was now out of circulation, but this didn't interfere with his respect for Thornberry's skill and military bearing.

The ability to lead men in combat and kill quickly and efficiently are sought-after skills in the military, particularly in small-unit combat teams where individual incentive and personal bravery exemplify the best in men. One cannot hide in a combat situation where only four men are involved, and four was the size of Rhodesia's basic combat unit. "My perfect stick," he said to Greg when they were back in the car, "would have you, Thornberry, and Barry Richards in it." He said it to let Greg know he was sorry that he had to eat like a servant, but he also meant it. The perfect stick never came together, however. Two of its potential members died tragically.

"What did Philip do before he joined the army?" Brigit asked. "He could have been a movie star."

"He was a high school teacher," Austin said, almost savagely.

"He looks like a high school student himself."

Austin didn't tell her that Philip was 29 years old and had started out as a Territorial but had found that he liked the Army and had decided to stay in. He didn't mention that Philip found sorting out terrs more exciting than teaching physical education to a bunch of schoolboys. All he said was, "You're too late."

She punched him playfully and said, "You're jealous."

This would be Austin's first opportunity to meet Philip's fiancee. He could tell a lot about an officer from the woman he chooses to marry. Carol Thornberry had to be some lady if her husband was as fine an officer as Philip Thornberry appeared to be. Would Brigit feel jealous when she met Carol? As if reading his mind, she snuggled against him in the backseat of the BMW. He wanted to take her there and then, and he knew that Greg wouldn't so much as look in the rear-view mirror, but Brigit was shy in front of the Sergeant and pushed him away. "Later," she whispered.

Major General Hickman was aware of Lieutenant Thornberry's leadership qualities but employed him as an aide far from the front where Philip longed to be. After working with him on the Harare raid, Austin wanted to work with him again, and Thornberry was positively desperate to stop serving tea and crumpets to generals. "Get me out of there, Colonel. I'll do anything."

In the luxury hotel on Lake Kariba they found Carol and Philip in the game room. He was teaching her how *chemin de fer* was played. If Austin expected a blushing bride, Carol did not fit the image. Mrs. Thornberry was bright, pretty in an athletic sort of way, friendly and outgoing. She worked as a teller for Barclays Bank and was obviously head over heels in love with Philip. They looked "right" together and should have enjoyed a long and happy life together. Unfortunately, the Fat Man had other plans.

The war was escalating daily. ZIPRA's leader, Joshua Nkomo, was favored by the Russians and his men were better armed and had access to more sophisticated weapons than did ZANLA. Nkomo was more determined than ever to put to rest the accusation that he was less aggressive than his tribal and political enemy, Robert Mugabe. He sent a message to a terrorist stick in Choma, and the wheels were set in motion.

The firing mechanism for a weapon not previously used by guerrillas was discovered in the bush about a kilometer outside the wire on top of a low kopje at the end of the runway at the Victoria Falls airport. The mechanism was identified as part of a Soviet-made SAM-7 (Strela) ground-to-air missile system. This was a direct copy of the US-built Redeye rocket issued to NATO countries, 4½ feet in length and weighing 25 pounds, a simple and easy-to-use one-man system, effective as it was deadly.

ZIPRA had launched missiles at South African Airways flights bound from Victoria Falls to Johannesburg's Jan Smuts airport on two separate occasions but, for some unknown reason, both attempts had failed, thus saving the lives of some lucky travelers and preventing an international incident. The "D" Notice kept reports out of the press, and most air travelers did not know their lives were in danger.

Propriety demanded that Brigit be given her own room, but when Austin came tapping at her door after an evening of dancing and drinking she wouldn't let him in. She had a headache, she said, but Austin believed that watching the newlyweds had upset her. *And she knows I'm married*, he thought, as he lay on his bed and stared at the ceiling. While he was brooding, the terrorists from Choma slipped quietly into Kariba.

The only animated person on the drive home the next day was Greg. Austin and Brigit hardly spoke and the tension was so great that when it broke they coupled desperately. *It's a carousel. I don't know what to expect.*

The following morning, as Brigit drove her car home from Austin's house, Philip and Carol Thornberry joined 56 other holiday makers and crew members departing Kariba on Rhodesia Airlines' four engine turbo-prop Viscount. The stewardesses on board the Viscount, Brenda Pearson and Dulcie Esterhuizen, started serving drinks to the passengers.

On the ground, a few kilometers from the end of the runway, the Choma terrorists watched the Viscount rise into the air. The group leader put the SAM-7 to his shoulder as the sound of the engines grew louder. The sun was at his back so the heat signature of the engines would be easy for the heat detector on the warhead to lock on to.

As the plane passed overhead, the leader squeezed the trigger until the first stop. When the target was positioned in the middle of the optical sight, he concentrated on the red glow of the light and waited, just as he had been instructed. Finally, the light went from red to green as the heat sensor in the nose of the missile locked on to the heat signature of the Viscount's engines. The group leader pulled the trigger back to its full stop position, and the deadly heat-seeking missile was on its way.

For seconds there was nothing, then a flash confirmed the hit. The terrorist stick dismantled the SAM-7 and melted into the bush.

The missile struck the exhaust pipe of the number three engine, and the warhead exploded, sending pieces of the rocket, large chucks of the engine exhaust and the trailing edge of the wing into the side of the aircraft. Fire broke out as fuel poured out of tanks in the wing.

"May Day! May Day! This is Captain Hood, Flight RH 825 from Kariba. There's been an explosion. I'm at 1500 feet and losing altitude fast. Do you track us?"

"This is air traffic control, Lake Kariba. We've got you, Captain. Keep talking."

Meanwhile, first Officer Beaumont was on the intercom, instructing the hostesses, calming the passengers, helping everyone prepare for the inevitable crash landing.

Desperately, Captain Hood and co-pilot Beaumont sought an open area for the emergency landing. "There! Down there!"

"I see it. Kariba, are you tracking?"

"We're with you, Captain. Describe the terrain, please."

At a clearing in the heavily bushed veld, Captain Hood brought the aircraft gently down. However, what at first seemed a miraculous textbook landing was suddenly violently altered, for in the middle of the open field was a hidden *donga*, a gulley, and on contact with it the plane broke apart, scattering passengers, crew and pieces of aircraft over the entire field like straw. A fire broke out in the main portion of the wreckage consuming Flight RH 825 and Second Lieutenant Philip Thornberry along with the pilot and co-pilot and most of the other passengers.

Eighteen people somehow survived the crash, including the newly married and just widowed Carol Thornberry and the two air hostesses, one of whom was in critical condition. The other hostess was badly injured, with a broken arm, but she was able to assist Tony Warne, a Territorial Trooper who was virtually unscathed, in gathering blankets and other items of warm clothing to comfort the wounded.

There was another newlywed couple on the plane and they, like Trooper Warne, were relatively unhurt. This trio decided to seek help at a nearby *kraal*, leaving five other survivors, including a young girl of four or five, to sort through the wreckage. These five were somewhat removed from where Carol Thornberry and nine other badly injured passengers were being attended to by the hostess.

"Halloo!" someone called from the bush.

"Over here!" the hostess shouted. "Thank God you've come!"

A party of Africans emerged from the bush and walked onto the crash site. Their leader called out to the ten badly wounded passengers, "Not to worry, we are here to help you," as they strolled up to the survivors.

Laughing, the leader took the injured hostess some fifty meters away and proceeded to rape her. Her screams and anguished cries alerted the group of five who were searching through the wreckage for other survivors, and they hid in the donga.

After the terrorists had finished with the air hostess, they brandished AK's and opened fire, killing the ten wounded survivors, including Carol Thornberry, with their assault rifles. Then, instead of sticking around to plunder the luggage and search the bodies for money and valuables, they forgot their training, panicked, and ran into the bush.

The trooper and the newlywed couple who were on their way to get help heard the gun fire and stayed where they were, hidden in the thick bush at the edge of the clearing. The five other survivors remained hidden in the donga.

It took almost eighteen hours for help to arrive. Eight badly shaken survivors were carried out. There was a village a few kilometers away from the crash site came, but none of the villagers had seen anything or heard anything. Neither the terrorists who fired the ground to air missile nor the rapists were apprehended.

Joshua Nkomo did not deny his part in the tragedy. To the contrary, he openly bragged about it in an interview with the BBC. He joked about how ZIPRA had opened the world's eyes to his people's new capability although he denied that his people had raped and killed the survivors.

White Rhodesia mourned, but press reports outside the country were subdued. No one cried out for vengeance. The Dean of Salisbury's Anglican Church referred to this "deafening silence" in his eulogy. "Nobody who holds sacred the dignity of human life can be anything but sickened at the events attending the crash of the Viscount Hunyani," he said.

The *Times* story made mention of "chickens coming home to roost."

A second Air Rhodesian Viscount was destroyed by a SAM-7 five months later. There were no survivors. In 1978, a Canberra bomber was lost while on a raid in Mozambique. This time it was ZANLA and Mugabe's men who fired the missile, but since the target was military it was fair game.

Rhodesia's leaders responded to the Viscount attacks in several ways. Sanction-busters were able to purchase a new paint that deflected heat, altering the exhaust's signature and making it more difficult for heat-seeking missiles to lock onto an aircraft's engine. Airport security was beefed up, with guards patrolling an enlarged perimeter around airfields. And civilian aircraft now took off and landed like military aircraft; instead of lifting straight off and descending slowly and smoothly onto the runway as was comfortable and customary, they spiralled in and out.

The worst was yet to come. Terrorists were learning how to aim before firing and had started downing military aircraft with small arms and machine guns. While no one in the military would admit the future looked grim, the award for optimist of the year went to the 7th squadron pilot who quit smoking for fear he'd die of cancer.

For once, Hickman and Walls were in agreement about what was needed: better weapons, newer aircraft, and Nkomo's head on a platter. They also agreed that if anyone could deliver the goods, Colonel Joe Austin could.

The only thing startling about all this was how openly it was discussed. MP's called for Nkomo's elimination on the floor of Parliament. A group of South Africans posted a 100,000 Rand reward for his death. No one suggested dropping leaflets. The war entered a new phase.

Worst of all, at least for Joe Austin, was the sheer audacity of the burglar who climbed over the wall surrounding his house on one of the rare nights Brigit was going to sleep over. Austin had sent Greg off in the BMW and told him to spend the night in the barracks at King George VI. The cook had prepared an elegant dinner before leaving the house.

They drank champagne and dined by candlelight. It was all very intimate and European. Austin picked a rose from the flowering bush in the garden and pinned it in her hair. He kissed her deeply, inhaling the rose's fragrance and the subtleties of her perfume, and when her body responded, pressing hard against his, he lifted her up and carried her upstairs.

In Austin's house, as in most split-level, ranch style Rhodesian homes, the bedrooms were situated along a protected corridor half a story above the main floor. At the end of the corridor was a grill that Rhodesians locked when they went to bed. This gate closed off the entire sleeping wing, securing it against attack. There were also burglar bars on all the windows, and most people slept with a gun nearby. Security, however, was not on Austin's mind as he unhooked Brigit's dress and slid it over her shoulder. He was not thinking about burglars when he took off his clothes and slid into bed beside her. He was removing her panties and panting with lust when someone suddenly screamed. There was a din and racket coming from the garden. The Rottweiler was lunging and biting and whoever was being hit was yelling blue murder!

In successive instants, Austin hit the floor, grabbed his .45, ran down the corridor, unlocked the grill door, dashed downstairs, followed the noise around the back, opened the back door, hit the flagstone, slippery with dew, and naked as a jaybird slid into the rosebushes and was ripped raw by the thorns. The burglar made it over the far wall and Austin limped back inside the house, leaving his libido in the thicket along with much of his skin.

The next morning, covered in mercurochrome, Austin inspected the compound. There was blood on the lawn in clots every twenty or thirty feet from one eight-foot white wall all the way across the compound to the other wall. Where Oso had hit and taken the interloper down there was more blood. Oso was waiting for the burglar even before he climbed over the wall. He sat there without making a sound, just waiting. As soon as the burglar hit the ground, Oso got him. Instead of turning around and scaling the wall the way he'd come, the fool had run across the lawn to the wall on the opposite side of the compound. Every twenty or thirty feet Oso knocked him down and started chewing on him. He scrambled to his feet, made it another twenty or so feet and got hit again. On the far wall there was a streak of blood eight feet high.

Enough was enough! A burglar with *biltong* for brains had gotten in the way of his love life, had embarrassed him with rose thorns, had riled his dog and bloodied his garden. War is war, but now the terrorists had gone too far and would have to pay.

9

New problems demand new solutions, but the sanctions the United Nations had imposed made it difficult for Rhodesia to purchase the weapons it needed to solve the problems brought about by an intensifying war. Therefore, a concerted effort had to be made to develop armaments in-country using materials at hand. Austin was involved in testing weapons that ran the gamut from sophisticated systems to Rube Goldberg contraptions. He adapted old weapons and designed new ones to meet the changing demands of Rhodesia's guerrilla warfare.

Roof-mounted devices were popular with farmers and lorry drivers. Designed to counter ambushes, one gadget consisted of 3/4-inch water-pipe barrels made to shoot 12-bore shotgun shells. While keeping his nose to the steering column, a farmer could dispense fifteen shots at once in a 360-degree circle around his vehicle by merely pulling on a rope suspended from the roof of his cab. The noise alone was enough to convince a prudent terr to keep his head down.

The 'Spider' was another locally-built rooftop device. This weapon consisted of three layers of pipe barrels with 12 barrels to the layer. It was fired by a hand-crank from inside the cab of the vehicle. By winding the crank like an organ grinder, a frightened farmer could fire thirty-six 12-bore rounds in about 1.5 seconds, enough to make even the most ardent terrorist think twice about charging.

One of the most ambitious projects called for the design and local manufacture of a submachine gun. The 'Rhuzi' was Rhodesia's simplified version of the Israeli submachine gun, the Uzi. Specifications for the Rhuzi were such that each and every part could be produced with the limited machine-shop capability available in Rhodesia.

Equipped with a 90mm cannon, the Eland was the basic armored military vehicle, but the only rounds available for this weapon were HEAT (high explosive anti-tank) and WP (white phosphorus). The HEAT had a fail-safe built into the fuse so that it would not arm closer than 200 meters to the tube. What was needed were old fashioned canister-type rounds, but sanctions made chances of getting these slim and bugger-all.

Lieutenant Bob Attenow, a wiry rancher as well as the commander of an armored unit, was complaining about army bureaucracy when Austin and Greg walked into the Ammo Box, the all-ranks pub built almost entirely of ammo crates. "They just delivered a shipment of blank rounds for the 90," Bob said, stretching out his legs and resting the heel of one boot on the toe of the other. "In return, I expect the Kaffirs will oblige us by using *mealy* instead of explosives in their landmines."

"Not bloody likely," Corporal Caruthers said, sucking on a Castle beer. "What in bloody hell are we supposed to do with blank rounds?" Attenow demanded.

"Fire your imagination, maybe," Austin said, taking a seat and signaling for a Hansa. "Could be those rounds are just what you need."

"Right," Caruthers said impudently. "We'll shove 'em up their bloody arses until they can't move and then we'll shoot the buggers as they try to hop away."

"Reminds me of how Grandpa Bass killed flies," Austin said and looked around the room like a promoter counting the house. "Tell you what, I'll bet I can kill gooks with blanks. Who says I can't and for how much?"

Amid spluttering and posturing from soldiers with hands stuck deep in their pockets, Attenow said, "One rhino."

"What?"

"You ever hunt rhino?"

"Can't say that I have."

"If you find a way to kill Kaffirs with blank rounds, I'll take you on a hunting trip you can tell your grandchildren about. If you fail, you buy every bloody man in here all the beer he can drink on a Saturday night."

"You got yourself a bet."

Before investigating what could be done with the blanks to make them useful, Austin inventoried the other combat arms of the Rhodesian army and discovered that they were still using 25-pounders left over from World War II. While quite handy in conventional warfare for destroying supply depots and other fixed targets, these howitzers were rarely used in guerrilla warfare because terrorists are usually mobile and don't hold fixed positions long enough for fire to be be brought down on them. The 25-pounders had separate charges for different ranges, including one called the Super Charge which was never used because engagements were rarely at a range requiring their extra power and because the guns used were old and thought to be unsafe with this charge.

Austin was watching a carpenter repair a leaking barracks roof when it occurred to him that Rhodesia manufactured its own nails. It wasn't much of a leap from a nail to a *flechette* and, bingo! he had the makings of a canister round. Several thousand *flechettes* were tested in a wide variety of sizes before Austin was satisfied he'd found the most effective weight and length for use in the 90mm. In the process of testing, he discovered that the powder charges used in the blank rounds did not perform nearly as well as the Super Charges, which worked like a charm. The blank cartridge casings were more than adequate to hold the Super Charges and a full load of *flechettes*.

Range tests revealed a kill zone of over 100 meters wide at 300 meters, exactly what the military needed to fill the void caused by the HEAT round. The canister round stopped working just where the HEAT started.

"I've used the blank cartridge casings with powder from the Super Charges to make these *flechette rounds*," Austin informed Attenow. "I think you owe me a rhino."

"The beer's on me," Corporal Caruthers shouted over the din at the Ammo Box that Saturday. "The Colonel has added a powerful new weapon to our arsenal."

"I'm of a mind to say we've all won," Lieutenant Attenow said, beer in hand. "And you're all invited to a *braaivleis* at the Attenow Ranch on Boxing Day. My ma will cook what the Colonel kills, and I guarantee you'll never eat better in your lives."

Austin figured on killing two birds on that hunting trip, for he'd been wanting to test still another weapon. The Jumbo was a privately-financed, government-supported automatic shotgun, a unique weapon designed by an American who had immigrated to Rhodesia and gone to work for one of the larger manufacturing concerns in Salisbury.

Designed for one purpose only, killing men in combat, the Jumbo was only 27 inches long. Built on the 'bull pup' principle, it held seven rounds in the magazine, plus one up the spout, and it could be fired one-handed like a pistol. As anyone experienced with magnum buckshot loads knows, this is a neat trick.

Austin took the Jumbo one step further. He asked an American hunter who was coming over on safari to bring a Diverter along. The Diverter is an attachment to a shotgun that looks like a duck's bill and is designed to make a shotgun shoot a horizontal pattern rather than round one.

In riot situations, a shotgun equipped with a Diverter,

instead of hitting one or two demonstrators at 20 to 25 meters, could hit five or six of them. There would be fewer projectiles per target, of course, but in a riot scenario the objective is to slow people down and remove the crowd's enthusiasm for attacking the police. Usually, one or two pellets of birdshot or buckshot is sufficient to get a demonstrator's attention and cause him to consider the advisability of changing direction and taking up new interests. Austin married the Diverter to the Jumbo and initial tests indicated it would work very well. At 25 meters with AAA buckshot (41 per round), killing or disabling hits could be expected on a seven meter frontage. AAA buckshot was ideal for the first two rounds, as contact usually occurred within 25 to 30 meters and then opened up. He decided to complement the AAA buckshot with Special SG buckshot (12 per round) for the next rounds and a rifled slug for the last round. Then he was ready to test the weapon under field conditions.

The Attenow Ranch was a large cattle ranch located not far from Birchenough Bridge on the Sabi river. Like all ranchers, the Attenows were experiencing an upsurge in cattle-rustling by local tribesmen who butchered the beef to feed visiting terrorists. Since the ranch was bordered on two sides by Tribal Trust Land and on a third side by Mozambique, the Attenow's had their hands full.

In fact, a report of a possible incursion forced Bob to turn the first day's hunting expedition over to his father, a bow-legged man who looked like a cowboy and wore a Stetson to heighten the affect. Austin and Greg would have preferred to join Bob's unit and ferret out terrs, but Bob insisted they bag at least a few bucks for the *braaivleis* and Harry Attenow, Bob's father, wanted to ask Austin all about cattle ranching in Texas, a subject the Colonel knew nothing about. "Sorry, old timer, I've never been a rancher."

"What d'ye want to know about it?" Harry asked. "I'll tell ye everything ye need to know."

A midsized kudu bull broke from cover, and a shadow

moved the other way. "I'm more interested in that buck," Austin said, taking aim.

One shot was all it took, and a fine buck fell to the ground. "Thet's one fine kudu," Harry said. "See that Kaffir over there? Might of been stalking that kudu. Might be a poacher. Hard to tell from here."

"I see him," Greg said. "Want me to stop him?"

Harry looked at the muscular American, then at the small, quick African. "You stop him? Hah! I'd like to see thet. He'll be in Nandi by the time you—"

Smoothly, Greg raised his Brno 7.62 sniper rifle and fired. The African fell to the ground. "Got 'im."

"Jesus! What'd you do thet for?" Harry screamed and jumped up and down.

"You told me to stop him," Greg smiled.

"I didn't mean permanently! Oh, brother, what am I going to do now? We'll have to fetch him to the hospital, I expect, and there'll be an inquiry. It's going to cost me, I know thet much."

"Hospital? That floppy don't need a hospital, he's deader'n *biltong*."

"You think so?" Harry ran over to the body and stubbed at it with his toe of his boot, then rubbed his hands gleefully. "He's dead all right. What should we do with him?"

"We don't have to do anything with him," Austin said. "We'll just report we shot a poacher."

"I think he's one of the mission Kaffirs," Harry said, lifting the corpse's chin with his toe. "I think I've seen him before. What are we going to do?" He ran in circles around the acacia tree beneath which the African's body lay sprawled, lost his hat to a branch and accidentally stepped on it. "Now look what I've done, and I just had it blocked."

"Let's bury him and forget it," Austin said.

"Thet's the ticket! We'll bury the bugger!" Harry whooped and ran to get a shovel from the Land Rover.

There was an ant mound nearby that a honey bear had burrowed into. A honey bear is an armored anteater and looks something like a big armadillo. Ant mounds in the low veld can be three meters high and as much as twelve meters in diameter, and the honey bear had dug his way into his favorite restaurant at a 45-degree angle. "Take his other arm," Austin said. "We'll stuff him in there. Unless you feel like digging a proper grave."

"He's too dead to care," Greg said, "and the day I dig a grave for a floppy will be my dying day."

They dragged the African over to the ant mound and stuffed him in feet first. It was a tight fit, and his head protruded from the top of the hole. Harry hit him over the head a few times with the shovel but couldn't hammer him in any deeper. "I got an idea," he said and ran back to the Land Rover, returning a minute later toting a jerry can of gasoline.

"What are you going to do with that?" Austin asked.

"You'll see," Harry said, and he poured the contents of the can on and around the body. Then, before Austin could stop him, he lit a match and tossed it on the makeshift grave. There was a sudden whoosh! and the African shot from the hole like a circus acrobat from a cannon and landed several yards away from the hole and burned and smoked for a minute or two.

"What in hell was that all about?" Austin demanded.

"I thought it would shrink him up some," Harry said dolefully and stubbed his toe in the African's smouldering face. "Stinks some, don't he?" The skin came away and some flesh stuck to Harry's boot. He scraped it in the grass to get it off.

"We can't leave him there, and we certainly can't report him as a poacher now, can we?" Austin shook his head. "A fine mess. Greg, climb that little *kopje* and make sure no one else is around. Harry, get your shovel."

"Reminds me of a Tom Mix movie," Harry said. "You remember Tom Mix?"

"Shut up and dig."

"It's his horse's name I keep forgetting."

Greg returned to report the area was clear. The corpse had cooled down and they were able to drag it by the feet and stuff it, head-first this time, into the enlarged hole. They packed the body down good and covered the hole. They walked around and examined it from several angles, then, satisfied that nothing showed, they loaded the kudu into the Land Rover and drove back to the ranch house. "I can still smell it," Harry said. "Can you?"

"You should take out a patent on that invention," Greg told him. "Call it a Kaffir launcher."

"Reminds me of the method Grandpa Bass had for killing flies," Austin said.

"You mentioned that once before. What was your grandpa's method?"

"He'd set a big pot of water on the stove. Then, when the water got to boiling real good, he'd catch a fly and toss it in."

"What's so special about that?" Harry asked.

"Waste a lot of gasoline the other way," Austin said with a straight face.

That evening, Mrs. Attenow grilled kudu steaks for Bob's unit, but Harry didn't have any. He said he wasn't hungry and thought the food smelled funny. Austin said he didn't smell anything funny and hadn't tasted anything so good since he left Vietnam. Greg had second helpings, too, but Corporal Caruthers outdid everyone and when he couldn't eat anymore wondered what Mrs. Attenow had planned for breakfast.

The next day, Bob asked Austin if he'd go with him to visit a *kraal* head on the Tribal Trust Land nearby. Like most farmers in the sharp end, Bob had a mine-hardened Land Rover that he used for travel around his farm. Greg rode in the back, and as they jounced along the dirt roads they watched for mines and possible ambush.

There was hardly any activity at the *kraal*. The old men watched their every move; the women grinding *mealy* never looked up. Greg pointed out that no children were present. "Let's get out of here," Bob said. "Something's wrong." Cradling their weapons, they retreated to the Land Rover and headed back home.

On the way back, Bob noticed cattle tracks crossing the dirt road. "There shouldn't be any tracks here," he said uneasily. "I don't have any cattle in this paddock, and I don't let the Kaffirs run their cattle on my ranch."

"Looks like someone drove a small herd this way," Greg said. "Better stop the car."

The road circled a small *kopje*, and Greg started walking to the top. Austin directed Bob to drive up the road about 1.5 klicks to where the road made a sweeping curve and wound back. "Backtrack towards me and try to pick up the spoor, in case it doesn't cross the road at the curve. I'm going to go around the other way. We'll meet in the middle."

Austin was carrying the Jumbo with the Diverter attached. Even with the attachment, the shotgun was only 29 inches long, and he carried it slung across his body just above belt level. He walked with his hand on the pistol grip of the gun and his trigger finger on the safety. To get the first round on its way would require less than a second and to fire all eight rounds would take less than three seconds.

He'd walked about half a klick when he came to a huge ant mound right in the middle of the track. He circled the mound and almost bumped into a CT walking around the other side with an AK slung across his chest in almost exactly the same fashion as his Jumbo. They froze, their eyes met, they went for their weapons, and Austin shot first. His gun was lying against his chest at a 45-degree angle from the normal firing position, and the full charge of AAA hit the terr full in the chest and he went down like a ton of shit.

Almost as quickly, Austin dropped down. He crawled around the ant mound looking for the rest of the terrorist's stick, but saw no one. Greg came charging, running low to the ground, tripping and rolling from the place where, halfway up the *kopje*, he'd heard the shotguns roar. Moments later, Bob pulled up, steering wildly with one hand, his Rhuzi in the other. Austin calculated that from where he had been standing to where the terr fell was exactly ten meters. Because he'd fired sideways, the gun had thrown a vertical pattern that blistered the terr from his navel to his sternum like the dotted line on a coupon. All 41 buckshot had hit him. When Special Branch came to pick him up, they reported that the only thing holding him together was his webbing: the vertical charge of buckshot had taken out his spine.

"They've got to be on the other side of that *kopje*," Greg whispered savagely. "Let's go after 'em!"

"They're halfway to Mozambique by now," Bob said. "Let's get the rest of my unit and follow the tracks." They piled into the Land Rover and tore back to the ranch. Within the hour, four vehicles and twelve heavily armed soldiers plus Greg and Austin were on their way to Mozambique.

They had no way of knowing that ZANLA had recently established a base camp close to the border town of Chioco, in Mozambique. It was to be a permanent camp, supply point and jumping-off station for incursion into Rhodesia. Bunkers had been constructed with connecting trenches, and there was no shortage of ammunition. FRELIMO troops were present to protect the town of Chioco and to provide moral support for Mugabe's troops. Unlike the guerrillas, FRELIMO soldiers were well-trained members of a regular standing army. They had never shown much enthusiasm for mixing it up with Rhodesian troops in the past; however, the ensuing battle was to prove otherwise.

Austin's unit crossed the border in slow pursuit, leery of landmines. They passed abandoned cattle that Bob recognized belonged to his neighbor and that had been stolen to mask the terrorists' spoor. The trail was easy to follow, and they followed it right into the ZANLA camp. Austin knew it would be prudent to return for more men and air support, but he could taste the combat and couldn't push himself away from the table. Everyone else felt the same way.

Before attacking, Austin divided his force into two units, one under his command and the other under Lieutenant Attenow.

Bob's callsign was given the responsibility for covering the left flank of the main assault, forming the long side of an 'L'. The fire Austin's people would direct on the terrs would give them two options: they could stand, fight and die or they could run, which was what they would most likely do. Running would bring them into direct contact with Attenow's flank, and at this point their options would be drastically reduced.

After the first attack, most of the FRELIMO troops retreated to protect the town and ZANLA troops went helter-skelter to protect their asses. However, several FRELIMO soldiers were holed up in the bunkers that had been bypassed in the initial assault, and they were now enthusiastically pouring fire into the rear of the assault teams.

Calling his team together, Lieutenant Attenow told them how they were going to clear out the bunkers and connecting trenches. Then he deployed his men and attacked bunker number one. First, he threw in a white phosphorus grenade. This stopped the outgoing fire. They could hear screaming from the FRELIMO troops upset about being burned by flakes of phosphorus which worked through their bodies in a most relentless manner.

There was a trench that ran from this first bunker directly to another one about fifty meters away. While his team poured covering fire into the second bunker, Attenow grabbed a bunker bomb and ran around the side. He pulled the pin and chucked it into the firing slit and waited. The bunker bomb used the same kind of fusing mechanism as hand grenades and should have gone off in four to five seconds. The bomb was a dud, however, and nothing happened, so Bob ordered one of his men to throw him another bomb. The second bunker bomb was tossed but fell three meters shy of Bob's position, so he dashed out to retrieve it and to bring it back to his relatively safe position at the side of the bunker. Firing stopped as Bob ran out, but when he picked up the bunker bomb and turned to run, his men heard the unforgettable *thuck*! of a high velocity rifle bullet hitting flesh. A terr in the trench had blindly stuck his rifle over the edge and fired off a full 30 round magazine. By sheer stupid blind bad luck, one round had hit Bob in the upper thigh and severed his femoral artery. He grabbed his thigh with both hands and tried to stop the bleeding, rolling meanwhile directly into the trench with the terrorist who had shot him. By the time his men had stormed the trench and sorted out the terr, Bob had bled to death.

Austin had to notify Bob's parents, at whose table he had so recently eaten. Mrs. Attenow cried; Harry Attenow slumped in his chair and aged ten years before Austin's eyes. Bob was posthumously awarded the Legion of Merit for his actions, and it was Austin's sad duty to present this to his parents as well.

There were no other RDF casualties. Fourteen terrorists were killed, sixteen including the terrorist beside one ant mound and the doubtful poacher inside another.

Austin was also able to recommend using Jumbos equipped with Diverters in ambush situations. Sanctions made it impossible to import Diverters, even though enough would fit into a single suitcase to take care of immediate needs. Unable to reward the patent holder for the ingenious device, Austin took his only sample to the manufacturers of the Jumbo shotgun and asked them if they could copy the device and make it available to the RDF as well as to civilians. "Can do, old chum," he was told, and within two weeks they had Diverters by the basketful. So much for sanctions!

"Now, if we can only find a way to acquire a few helicopters," O'Brian said.

"Actually, I've been thinking the same thing," Ted said, "and I've an idea. It's a bit risky, but I think it will work."

"I'm all for it!" General Walls said, rubbing his hands.

"I'll hear it out," General Hickman said, "but I'm sure it's not at all feasible."

"Don't forget world opinion," Ken Flowers added.

"Gentlemen, gentlemen," said Sutton-Price, checking his watch.

Austin just smiled.

Rhodesia's beleaguered aircraft were held together with the finest chewing gum and baling wire. There were fewer than fifty Hunters, Vampires and Canberras in the air force, and at any given time only half were airworthy. The most important weapon in Rhodesia's air arsenal, however, was the helicopter, and Rhodesia had precious few of them. Maximum operational strength was approximately thirty Alouette choppers, and with each passing year combat-ready choppers grew more and more difficult to field. Not only were the Alouettes old, they could carry only four men with gear. Therefore, in probably the only war ever fought where available transport dictated the size of the basic operational unit, there were four Rhodesians to the stick. To compensate for this, the available firepower was heavier than that of any similar size unit ever fielded. Each stick had a MAG machine gun and three FN 7.62X51 (.308) automatic rifles and could lay down an impressive volume of fire.

Sanctions made it impossible to purchase aircraft on the open market so, when Ted Sutton-Price discovered that Israel had 15 Bell helicopters it might be willing to sell, unusual methods of procurement were found. While Israel was not, in principle, adverse to climbing into bed with Rhodesia, she would only do so when no one was looking. Worried about her reputation, Israel was afraid the U.S. would stop favoring her funding requests if word got out she was dating Rhodesia. Since few other countries would ask them out, Rhodesia, South Africa, Israel and Taiwan danced cautiously with one another, ready on a moment's notice to repudiate their partners should one of the major western powers wish to cut in.

Although Israel was willing to sell helicopters to Rhodesia, a go-between was necessary, someone trusted by both sides, a pragmatic military officer, preferably an American. Someone, for example, like Colonel Joe Austin.

"We'd like you to go shopping for us," Ted Sutton-Price told him when he was summoned to a meeting in the Milton Building. "It's all very hush-hush."

"It's a delicate operation," Hickman said, "and I'm not sure how feasible it is."

Group Captain Walsh of the Rhodesian Air Force had been asked to join them, and he smiled disarmingly and said, "It's the best chance we have for bringing this war to a successful conclusion."

"Yes," Hickman said, "and you might be the man for the job. You know aircraft and you follow orders. This job requires someone able to maintain a low profile, keep a stiff upper lip, and exercise sound business management."

"We cannot use a Rhodesian national," O'Brian said emphatically. "Colonel Austin is the logical choice."

"Perhaps you're right," Hickman said, but turning to Austin he added, "I must say that my first choice was the man you knew in Australia as John Smythe-Jones."

"Oh, yes, I remember Samuel," Austin said. "A man who knows how to keep his cover. He'd hold his own with the CIA and KGB for about, oh, thirty seconds."

"My sentiments precisely," General Walls said. "Major Cuttingham is better suited for business negotiations than for sanctions busting."

"I'm sure they'll be able to work together," the Prime Minister said. "Personalities aside, what's your opinion, Ken?"

Flowers put his hands together on the table, then nervously tapped his index fingers against one another. "I don't like anything about this affair, but if you're dead set on it then without a doubt Joe's our man." Intertwining the rest of his fingers, he pointed the index fingers at Austin. "If there's a leak, we will have lost a good friend as well as ten million dollars."

"I didn't think you liked me," Austin said teasingly.

"I was referring to Israel," Flowers snapped.

"Then if there's a leak," Austin said, staring defiantly at Flowers, "it will have come from somewhere else in this room."

"There'll be no leaks, gentlemen," Ted said. "The future of Rhodesia depends upon it. With these helicopters we'll be able to quadruple the size of our lift capability. Now, if there are no further questions, we'll adjourn this meeting. I'll meet with Joe later to discuss the specifics."

A week later, Greg drove him to the airport and Austin boarded a Boeing 707 non-stop flight to Berne. His diplomatic passport was cursorily examined in Switzerland, but his baggage was not, and he entered Europe carrying an Astra 700 .22 Automatic, a pistol that while rather cute and quite small was not very effective. *What we like in women we hate in weapons.*

From Switzerland, he booked train passage to England via Paris. He dined alone, engaged no one in small talk, and arrived in London mid-morning of his second day on the continent. He wanted to buy some good footwear and a Carnaby Street hooker, but these things would have to wait until business was finished.

First he had to find a way to order the Israeli helicopters. He then had to pay for them and ship them to Rhodesia without anyone finding out where they were destined. This would not be easy. Fifteen helicopters together with spare parts were a bit bigger than a bread box!

After checking into the Tower Hotel, Austin placed a call to Samuel Cuttingham. "Hello, Major! This is Mr. Smythe-Jones. Do you remember me?"

"I'm not sure I—"

"Good! I was hoping you'd join me for dinner. I realize the Harbour Restaurant's a bit out of the way, so I thought we could pick up a couple of burgers at Wimpy's and feed the pigeons in the park."

"How ghastly! I'm sorry but I always dine at my club."

"The Explorer's, I believe. Is that right?"

"Yes, how did—"

"All right, you've twisted my arm, the Explorer's Club it is. What time shall I meet you?"

"I always dine at seven, but this is—"

"An unexpected pleasure, yes," Austin said, mimicking the Englishman's very proper accent. "You'll have to give me directions, but I know you'll be very interested in a certain proposition that some mutual friends have up their dickeys, what?" He kept from laughing by remembering what General Hickman had said about keeping a stiff upper lip.

Major Cuttingham reluctantly agreed to the meeting and gave Austin the address of his club. The English Major was wearing out the carpet in the anteroom when the American Colonel arrived dressed in a sports jacket and contrasting trousers, not the sort of dress normally seen in an English gentlemen's club. The Explorer's Clubhouse was a stuffy place, massive stonework outside, mahogany and leather inside, with stiff portraits in dark oils on the walls. "Burnt umber has always been my favorite color," Austin said.

"Could you speak a bit more softly? Cuttingham asked, leading him into a somber room that bore a greater resemblance to a library than it did a dining room despite the presence of serviettes and cutlery on the tables.

"More than happy to, old bean!" Austin boomed, then added in a lower voice, "but we'll talk business later, eh?"

"Yes, quite," the Major said, relieved. "Is this your first trip to the Mother Country?"

"Not at all. I was stationed in Germany for a number of years, and every leave I'd head straight for London."

"The theatre, I expect?"

"No, the chicks."

"Chicks?"

"That's right," Austin said, "chicks, quail, birds. English birds are ready for Freddy faster than other European women, you know. English men don't like to do it very much, eh?" Austin laughed, making short jabbing motions with his fist.

"I wouldn't know, I daresay!"

"I guessed as much. So, what's good to eat in this dump?"

"Decorum," someone at the next table said stiffly.

"I don't eat fish," Austin said. He was having a grand time.

"The mutton is usually first rate, but please lower your voice." Major Cuttingham ordered and dinner was brought promptly, but the Englishman took little pleasure in his food this particular evening and ate quickly. His American friend, however, had something to say about every dish and if he thought his comments clever or pithy he repeated them to the waiter as well as to nearby diners. When they had finished, Austin tried to prevent Cuttingham from signing the check and demanded a bill be brought to him in dollars and cents. It took Cuttingham a good five minutes to explain that cash was not accepted in a gentlemen's club. Austin finally let him off the hook and they got into a cab. He gave the driver directions and shut the communicating window.

"This has been most embarrassing for me, Colonel Austin," Cuttingham said, "and I must insist that—"

"We are going to be partners, you and I, Major, in a most enterprising enterprise."

"I don't know what you're talking about and I am certainly—"

"I figure we can wrap everything up in a month and your share will be, let's see, ten thousand pounds. You could use ten thousand pounds, couldn't you?"

"I am not a per—" Major Cuttingham was caught with a mouthful of air and he exhaled forcefully, then coughed until he was red in the face. "That's a great deal of money for a month's work, Colonel," he said when he had recovered, "but I am not in your line of work and I—"

"If you were in my line of work, I'd fire you. For your own good, of course. No, what I want you to do is form a legitimate company. You know how to do that, don't you?"

"A company? What sort of company?"

"A company to represent a South American logging firm."

"A South American logging firm?"

"Bolivia, to be precise. They've got a log jam there you wouldn't believe. They can't even dynamite that sucker."

"I thought you were working for Ian Smith. What are you doing with a Bolivian log jam? What is a Bolivian log jam?"

"It's worse than a sticky wicket. WD-40 won't touch it. The only way to unstick a Bolivian log jam is with helicopters. Helicopters, you see, are used to lift hardwood logs out of the jungle and take them to pick-up points where they can be transported to the mills. And that pleases our friends in Salisbury no end."

"Rhodesia is interested in hardwood?"

"Just the helicopters."

"I see." A glint in the Major's eye informed Austin that Cuttingham not only understood but was intrigued by the idea. "And where do *we* obtain these helicopters?"

"We buy them."

"From whom?"

"Let's see who wants to sell them to us. First, we've got to open some bank accounts. I have a letter of credit from a Swiss bank in the amount of ten million dollars U.S." Austin extracted a certificate from his inside coat pocket and waved it in front of the Major. The breeze, or the size of the check knocked Cuttingham back against his seat.

"Shall we discuss this at my house?" the Major asked. "Over a brandy, perhaps?"

"An excellent idea," Austin said. "We're almost there."

Cuttingham looked out the window as the cab turned onto Grosvenor Square. "How did—"

"How did I know your address? You're listed."

"How did you know I would be interested in your uh, unique proposition?"

"I know your bank balance, too."

And so, in a matter of days an office was opened, a bank account established, and a secretary hired through a storefront employment agency. The La Paz Lumber Company was in business. *Requests for Quotations* on the purchase of heavy equipment and helicopters were published in appropriate newspapers and, before long, L.P.L.C.'s only employee, dowdy, plump Pauline Sanders, was besieged by principals and sweet-talking brokers with cranes, tractors and helicopters for sale and lease. Calls came in from all over the world, and Pauline dutifully noted the terms and particulars. At long last, a decision was made.

"Miss Sanders," Major Cuttingham said, "the directors of L.P.L.C. have decided to award the contract for the purchase of used helicopters to the Government of Israel, pending inspection and approval by trained personnel, etcetera, etcetera."

"Very good, sir. And the cranes?"

"What cranes?"

"For the log jam, sir. From whom shall we be buying the cranes?"

"We no longer require cranes, Miss Sanders."

"I see, sir."

"Effective next Friday, we will no longer be requiring your services, either."

"Was it something I said, sir?"

"No, your work has been most exemplary."

"It's the wogs then, isn't it sir? The Pakistanis and that ilk. They work for next to nothing. It's hardly fair, is it?"

"They are not long, the days of empire, Miss Sanders. I'm glad Queen Victoria did not live to see what has become of the Commonwealth."

"She would've been awful old, sir."

Group Captain Walsh sent a couple of Blue Jobs from the Rhodesian Air Force from Johannesburg via Frankfort to Jerusalem to inspect the Bell Helicopters prior to their purchase. The pilots were concerned about the lack of adequate spare parts. To keep the choppers in the air, considering the heavy use they would be getting, spares were vital. But merely getting the new toys was cause for celebration. The problem of parts was left to be sorted out later. Word reached Austin in London to conclude the deal as quickly as possible, pay for the choppers and send them on their way. He called the Israelis and arranged to meet them the following morning to provide shipping instructions and obtain registrations in exchange for payment in full.

Just before leaving the offices of the La Paz Lumber Company, Austin received a call from Ken Flowers. "I'm glad I caught you, Joe. There's been a slight change in plans. You're staying at the Tower, isn't that right?"

"Yes."

"Send someone round to pick up your things and check into the Mayflower Hotel instead."

"Why? I'll be flying home in a couple of days."

"Yes, well, you see, the Israelis are staying at the Mayflower, and in the event that negotiations drag on or new meetings need to be scheduled, it would be much more convenient if you were near to hand, don't you think?"

"Everything's been going smoothly," Austin said, surprised by Flowers' sudden chuminess. "I don't expect there'll be any problems at this stage."

"Yes, well you never can tell, and we're anxious that everything gets done just as soon as possible. I've rung up the Mayflower and they're expecting you. Call me tomorrow to confirm the arrangements, will you?"

"Well, all right." What was going on? What did Flowers know? Something was in the wind, he could tell from Ken's voice. Why had he called rather than his secretary? Did the Israelis want more money, sensing the Rhodesians were eager to buy? No, they'd always known Rhodesia wanted the Hueys, and they were already getting top dollar. It was something else, something personal, but Austin didn't know what. He made sure his Astra .22 had one up the spout before taking a cab over to the Mayflower.

Without checking in, Austin went to the pub for a quick one. There would be no meetings that day, and he needed to take the edge off. In a corner of the bar, he saw someone who looked familiar, someone in the business, and he was trying to recall where their paths had crossed and whether it was a positive or negative passing of the ways when the man spotted him and sauntered over. "Colonel Austin, is that you?"

"Jim? Jimmy Fellowes, now I recognize you. How are you?" This was a welcome surprise. Jim had been the head security man for the Southern Sun hotels in South

Africa. A heavyset man with jowls like a bulldog, Austin recalled that he'd once shot a demonstrator for painting graffiti on the walls of his hotel. "What are you doing in London?"

"I'm working here now, Joe. I've been here a little over a year. It's a cushy job. I got too old for that other stuff. Always looking over your shoulder. Here, as violent as it gets is the occasional belligerent drunk. Speaking of which, let's have a drink and swap some talk of the old days. How's Greg?"

"Same as ever. Always looking for someone new to kill." They laughed, and memories chased after one another like beers after whiskey. One drink led to another, and the evening passed all too quickly. They drank to Greg and to Lieutenant Attenow and to Philip and Carol Thornberry. By the time good friends had been toasted and absent friends mourned, Austin was sloppy and Jim was soused. "Time to call it a day," Austin said, gathering himself to his feet.

"What room are you in?"

"I don't even know. My key's still at the desk. I'm registered as A. Jones. Oh, that reminds me, I've got to send someone round to the Tower for my baggage. They don't know I've checked out."

"You can call from your room. I'll get your key for you. Wait right here." In a minute, Jim was back from the lobby. "Room 424. Come with me; I'll tuck you in."

The elevator made Austin queasy, but, fortunately, they only had four floors to ascend. His room was in the old section of the Mayflower. Like all old London hotels, the rooms were tiny and the halls were narrow. Austin was a big man and Jim was even bigger, so they walked unsteadily in single file down the carpeted corridor with Jim leading the way and talking over his shoulder. They were almost to Austin's room when a door opened and a well-dressed black man with a Scorpion Machine Pistol stepped into the hallway and fired a four round burst that pushed Jim back into Austin. The assassin ducked back into the room and slammed the door shut.

Blood was seeping from Jim's body. He took two staggering steps forward and collapsed. "Jesus, Jim," Austin said, "I'm sorry. Those bullets weren't meant for you."

Then it was stop action, slow motion, followed by gaps in consciousness. Austin watched himself step over Jim's body so he would leave no bloody footprints behind. He watched himself retrieve the key lying on the carpet. Gun in hand, he tested the doorknob of the room into which the killer had disappeared. The door swung easily open, and Austin ducked inside, ready to fire, but no one was there. A window across the room was wide open and into it neon light poured obscenely. He ran to it and leaned out just as the gunman dropped from the fire escape. Austin didn't remember climbing out the window, didn't remember the descent, but when he reached the ground and realized where he was, the killer was nowhere to be seen. He hadn't been able to fire a single shot.

Austin hailed a cab and took it to the Tower Hotel. Locking himself in his room, he drank from the bottle of scotch he'd bought for General Jamison. He was sure the General would understand. He drank himself sober and a little before dawn he fell asleep, fully dressed. The phone woke him at eight the next morning. It was the Israeli negotiator wanting to change the venue for that morning's discussion because there'd been a disturbance at the Mayflower.

"Why don't you come over here," Austin suggested.

"We'll be there at nine."

"Take your time," Austin said.

He showered and shaved and drank several cups of black coffee and was ready when the Israeli team arrived. There were no new obstacles to negotiations, and by noon the helicopters belonged to the La Paz Lumber Company with delivery by Israeli freighter confirmed for the first of the month. Everyone shook hands and parted the best of friends.

Now Austin wanted to know who had set him up. For some time, he had felt there was a leak in the upper reaches of the security network. The opposition had been getting too lucky. Operational decisions and policy decisions were passed by the Overall Co-ordination Committee which always included the Prime Minister's representative or Ian Smith himself, General Walls, the Commissioners of Police, the Director of Central Intelligence and anyone whose expertise was required. Someone in this select group had tried to kill him, and the leading candidate was Ken Flowers.

Before returning to Salisbury, Austin shut down the office. Checks were written and accounts closed. Major Cuttingham bought a round at the club which Austin thought was jolly sporting of him, and Pauline Sanders wrote a letter to the *Times* assailing the current immigration policies. With licenses and legalities out of the way, and with end-user permits in the proper hands, the choppers were shipped to South America by way of Durban aboard an Israeli freighter. Somewhere off the coast of Africa they fell off the ship. Since L.P.L.C. was no longer in business, there was no one to mourn their loss, and, since the choppers had not been insured, there was no insurance agency to ask difficult questions.

Upon his return to Rhodesia, Austin tried to convince Sutton-Price and General Walls that he'd been set up by Ken Flowers, but they refused to believe it. Joe was the new guy on the block while Ken was part of the old boys' network. "I can't *prove* there's a traitor in the crowd," Austin told Greg and Brigit a week after he'd returned, "but I know in my bones that there is one, and I want your help in nailing the bastard."

"I'll keep my eyes and ears wide open," Brigit said.

"He'll make a mistake," Greg said. "All we've got to do is make sure that we don't make any."

The Blue Jobs set up a training program for the Hueys and rushed them into active duty within days of their arrival in Rhodesia. In the Armoured Car Regiment there was an American Captain named Bill who claimed he was one terrific helicopter pilot. Bill had spent more hours in a Huey than anyone else in Rhodesia, so he was asked to test them after they were assembled to make sure everything was okay. Austin and Greg were at New Sarum Air Base for the first flight. After the Blue Jobs had checked out the first chopper, Bill lifted the chopper in the air and promptly pranged it!

Of course, Bill was mortified. He was afraid Austin would court martial him or, worse, make him reimburse Rhodesia a quarter of a million dollars for the chopper. He was trying to calculate the number of years he'd have to serve without pay to make up for the Huey when Austin told him not to worry about it. "You may have cost us a chopper, Captain, but you've solved our spare parts problem."

11

"We went into Mozambique at Pungwe with absolutely no air cover," Ted said, cupping a match to his pipe though there was no breeze in the Milton Building boardroom, "and we caught them with their knickers down. There's no telling what damage we can inflict with proper air support."

"We were lucky," Ken Flowers said brushing a speck of dust from his coat with the back of his fingers. "The ruse worked in Mozambique. They weren't expecting funny business so they swallowed the bait and took our lads for FRELIMO troops. We won't get away with that stuff in Zambia, if I know anything about Josh Nkomo."

"Don't overlook the "K" Factor." This gem of wisdom coming from Courtney, Chief of Special Branch, a lanky academician. "Kaffirs don't learn from experience, at least not the ones we've caught."

"Hah!" General Walls snorted. "They're all the same, and I wouldn't give a dollar for the lot." He raised his head and looked about the room to see if anyone dared disagree.

Ian Smith rose from his chair at the head of the yellowwood conference table and limped over to the wall map. He ran his index finger over what had once been Northern Rhodesia. His face was grave; he looked tired. He looks defeated, Austin thought, but so far we have won every battle.

"I put the question to you gentlemen," the Prime Minister said, tapping the pointer against the map. "Should we attack 'Freedom Camp' and risk engaging the Zambian Army and Air Force, or should we settle for interdicting however many terrorist groups we can of those that ZIPRA now sends against us with seeming impunity?"

"Settle, sir?" Ted ask raising his arms, "I can't speak for the others, but this Rhodesian will not compromise his beliefs, regardless of the risks involved. I can assure you of *that* with impunity! He swung his arms across his body. "I only wish I could lead the men into battle!" He would be cool in the face of fire, Austin thought, clean and well-manicured and home in time for the seventh race.

"If you put it that way, sir," Ken Flowers said archly, "how can we do anything but commit every able-bodied man to the fray." And Ken would *never* go anywhere that suits were not *de rigeur*.

"I believe," Ian said mildly but forcefully, "that every man, women, and child is already totally committed."

"I was speaking militarily, not ideologically," Flowers said, scratching his lip. "However, if I'm being cast in the role of devil's advocate, may I remind the assembled of the number of young men who have recently decided to visit England, or has London suddenly become the fashionable place to go in winter?"

"Every nation has its quota of cowards," Ian remarked evenly. "They'll be back in time to drink the champagne. The question, gentlemen, is what are you prepared to do in order to achieve victory."

"Whatever it takes," Ted said, and then everyone except Austin and Flowers rapped their knuckles on the table and shouted, "hear, hear!" When they had finished congratulating themselves, Dieter Von Neukirk, the Minister of Information, rose to his feet.

The tall, stoop-shouldered Afrikaner glared at his colleagues from beneath bushy gray eyebrows and said, "The Vest, gentlemen, tink first about vat the Vest vill say if ve inwade Zambia!"

"They von't say 'Good vork!'" Austin said.

Walls chuckled phlegmatically and leaned over to poke Austin in the ribs, but Ken and Ted shook their heads. "Really not on, Colonel" Flowers said disapprovingly, though Dieter didn't seem to mind.

"Precisely!" Dieter said, pointing at Austin. "The Americans could make it wery difficult to conduct business."

Ian leaned over the table and supported himself on his fists. "If we worried about what the West says, we would have had our necks wrung a long time ago. We can no longer tolerate savage attacks on civilians. We can no longer accept the barbaric murder of innocent airline passengers. We have the right and duty to protect ourselves and to punish those who threaten our citizens, no matter where they run, no matter where they hide. If Zambia will not stop the terrorists who launch attacks against us from within her borders, then the consequences must rest squarely upon her shoulders. If anyone disagrees let him speak now!" No one did, and in this way it was decided to launch the largest military undertaking of the Rhodesian War and hit Nkomo's camps deep inside Zambia.

ZIPRA's largest military encampment was located near Westland Farm, some fifteen kilometers from Lusaka, the capitol of Zambia. 'Freedom Camp,' as it was called, was not only home to 4,000 terrorists, it was also the Central Operational Headquarters for ZIPRA's military wing. Here, the planners and perpetrators of the attack against the Viscount would be found. Because a successful attack against Freedom Camp might cripple Nkomo's entire war effort, Walls and Austin worked overtime considering responses to possible Zambian military interference.

When the final battle plans were forwarded to Com-Ops for consideration, Walls recommended hitting Mkushi Camp and CGT-2 at the same time as Freedom Camp. "In for a penny, in for a pound," he said to Ian by way of explanation.

Mkushi Camp was 125 Kilometers north of Lusaka, 93 long miles away. "Aerial recon indicates facilities to house and train about a thousand terrorists," Austin added.

"And the camp you call CGT-2?" Ian leaned over the maps spread on the table.

"Communist Guerrilla Training Camp? That's not our name, sir. That's what ZIPRA calls it. We never call the bastards anything nicer than 'terrorists'.

"Well said. Communists have always known that language is a powerful weapon. Mao raised an entire army on slogans. We can also learn a thing or two from the way the Matabele spirit mediums cast their spells."

"You don't believe that hocus-pocus bullshit, do you sir?" Walls asked, astonished.

"Of course not, but it demonstrates how susceptible the African is to symbolism. How many terrorists are at CGT-2?"

"We estimate four thousand."

"That's a total of approximately nine thousand bad guys," Austin said, "not to mention support that might be forthcoming from the Zambian military."

"Can we keep Zambia out of it?" Ian asked.

"I think we can," Walls said.

"Good, that will reduce the odds somewhat," Ian smiled.

Austin rubbed his hands in anticipation of the joint operation. The SAS, RLI and Air Force would all be working together, and each link was vital. At peak strength, the SAS never had more than 270 men, including Territorial troops and administrative personnel. The entire Squadron would be used in the operation, but the RLI would use only one of their Commando units. The short straw had been drawn by 3-Commando, which committed 160 RLI troopers, officers and men to the operation. The Air Force would attack Freedom Camp with two Hunter jets, four Canberra bombers, and four K-Cars. Obsolete even by Rhodesian standards, a Vampire fighter of a type used by the British Air Force thirty years earlier would attack Mkushi along with one Lynx (a twin engine Cessna) and four K-Cars. If the strike at Freedom Camp proved successful, the planes used in that raid would fly back to base, re-arm, then supplement the feeble Mkushi strike force. "If we include *all* the flight personnel that will take part in the operation and add in the SAS and RLI troops the good guys still number fewer than 500. The odds are almost twenty-to-one against us."

The Prime Minister wasn't deterred. "That's the kind of odds that the 'good guys' thrive on, isn't it?"

"Yes, sir!" Austin said. "It's the sort of challenge that separates the men from the boys."

On the day of the raid, Squadron Leader Chris Dixon, the Canberra bomber commander whose call sign was Green Leader, called the Lusaka International Airport. The airport's control tower radar covered all of Zambia and the air traffic controller maintained direct contact with the Zambian Air Force at Mumbwa. "Lusaka Tower," he began, "this is Green Leader. I have a message for the Zambian Air Force station commander at Mumbwa. Are you ready to copy?" From Dolphin 1, the Rhodesian command Dakota carrying Air Force Group Captain Norman Walsh along with General Walls and Colonel Austin, the commanding officers monitored Dixon. His voice sounded authoritative but neutral. "Do you read me, Lusaka?"

The air traffic controller at Lusaka sounded testy and unsure of himself. "This is Lusaka, uh, Green Leader. I read you. What do you want?"

"We are attacking the terrorist base at Westland Farm at this time. This attack is against Rhodesian dissidents and not against Zambia. Rhodesia has no quarrel—*repeat*, no quarrel with Zambia or her security forces. We therefore ask you not to oppose or intervene in our attack. Do you copy?"

"I copy."

"We are orbiting your airfields at this time and are under orders to shoot down any Zambian Air Force aircraft which in defiance of our request attempts to take off. Do you copy?"

"Copied. We, uh, there are two civilian aircraft scheduled for takeoff . . ." The controller's voice broke. There was noise in the background, an argument or shouting.

"This is Green Leader to Lusaka Tower. We have no objection to civilian flights, but advise you to stand by on that. We cannot at the present time guarantee safe passage and require that you hold all flights for a short while, half an hour or so."

The Lusaka air traffic controller did not respond, but no planes lifted off and for the next thirty minutes the Rhodesian Air Force maintained control of Zambian airspace while the joint forces pounded the ZIPRA camps north of the capitol. Walls and Austin paced the narrow confines of the command headquarters inside the Dakota, their fingers crossed, every squawk of static from the radio pulling them towards the control panels. A billowing cloud of black smoke, clearly visible in Lusaka, rose from what had once been Freedom Camp. Hundreds of terrorists—wounded and dying, or frightened and blindly fleeing, or armed with AK's and futilely firing into the air—abandoned the burning camp for the safety of the bush. From the air, scores of bodies could be seen splayed on the ground inside the camp before the smoke obliterated everything and command had to rely solely on radio transmissions.

The Blue Jobs were finishing the raid at Freedom Camp and starting the next phase when a Kenyan civilian aircraft from Nairobi was spotted approaching Lusaka. Green Leader was no longer in range, so Group Captain Walsh took over the transmission. The Kenyan pilot was told to orbit the airfield and asked who had priority.

A subdued air traffic controller replied, "Well, I think the Rhodesians do at this time."

"What in the hell—" General Walls sputtered. He almost tore the mike away from the Group Captain. "Give me that bloody... Lusaka this is the Commander of the Rhodesian Forces, callsign 'Sunray', do you read me?"

"Loud and clear, Sunray."

"Good! I want you to wind your neck in, do you read me?"

"I take orders from the Zambian Government," the air traffic controller said, "and my orders are—"

"Bugger your orders!" Walls bellowed. "Put me through to someone in the government, a minister or the president, if he's not too busy eating *sadsa!*"

"Right away, sir," the controller said. A minute later he was back on the radio "Sunray, I have been ordered to inform you that you are in violation of Zambian air space. Abort your mission immediately."

"Put me through to the *burumba* who gave you that order."

"He declines to speak with you."

"Then I'll wait!" Walls said. "I've got all day."

When the air attack on Mkushi was over, Group Captain Walsh contacted the Lusaka airport. "We're done; you can carry on now," he instructed the controller. Then he signed off by saying, "Have a nice day!"

"What a way to fight a war!" Austin told Walls. "You had a sovereign foreign country eating out of your hand."

"It's all in the approach," Walls said gruffly. "If you sound like you know how things are done, people will generally do what you tell them. A Peace Corps Volunteer told me you chaps teach courses in this approach. He said it's called 'EST'."

He wondered if General Walls knew that the PCV had been eaten by a croc. He probably did, Austin thought: the General had a droll sense of humor.

The attack went as planned. The Hunters hit Freedom Camp with 1000-pound bombs at exactly 0830 hours when the entire camp was in formation for roll call. The Canberras followed with Alpha bombs, a homemade product designed for this type of operation. Then, from opposite directions their 20mm cannons loaded with high explosive, the K-Cars bore down on the stunned terrorists on the parade ground. "They didn't know which way to run," a pilot reported, "so they ran in circles until we came around to give them another dose."

When the aircraft finished destroying Freedom Camp, the fixed-wing units returned to Rhodesia to refuel and re-arm, while the helicopters landed at a supply base set up inside Zambia about five minutes flying time from Freedom Camp. Because of the slow air speed of the Alouettes, there wasn't time for them to return to Rhodesia for fuel and ammunition. Walls and the Air Force had gambled that the resupply depot would go unnoticed while bombs were dropping nearby, and the gamble paid off.

As the last of the Rhodesian aircraft left Mkushi in flames, SAS paratroopers were falling around the camp like rain. A few minutes later, helicopter-borne SAS troopers landed, and groundwar fighting began!

The Mkushi terrorists fought with a savagery unrivaled by the other camps, but it was not until they were finally subdued that the Rhodesians learned why. Mkushi was a training camp for women! They were all dressed in camo uniforms, and all had webbing and rifles. These brave fighters inflicted heavier casualties than the forewarned terrorists at CGT-2.

The RLI target at CGT-2 was not hit until all the SAS had landed at Mkushi, which eliminated the possibility of surprise. To make matters worse, the first helicopter drop was off-target. The choppers were forced to go back to refuel, then return to drop the SAS at their designated landing zones, which delayed the attack until well after the initial shock of the preliminary air attack had worn off. When the RLI paratroopers hit the silk, they were greeted by strings of green tracers. Fortunately, all operational jumps in Rhodesia were made at 500 feet and, at this low altitude, it doesn't take long to hit the ground. Of course, if you're hanging there, it *seems* to take forever, and lots of thoughts can cross your mind while you're being shot at floating down from 500 feet. Thinking rarely helps a combat soldier pursue his duty with vigor and, coupled with the lack of surprise, the final task of the day did not meet with the success of the two earlier raids. The terrorists melted into the bush and were not pursued very far.

The SAS at Mkushi came across a well-stocked library and gathered more high-level documents and plans than Special Branch had previously had the pleasure of studying. They also destroyed an enormous underground armory and would have been welcomed home as heroes by the jittery ministers had the camp not been a training base for ZIPRA *women*. If the press enjoyed a field day after Pungwe, what would they have to say about Mkushi? General Hickman and Neukirk were already sweating when Austin came up with a simple, foolproof tactic. "Before we give the place back to Zambia and ZIPRA to decorate with borrowed refugees, let's hold a press conference in Mkushi."

"Ridiculous!" Ken Flowers stormed. "We can't bring the press into a war zone. It's really not on!" There are ladies in the press corps."

"Like Kitty Canty?"

"Precisely."

"She'd love it. Locker-room analysis and landing zone interviews are her style." Pretending he was holding a microphone, Austin put his fist to Flowers' jaw. "Tell me how you felt when you saw your buddy cut to ribbons."

Flowers pushed his hand away. "I fail to see—"

"I know that," Austin interrupted. "Listen and learn." Turning to the Prime Minister, he pressed his point. "Mkushi has been secure since 1600 hours. At present, only clean-up operations are underway. By tomorrow morning, the place will be relatively quiet and orderly. Let's bring the press in *before* Nkomo and Kaunda have time to stage their stories. Let's show the world what a terrorist base looks like before its turned into a child care facility."

"What's your opinion, Teddy?"

"I think it's a splendid idea, and I'm prepared to wager that it will work!"

"The kiss of death," Austin said to General Jamison that evening over dinner. "Ted hasn't picked a winner in months."

"What did General Hickman think of the plan?"

"He said it would be 'jolly good' if it worked!"

"And if a reporter is shot, he'll blame it on you."

Austin smiled. "If I can choose the reporter, I'd be only too happy to take the heat."

"It doesn't work that way, I'm afraid."

"Just another injustice life foists upon us, eh, General?"

Jamison's spirits were on the mend, and he seemed his old self again when he recommended the plum pudding. "The chef at Tiffany's is rather proud of his plum pudding, and I daresay I've had worse. Why in Rangoon before the war I once. . . ."

12

After seeing Jamison safely home, Austin and Greg drove over to Samantha's Disco to assess the mood of the foreign reporters who frequented the nightspot. Most of the patrons were celebrating, but Austin couldn't determine whether Rhodesia's offshore victory against guerrillas, a sports triumph over South Africa, or life in general motivated the revelers. At a corner table he spotted Brigit and Kitty, but the reporter abandoned her seat when he approached. "What's eating her?" Austin took Rhoda's chair, then took the cigarette lighter from Brigit's hand and lit her cigarette.

Brigit inhaled deeply, blew the smoke out slowly, and held on to his hand when he returned her lighter. "Kitty said you and General Walls ordered a massacre of Zambian women today."

"That's a crock of shit! Excuse my French, but it eats my butt the way that broad has the nerve to enjoy the comforts of Salisbury while badmouthing the government that allows her to indulge herself in comparative safety. There's a war going on, in case you hadn't noticed, and your friend is acting more and more like a mouthpiece for the communists!"

"She's not my friend," Brigit said petulantly. "In fact, I wish she would stay away from me. I prefer the company of young officers."

"Terrific."

"Well, you can't expect me to sit by the phone waiting for you to call—"

"Hey, hey take it easy. I've been tied up for weeks working on today's raid, but it's finished now, and I'am all yours."

"You could have said something." She stirred her frothy drink with a pink straw. "I thought there was another woman."

"There's no other woman." Tentatively, he touched on the subject they'd studiously avoided. "There's no woman anywhere."

"Oh?" She took another long drag and looked at him from beneath lowered eyelids. "Did something happen to Sophie?"

She even knows her name, he thought. "She's filed for divorce." She waited for him to say something else, but that was as far as he was prepared to go. She lit another cigarette from the one still burning. "Why are you smoking so much?"

"Am I?"

"Are you going to answer every question with another question?"

She looked up at him then, and he saw there were tears in her eyes. "You're going back to Australia, aren't you? You're going back to your wife."

"It never even crossed my mind."

Her eyes widened. "You are not going to contest the divorce?"

"Whatever gave you that idea?"

"You don't call me. You don't tell me what you're doing. I think you don't care for me anymore."

"Of course I—" He stopped and extinguished her cigarette, then looked directly at her. "I'm not going to be ready to marry again for a long time, Brigit, if that's what you're thinking. I don't want to mislead you. My work is—"

She interrupted him with a kiss. "I know, I know, don't say it."

He kissed her back. "I've already forgotten what I was saying."

"I missed you."

"Let's go to my place for a drink. It suddenly feels very crowded here."

"All right," she whispered. "I haven't seen Oso in weeks; I bet he's forgotten everything I taught him."

"I certainly hope so," Austin said, helping her on with her coat. "Let's find out."

"I don't want *him* to come," Brigit said, tossing her head in the direction of the bar where Greg was settling up with the bartender. "He frightens me. I think he listens when we're together."

"All right, we'll take your car."

When Austin told him he was on his own for the rest of the night, Greg protested. "Sir, the last time you went somewhere without me, someone tried to take you out."

"That was in London, we're in a civilized country now."

"Make sure Oso isn't chained. The garden boy ties him up when we're not around."

"You know what, Greg? Sometimes you remind me of my mother."

"I'll take that as a compliment, sir."

"No one else would. Don't get too drunk."

"My ma used to tell me that."

"Terrific. Pick me up in the morning at 0700. We're flying to Mkushi to meet the press."

Austin took Brigit's car keys and unlocked the passenger door of her MG. It was a warm evening, so he let the top down and drove slowly through the quiet Salisbury streets. Greg would have a shitfit if he knew, Austin thought, but so what? If I am meant to die, so be it. But there was no attack on this night, and they reached Austin's house without incident. As the house boy was closing the gates, Austin saw the white BMW slowly pass the driveway. "The sonofabitch tailed me," he said to himself, "and I never saw him." Chuckling, he pulled the MG into the garage and walked around to help Brigit out. "Greg's gonna give me hell for riding with the top down."

"I saw him following us," Brigit said. "I thought you'd told him to do it."

"I must be getting old. I didn't see a thing."

"Maybe you had something else on your mind," she said shyly.

He led her inside the house. "Maybe I did."

If Brigit was shy and insecure when she was dressed, she was bold and wanton naked; and Austin learned why she hadn't wanted Greg around. Her soft moans became pinched cries when he entered her, and when she came her screams could be heard for half a kilometer.

The next morning, Brigit accompanied Austin and Von Neukirk to Mkushi where over a dozen representatives of the world press had gathered. The reporters were helicoptered in and permitted to wander around so they could see for themselves that the base was indeed a terrorist training camp. A woman prisoner was brought before them for questioning. Her name was Phinah Malaba and, except for her AK, she was dressed in full battle gear, just as she was when the SAS had captured her. Austin would have liked her to show more defiance, but prisoners of war couldn't be scripted overnight and Phinah appeared frightened and withdrawn. Still, she answered questions honestly, if in words of one syllable, and there was little doubt that she was exactly what her captors represented her to be.

A captured male instructor provided information that the original estimate of 1000 terrorists at the camp was off by fully as many, for in addition to 1000 trained terrorists an equal number of new recruits had recently arrived. Training for women lasted six months and included bayonet drill, small unit tactics, and small arms training in handguns, rifles and machine guns, including the 12.7mm heavy machine gun. Advanced courses in urban warfare, ambush and military administration were offered to promising post-graduates.

After the reporters were ferried back to Rhodesia, the ground troops started to pull back and, in so doing, finally encountered the Zambian Army. A day late and a dollar short, the Army column lacked the sense of their Air Force compatriots. They neither looked the other way nor hightailed it to safety.

Spotted while they were still several miles away from the camp, the column had no tricks to play and didn't try to mask their intentions. The Rhodesians planned a little welcoming committee for the 64 Army, 17 Police and 12 ZIPRA Officers marching toward oblivion. The SAS picked the spot, deployed their troops, and waited in ambush. It was over before it even began.

The actual fighting took ten minutes. In addition to 47 dead, the top ZIPRA logistics officer was captured. Special Branch interrogated him and found him both valuable and pliable. He turned out to be the real prize of the battle, a coup for intelligence and a source of vital information about ZIPRA's military administration, tactics, bases and personnel.

A jubilant Ian Smith tallied the score. "Freedom Camp: 900 killed, 600 wounded. Mkushi: 600 killed. CGT-2: 52 killed. Our casualties: two killed, four wounded. Rhodesia is in your debt, gentlemen, for a job well done in these trying times." Austin noticed that Ian did not limp when he left the room this time.

And so ended the most ambitious undertaking of the

war to date. The only sour note of the campaign was the report in the *New York Times* and other foreign papers that Rhodesia had invaded Zambia to attack refugee camps where innocent and unarmed women and children were massacred. To no one's surprise the most vituperative articles carried Kitty Canty's by-line.

"To hell with them!" Ian shouted.

"Here's to us and to hell with the rest" echoed the Armed Forces in all the pubs in Rhodesia.

Brigit was having trouble with a Breather, but she wouldn't let Austin trace her incoming calls. At first she said the creep was calling her nightly, but when she saw how overwrought it made him, she said it had only happened a few times. He suspected she was minimizing the frequency of the calls out of fear that he would quickly locate and just as quickly dispatch the pervert, and he couldn't understand why she was trying to protect the creep.

"I'm not trying to protect him." Exasperated, she clipped her words like a teacher explaining a simple procedure to a dense pupil. "I just don't want you to kill him."

He still couldn't understand. They were at the Salisbury Snake Park, which Austin felt was a fitting place to talk about slime who whisper obscenities in the dark to girls who sleep alone. "People like that don't deserve to live," he said, more to himself than to her. They were standing in front of a cage in which an enormous python lay coiled. "You know him, don't you? He's an old boyfriend or something. Who is he? Just give me his name."

"I don't know who he is. Everything to you is this or that, black or white."

"If it's that Kaffir who's been hanging around Kitty, I'll kill both of them."

"You sound just like Greg. Look, forget it! Forget I asked to borrow Oso! Forget the whole thing!" Stamping her foot and tossing her hair, she wanted to storm off, but Austin caught her by the arm. A cobra lifted its head to flick its tongue, then settled lazily into itself.

"I won't kill him, just tell me who he is."

"Joe, I don't know. Someone playing a game. I shouldn't even have mentioned it to you, but I thought I'd feel safer if Oso stayed with me for a few days."

"That's fine. I have no problem with that. But it's not going to solve the problem."

She stamped her foot again. "There's no problem. Certainly not one that requires drastic measures."

"You don't know that, honey." *God, she looked good.* "It's not how you felt when you called me this morning."

"I'm sorry I did." She fumbled in her purse for a handkerchief.

"Come on, you don't mean that. Who else would take you to the Snake Park after lunch?"

She giggled, then shuddered. "Now, there is what I would call a problem." She read from an exhibit sign posted in front of a walled pit containing a huge, thick snake with a head the size of a soft ball: "The Gaboon Viper (Bitis gabonica) is the heaviest snake in the viper family. It may grow to a length of six feet. While there are several members of the viper family that grow considerably longer than this, none are as heavy as the Gaboon Viper, which also boasts fangs nearly two inches long, longer than any other snake. These fangs enable it to reach deep into well-blooded muscle where it can inject as much as two ounces of venom per bite, making the Gaboon Viper one of the most deadly snakes in the world."

"General Jamison told me that in Rhodesia there are 26

venomous snakes of different species per *acre*." Brigit uttered a little cry and looked quickly around her. Austin took her arm and led her to the next exhibit area. "When you consider that there are many more species of nonvenomous snakes than venomous ones, you would expect to see or run into a snake at every turn, but it's unusual to see a snake of any kind, even in the *bundu*."

"They're very clever," Brigit said.

"And very shy."

"Don't look at me like that; everyone's watching."

"Don't be silly; no one's watching."

"Oh, look at these little ones. They're cute."

"Cleopatra's darlings."

"Why do you call them that?"

"The asp, or horned viper, was the symbol of Egyptian royalty. Legend has it that Cleo killed herself with one." Austin ruffled the hair at the back of her neck. "In the bush, the average snake is no more anxious to meet you than you are to meet it. The exceptions are certain members of the pit viper family that are just too damn lazy to move: the horned viper and the puff adder, in particular. In Africa, more people are bitten by the puff adder than by all other species combined because they're too lazy to get out of the way and are so well camouflaged that people don't see them until they've stepped on one. No matter how lazy and well-meaning, no self-respecting snake likes to get stepped on."

"So the lesson is to look where you step?"

"That's true even in places where there are no snakes."

"Or breathers." She took his hand. "Joe, I'm 26 years old and I've been taking care of myself for years. Why don't you trust me?"

"It's my job not to trust people." He kissed her hair and felt its softness against his cheek. "I just don't want anything to happen to you."

"These anonymous callers never do anything. They're

afraid to meet a woman face to face. They say their dirty words, 'Pee-pee, poo-poo,' to the telephone and hang up with their heart beating like a hummingbird's."

"I thought he just breathed."

"I mean in general; I'm not talking about my caller."

"*Your* caller? He hasn't said a word to you but already there's a relationship."

She laughed. "I think you're jealous of my breather."

"That's ridiculous."

"No, I think I'm right."

"That's like me saying you're jealous of Greg."

She shuddered. "Jealous? No, that's something else. Greg reminds me of a snake, the kind that falls on you from a tree."

"A boomslang?"

"I don't know. Maybe it's the color of his eyes. I've never known anyone with aqua eyes."

"Lots of gunfighters in the old west had pale blue eyes. You know who he reminds me of? My grandfather."

"Was he a cowboy?"

"Grandpa Bass was a U.S. deputy marshal in the Oklahoma Territory and the first elected sheriff of El Reno County when Oklahoma became a state," Austin said proudly. "He rode with Teddy Roosevelt's Rough Riders and killed his last man in Compton, California at the age of eighty-one."

"Over a woman, I bet."

Austin laughed. "Over a chicken, actually. He used to sleep with a revolver under his pillow. He kept an 1897 Winchester pump shotgun in the corner. Someone was stealing his chickens, and one night he caught the thief sneaking into the hen house. He killed the fucker, returned to bed and went back to sleep. When they found the body next morning he hardly remembered shooting him."

Her eyes were wide open. "The police didn't do anything? They didn't arrest him?"

"They weren't too happy about it, as I recall. The zoning ordinance didn't allow folks to raise chickens in that part of Compton. They took his shotgun away and told him to leave town."

Brigit clapped her hands. "They said—" She tucked her thumbs into her waistband of her dress and tried to affect a Texas accent—"'Git out of town, podna, otherwise we string you up.'"

It cracked Austin up. "Something like that."

"You loved him, didn't you?"

"Grandpa Bass gave me my first object lesson in honor. When I was about six there were two boys, the Ralston twins, who used to hassle me. I can't remember why. One day, I caught one of the Ralston boys alone and beat him up, but I knew I couldn't whip both of them, and I knew both of them would try to get me after school. Soon as the bell rang, I hit the door and ran home. I looked back once and, sure enough, they were on my tail. I made it inside my yard and slammed the gate. I was safe then, so I got to taunting them, unaware that Grandpa Bass was on the porch. He saw what was going on and came down and beat my butt, and then sent me outside the gate where the Ralston twins beat my butt a second time. When they got finished, he cleaned me up and I'll never forget what he said. He said, 'there ain't no disgrace in getting whupped, Joe, but when you run away, even when you are outnumbered, there's disgrace for sure in that.' I've been whupped a time or two since then, but I've never run away from a fight."

"That's why you are in Rhodesia?"

"And outnumbered again," he laughed. "Can't teach an old fool new tricks."

"And Greg? Why is he here?"

"He just likes to kill. He was a sergeant in the Marines, a member of Ambassador Bunker's personal bodyguard in Saigon. You have to be real good to serve in that capacity, and Greg's one of the best. He doesn't make a good civilian, though. After his discharge, he went home to

West Virginia and waited for a deputy's job to open up. He got into a few fights, one of them with the sheriff, which diminished his chances of employment considerably, so he came to Rhodesia and joined the SAS. You don't think he's the breather, do you?"

"No, I don't think he likes girls. I don't know, Joe. I would just feel more safe with a watchdog in my bedroom. You have Greg to protect you."

"I'll bring Oso to your place tonight. You ought to think about getting a dog of your own."

"Maybe you're right. You're sure you don't mind?"

"No treats and no doggie tricks, okay?"

"I promise."

"Okay. Now let's get back to work before someone misses us."

The house the Rhodesian Government had given to Austin was built on the side of a small hill. Beneath the main part of the house was a garage and two small rooms that had been made into living quarters for Greg. When no one else was around, they were on a first name basis, for not only were they both Americans with service in Vietnam, they both enjoyed competitive shooting and spent more time together than most married couples.

One of Greg's duties was driving Austin back and forth from home to office. Greg's military training led him to explore random routes to frustrate possible assassination attempts, but Salisbury was not a large city, there were only a limited number of traffic patterns, and the terminus was always the same, so he had developed strategies to counter various ambush scenarios. When they left the Earl Grey Building, Greg would call home and give the servants their estimated time of arrival. Fifteen minutes prior to their arrival, the cook would unchain Oso, and the sixty-kilo Rottweiler would make a circuit of the property to sniff for uninvited visitors. After Oso completed his search of the area, one of the servants would come down to open the gates for the white BMW when Greg drove up and blew the horn.

The African servants, who had all been vetted by the Police before being hired, were terrified of Oso and called him the black lion. Austin had trained the Rottweiler not to take food from anyone who did not give the proper command. This was to protect the dog from being poisoned by terrorists or burglars. Absent poison or narcotics, no interloper in his right mind would come within sight, sound or smell of a trained Rottweiler, so ambush at home was highly unlikely with Oso on guard.

Work did not demand that Austin or Greg wear a uniform during the normal business day. In fact, Ted Sutton-Price requested that uniforms *not* be worn during meetings at his or Ian's office. Walls grumbled and Hickman said it was highly irregular, but they complied. Although Rhodesia was very British, formal business wear was also not expected. Slacks and sports coat with tie were considered appropriate except for formal occasions. Safari suits were generally considered acceptable business attire when worn with long pants. Only Sandhurst graduates like Sutton-Price and Ken Flowers wore dark suits and school ties every day.

Regardless of what he was wearing, Austin also carried his Colt Combat Commander. Armand Swenson had customized his .45, and Austin had slogged this weapon through salad days and dog days in Cambodia. It was now as much a part of his dress as shoes and socks. Greg trusted in a Colt Gold Cup that Austin bought for him. They each carried two spare magazines, and Greg also carried a briefcase containing a Beretta Model 12 9mm submachine gun loaded with a thirty round magazine and two additional thirty round magazines. To complete their armory, they kept a 12-bore automatic shotgun in the car, beneath the front seat (rather than in the trunk where it would be inaccessible in an emergency). These weapons were not part of a field kit but standard for social occasions in Salisbury and trips within Rhodesia, so even with Oso gone for a few days and terrorist activities on the increase, Austin and Greg were far from unprotected.

They were almost proven dead wrong two days later after a night at the Ammo Box. The club of the Armoured Car Regiment welcomed senior enlisted men and officers and had been Bob Attenow's home away from home. The place was full, the lies thick as Rhodesian *filet mignon*, and every drink was a double. Greg was awash in pilsner when they left for home a little after 0200. Austin was comparatively sober, so he drove. Considerate of the sleeping neighbors, he did not honk the horn when he pulled up in front of his driveway. Greg had dozed off in the passenger seat and, rather than disturb him, Austin got out of the car to open the gate.

In outfitting the BMW for ambush, Greg had removed the bulb from the dome light, because when the door was opened at night the light made the passengers perfect targets. This saved his life as surely as his overindulgence got *him* shot rather than Austin, who was unlocking the gate when all hell broke loose.

Perhaps the terrorists had also nipped away the night waiting for the Americans to return home, because the driveway and gate posts were illuminated by a full moon, a sniper's moon, and Greg was a slouching, if not a sitting duck. Nor were the assassins inexperienced, for they lay in waiting behind the bushes on the same side of the gate rather than on both sides where they would be firing into one another. When Austin pulled haphazardly into the driveway, two terrorists emerged from the bushes at the front left fender of the car, while the third appeared near the rear left fender. Austin had not turned into the driveway straight on, so instead of sitting perpendicular to the gate, the car was at a slight angle, with the rear of the car to the right of center. When Austin got out to open the gate, the right front fender of the BMW was between himself and the terrorists on his left while the third man was separated by the entire expanse of the vehicle.

The first terrorist opened fire with his AK, punching several holes in the left front fender, knocking out the headlight and winging Greg who reacted to the initial burst by diving into the well beneath the dashboard and grabbing for the briefcase. The second terrorist could not get off a shot without endangering the first, but the third let loose a burst from behind the car that stitched the left front door, broke the side window glass and the windshield and put a hole in the roof. No one paid any attention to Austin who rose from behind the right front fender to take out the second terrorist with a round from his .45. Austin's second shot creased the terrorist who had winged Greg and who was now firing wildly across the car and into the bushes alongside the right gatepost.

With attention diverted from him for the moment, Greg rolled out the left front door, the passenger side on British roads, instantly sober and with the Beretta in hand. Austin had fallen flat on the driveway behind the right front tire and was crawling around the BMW trying to find where the gunman he'd wounded had hidden himself.

Shielded by the car door from the action in front, Greg fired a burst at the third hitman who zig-zagged across the road and dove into a drainage ditch. The ditch, designed to drain large quantities of water in the rainy season, was perhaps two feet deep and three feet across. Bent low, Greg followed his assailant and took cover in the same ditch but on the other side of an intervening driveway. Another figure reached the ditch two driveways down from the terrorist in the middle, who now reacted to a new burst of fire near the BMW by lifting his head and shoulders and releasing a blast that peppered the car but hit no one. Greg had him dead to rights and triple-tapped him with the Beretta. Then he crawled out of the ditch and around the driveway in pursuit of the last terrorist.

Meanwhile, the lead terrorist, the first one shot, discovered he wasn't dead. Startled by the burst from his buddy across the road, he decided he was too exposed to continue lying where he was. He saw Greg climb out of the ditch and he fired one round, hitting Greg in the calf, before Austin came around behind him and shot him through the neck. Bleeding from shoulder and calf, Greg threw himself into the ditch next to the floppy he had killed and about thirty feet from where the remaining terrorist had taken cover.

Greg's proximity was apparently more than the third assassin could handle and, deciding that enough was enough, he jumped up and took off down the ditch. In his panicked flight, he failed to consider that the drainage ditch abruptly ended at every driveway to enable cars to pass over and that there was a steel culvert under each driveway to enable water to flow through. He hit the culvert knee-high while going full speed. The law of inertia forced his upper torso in one direction while the law of mechanics brought his lower torso to a full stop. As he tried to gather himself up for another try at mounting the driveway, Greg hit him with a burst that started at his right thigh and ended at his left shoulder.

All was silent for a half a dozen heart beats. Austin made sure the man he'd shot was thoroughly dead, then shouted to Greg that he was coming over. Lights were blinking on in the nearby houses, and the first faint sounds of a siren could be heard. Bent low, alert for any movement, Austin was cautiously crossing when a vehicle roared to life and came careening towards him! Austin was a fighter, not a runner, but he took the rest of the road like an Olympic sprinter and dove into the ditch beside Greg just as a Land Rover hurtled past, the driver steering with one hand and firing wildly with the other. Greg emptied the Beretta at the vehicle without slowing it down.

Then it was over. Austin removed Greg's belt and made a tourniquet that he placed above the knee. That stopped some of the bleeding. Greg's only response was,

"So much for letting the neighbors sleep." For some reason, this struck them both as the funniest thing Greg had ever said, and they were still laughing when the police arrived.

14

Greg spent a few days in the hospital reading magazines and receiving visitors. Austin emerged from the fracas without so much as a scratch and spent the first morning at the Police Forensics laboratory. Ballistic tests on the brass fired from the Land Rover indicated that the weapon it came from was an FN issued to Corporal Ncobe, a BSAP deserter who was now confirmed as the sole surviving member of a terrorist stick whose other members were awaiting identification in the morgue. The day after the attack, General Jamison accompanied his daughter's servants to the large, cold green room where the bodies were laid out on slabs. The servants confirmed that the three Africans were the same men who had killed little Samantha.

That evening, while Austin was playing gin rummy with Greg at Salisbury General Hospital, Fitzgerald called to inform him that the police had located an abandoned, bullet-riddled Land Rover near Inyanga in the Eastern Highlands. A search was being mounted by his tracker friend, Sergeant Barry Richards. Would Austin like to join the search?

"What a question!" Austin retorted.

Inyanga borders on Mozambique in an area of large tea estates between five and six thousand feet above sea level. The climate is perfect for growing premium tea.

The tea estates were beautifully maintained, with tea hedges meticulously trimmed and manicured. The estates were labor intensive, even by Rhodesian standards. Rhodesian farms and industrial plants used many more workers than their modern, mechanized counterparts in the West, where wages were higher and labor-saving devices more accessible. The British tea estate in the colonial highlands was as much a symbol of the Empire as the soccer field and cricket pitch, and similar estates could be found in Kenya, Ceylon and Malaysia.

The number of native workers, as well as the proximity of a hostile foreign country, made the estates a center of terrorist activity. There were a thousand places where Ncobe could hide, hundreds of *rondavaals* where he would be welcome, if he had not already crossed over into Mozambique. Finding a native willing to talk would be impossible; forcing one to talk would not be easy, for the laborers had been thoroughly intimidated by terrorists who were in no way adverse to employing the most barbaric methods of ensuring silence, if not loyalty. It was believed that only a similar display of cruelty could hope to loosen the tongues of the local *kraal* chieftains. Fortunately, Sergeant Richards knew a few tricks guaranteed to impress the natives. In addition to being fluent in Seshona and Sindebele, a renowned tracker and perhaps the greatest living elephant hunter, Richards was an ornithologist and herpetologist of some repute. On his farm near Que-Que he had built the largest privately-owned aviary in the world. He had rescued pygmy geese from the brink of extinction, and he milked mambas as a hobby. He was truly a Renaissance man of the nuclear age. Austin had taught him to shoot competitively and had spent many pleasant evenings on the farm with Barry and his wife, Annette, drinking beer and watching hippos emerge from the river to graze on the lawn.

At a village adjoining a tea estate near the spot where Ncobe had abandoned the Land Rover, Richards had all the men line up outside their *rondavaals* for interrogation. He asked each man if he had seen the driver of the Land Rover and, as Austin expected, he got no results. After conferring with Austin and the three men in his stick, Richards selected an African whose eye movements betrayed uncommon fear or uncommon knowledge and had him bound fast to a chair. "Keep questioning him," Richards said. "I'll be right back." Then he borrowed a burlap bag and drove over to the tea estate.

As with most estates, after the land had been cleared on this place and mile after mile of tea planted, cane rats had infested the cleared, leaf-covered terrain. Rats are on the food chain of snakes, and the highly venomous puff adder, like most vipers, has a sweet tooth, or fang, for rats. Richards soon returned with a fat and sassy snake which he clutched in one hand and held in front of the bulging eyes of the bound African.

The African strained back in his chair, then tried to evade his destiny by bouncing the chair around the dirt floor of the *rondavaal*. In an enclosed circle with a diameter of less than fifteen feet, one soon exhausts the possibilities of escape, and Richards let the African wear himself out before asking, in perfect Seshona, "Where is Ncobe hiding?"

"Ndatembwa knows no one named Ncobe." He was soaked in perspiration and his eyes flew around the circle like a trapped bird, but his closely-watched neighbors, men who had been ordered into the *rondavaal* to witness the interrogation, kept their eyes fixed on their own feet and the Rhodesians were laughing at the sport and showed no inclination to come to his aid.

"Ndatembwa knows where the terrorist who abandoned the Land Rover is hiding," Richards persisted, bringing the viper within inches of the native's face. The snake's fangs were fully extended; venom dripped from them onto the African's shiny hairless chest. Held helpless, the enraged puff adder coiled and uncoiled and flailed its scaled body against Richards' forearm.

"Ndatembwa swears he knows nothing of this man." The African's chin was buried in his neck and he tried to draw the rest of his face inside as well, like some yogi contortionist, but the hand that held the snake kept coming closer. Now Ndatembwa couldn't move in his chair. Richards' men had him pinned on either side. The viper was staring into his eyes, and hatred was dripping from its black eyeslits like the venom that dripped from its fangs. Ndatembwa couldn't tear his own eyes away, couldn't respond to the questions that the *manigi* kept asking, couldn't even scream when the snake hit, withdrew, then hit again and again, the fangs injecting him with venom, the venom etching and filling his tissues.

As Ndatembwa jerked in his death throes, the Africans in the *rondavaal* threw themselves on their knees, pleading and gibbering. The Rhodesians left them there. Richards tossed the fatigued puff adder on the floor in the midst of the terrified Africans before exiting, and the Rhodesians then drove to the next *kraal*, but the results there were much the same. "This isn't working," Richards said. "We've got to make the chiefs work for us. I think I know how to do it."

The tracker was not present when Austin summoned the *kraal* chief of the third village for an interview in front of his assembled people. "What is your name?"

"Chiritza, baas," the bony chieftain said, standing erect and trying not to tremble. The bush telegraph system had already alerted the chief to their interrogators rapport with snakes.

"What are the names of your sons?" Austin asked.

"Jemma is the name of my oldest son," Chiritza said, indicating a teenaged youth who was watching the proceedings, "and Wasiya is my youngest son." He pointed his stick at a two-year old in the arms of a thick breasted woman.

They kept up a desultory conversation, Austin asking about Chiritza's daughters and grandchildren and the chief answering in few words, impatient, but also fearful. "Ncobe is the name of the man we are searching for, Chiritza. He is a dangerous man, a bad man, and he is hiding nearby. Have you seen him?"

"Chiritza see no one, baas."

Austin turned at the sound of an approaching vehicle, shielding his eyes against the midday sun. "Do you know Chief Tembanie who lives in the village from which this Land Rover is coming?"

Chiritza was on guard against any association that might involve him in possible criminal activity. "I stay in my own *kraal*, baas. My people harvest tea leaves and keep to their business."

"Chief Tembanie also had a son like your Wasiya," Austin said as the Land Rover came closer, then passed by. "He would not help us and now look what has happened!" Strung on a frame at the back of the vehicle swung what looked like a child's body. It had been skinned and tied like a sail between the poles with its arms and legs outstretched and tied off. "If you do not want this to happen to Wasiya, you will find out where Ncobe is hiding. We are going to the Police Station for tea. We will come back for Wasiya this evening if we have not heard from you." And with this Austin and Richards' men said goodbye and left the village.

Back at the station, a message was waiting for Austin from Superintendent Fitzgerald. He called back. "What do you have for me?"

"Ever hear of Rex Nhongo?"

"Can't say that I have, Marv."

"He's one of Mugabe's top aides, and we've received a report that he's on his way from Mozambique to Inyanga to convene a meeting of terrorist group leaders."

"That's where we are."

"I know. We were wondering if you'd mind laying out a welcoming party this evening."

"I'm on another assignment."

"Perhaps you could attend to Nhongo first. We'd really like to have a chat with him."

"You've got it, my friend."

"The BSAP is sending a Police Superintendent from Umtali to assist. Jock will be able to identify Nhongo for you. If we find out exactly where this *indaba* is to take place, I'll contact you. Meanwhile, see what you can sniff out, but don't let on. Nhongo is twitchy."

They had finished lunch and were mulling over the news when Jemma, Chiritza's oldest son, appeared at the door of the Police Station with news that Ncobe was headed for an *indaba* at a tea estate several miles the other side of Inyanga. It had to be the same meeting!

When Jemma left, Austin called Special Branch and received permission to mount an ambush. Nhongo was one of the cleverest and most aggressive of Mugabe's military leaders; capturing him would be a major coup. To allay any suspicion of attack, Austin asked Walls to remove all RDF troops from the area. He would go in with just the Police Superintendent from Umtali, Richards and his three men.

"Greg is gonna be real miffed about missing this one," he told Barry as they climbed into the back of the camouflaged Mercedes Unimog truck that would take them to the meeting site. "I heard he got shot. How is he?"

"Bored. By the way, what happened to you this morning? I was running out of things to say to old Chiritza."

"Sorry about that. Baboons are hard to find in this part of the country."

"So it *was* a baboon, I was almost afraid to ask."

"It did look real, didn't it?"

"Chiritza thought so; that's what counts. What gave you the idea?"

"In order to graduate from the Sniper Training Program, you've got to bring back a *babijaan*. Skinned, they look just like a Kaffir baby."

They stopped in Inyanga to pick up a heavyset man in a poncho. "You must be Jock," Austin said.

"Colonel Austin, I've heard a great deal about you."

"Don't believe a word of it." They shook hands and Austin introduced the Superintendent to Sergeant Richards, Corporal Dawson, and Troopers Thomas and Upshaw.

"Are you the Sergeant Richards that mucks about with snakes?" Jock wanted to know.

"The very one," Austin said. "He had a couple of chiefs pissing in their loincloths this morning."

"It's interesting," Richards said, "that the average Kaffir isn't nearly as afraid of the Gaboon Viper as he is of the puff adder or the mamba, but the Gaboon Viper is just as lethal, if not more so."

"Why is that?" Austin asked.

"Africans believe the Gaboon is a well-disciplined snake that bites only to feed. They think you can talk a hungry Gaboon into eating your lunch instead of eating you."

"Is there any truth to that?" Jock wanted to know.

"To my knowledge, no one has ever tried to reason with a Gaboon or any other snake they encountered along the way."

Dawson gasped. "If I met a snake in the bush, I wouldn't engage it in no bloody conversation, believe me. By the time I came down from where I'd jumped, I'd be headed in the other direction with my legs churning like a bicyclist."

"Which is exactly the way most snakes would respond to meeting you," Richards allowed, "and the way Nhongo and Ncobe are certain to react if they get wind we know about their *indaba*."

"That's why there's only the six of us," Jock said. A Superintendent in the BSAP holds a rank roughly equal to an Army Major. Austin outranked him and was therefore in command of the small party, but Jock was no stranger to field ops and kept them entertained during the long, slow ride in the Unimog. "The smaller our group the better the chance we won't be detected," he said, betraying by the burr in his accent his Scottish origin. "If we encounter more than we can handle, we can radio Umtali for assistance. They're standing by."

"Our objective," Austin reminded his stick, "is to capture Nhongo and, if possible, Ncobe. If we can't take them alive, kill them, and with them take out as many of Nhongo's group leaders as possible. But remember, it's quality, not quantity that counts this mission."

"That's correct," Jock said. "We've tried to catch this Nhongo chap before and he always seems to find a way out in the confusion."

"There will be *no* confusion this time," Austin promised. "Just the six of us and two CT's. Don't count on anything else."

"One thing we can't count on," Richards said, "is air support." It was mid-summer, Rhodesia's rainy season. At their altitude, the rains and dense fog made any air operation impossible.

"We won't need the Blue Jobs," Austin said. "This is a snatch operation, not a major contact. Or so we hope."

"Amen," added Corporal Dawson.

Before leaving Umtali, Jock had met with the local RLI Commander and coordinated call-signs and an overall game plan. If Austin's stick ran into more than they could handle, RLI reinforcements would move into place within a couple of hours. It was the best they could do and everyone hoped it was more than Austin would find necessary.

Even had the visibility not been close to zero, aircraft would not have been used in this operation. Austin was entering into an area heavily influenced by terrorists, if not in their outright control. Locals would notice a helicopter insertion at once and spook the twitchy Nhongo and his party. It would have also been impossible to walk in from any great distance, for the *mujibas* were certain to pick up the spoor, no matter how careful they were, and the mission would be blown. Instead, the insertion would be accomplished using a technique developed by the RLI Territorials.

The Unimog had been modified as a mine-proof troop carrier. The entire stick was riding in back. They rumbled slowly towards their ambush site over a dirt track that passed for a mountain road.

The locals would have noticed immediately if the vehicle stopped, for this was a dead give away that something had been delivered or somebody had gotten off the truck. However, no notice was taken when a truck slowed down or went into a lower gear to climb a steep grade. When the Unimog geared down to climb a sharp incline that was within one klick of the ambush site, Austin and his men rolled off the back of the moving vehicle.

It was raining like a cow pissing on a flat rock. Steam was rising from the terraced fields; it would be impossible to follow their spoor. The price they paid was being covered with mud from the moment they rolled off the truck onto the dirt track until they took up their position on the tea estate where the terrorists were scheduled to meet. They immediately got off the road, sloshed through a *donga* to a thick patch of acacia, then clambered through fences and tea hedges to a concealed site near the junction of two roads.

This was where Nhongo was supposed to be transferred from the guides who had brought him in from Mozambique to Ncobe and the local group that would furnish him security and guide him to the *indaba* site somewhere on the plantation. The transfer would probably occur at dusk, in about four hours, but it could happen at any time.

The location offered no high terrain or prominent feature that would allow for a classic ambush. They were on the edge of a cultivated field. The tea plants were about four feet high and planted in precise rows that followed the contour of the hills. The rows were only about eighteen inches apart, and this was the only cover available. Whoever selected this site for the transfer knew what he was doing; Austin would have to make the best of a bad situation.

The weather at least was on their side. The rain had turned to a heavy mist, with visibility down to twenty feet. It was like being inside a cloud, but what at first seemed a stroke of good fortune was soon to become a tragic problem.

Austin placed his people in an 'L' ambush, with Jock at the top and Richards at the right flank, near the road and about three meters from his own location at the base of the 'L'. From his position, Austin could trigger the ambush and control the stick. As they were moving into position, a truck rumbled down the road and everyone dropped to the ground. Suddenly, an inhuman scream froze everybody where they were.

It came from Austin's right, and the Colonel ran past the MAG man to Richard's position. The tracker jumped up, took one step towards Austin and screamed a second time. Then as if someone had pulled a switch, he became completely calm. "Colonel, I have just been bitten by the biggest bloody Gaboon Viper you have ever seen." He took hold of Austin's shoulder, the tightness of his grip his only expression of discomfort. "I fell on top of the bugger and didn't have time to offer him my sandwich," he laughed.

Any thought of ambush or capture was now out of the question. Austin called in his people and had them look for the snake. It hadn't moved, and Richards hadn't exaggerated. It was the largest Gaboon Viper any of them had ever seen, a beautiful specimen the color of autumn leaves and over six feet long with a head as wide as Austin's fist. The snake had bitten Richards in the upper thigh first, and, when he'd jumped up, the snake had bitten him again just above the ankle. Corporal Dawson hacked its head off.

The collective wisdom at the time was to inject the snake-bite victim with Cortisone to combat shock, and then to watch for symptoms of envenomation. It is not commonly known, but the injection of venom by a poisonous snake is a voluntary act, and fully twenty percent of all venomous snake bites are without venom. Since antivenin can have adverse side effects due to allergic reactions, caution is advised. Only if envenomation occurred would Austin allow himself to inject the antivenin. The standard dosage was two vials of the serum that each man carried in his first aid pack. Manufactured in South Africa, the serum was a polyvalent that was supposed to be effective against ten different poisonous snakes commonly found in Rhodesia.

While Jock got on the radio and summoned assistance, Austin and the Territorials tried to make Richards as comfortable as possible. It took less than fifteen minutes for envenomation to become obvious. Austin injected Richards intravenously as he had been instructed. The hunter, tracker, breeder and snake handler did not appear to be in shock, but, to be on the safe side, Austin started an IV drip. While this was going on, Jock tried calling for a medevac chopper to airlift Richards to the hospital in Umtali, but the ceiling was zero, nothing could get off the ground. Police headquarters in Umtali assured them that surface transport was on the way, but their best guess was a two-hour ETA. Austin's insistence that the area be cleared to prevent compromise of the operation was working against them.

"It feels like there's a great weight on my chest," Richards said, "and I'm having trouble breathing." He reported this like a scientist noting phenomena. His leg was swelling fast; his ankle was now as thick as his thigh.

It looked like every blood vessel in his leg had ruptured and the entire leg was blood-engorged. "I once saw a man's leg split open like a sausage," Richards said. "You could see the femur and tibia." Then, off-handed, "I'm dying, you know."

"You'll be all right," Austin said. "We'll be drinking beer again and watching the hippos mow your lawn."

"I've blown the entire operation, chaps. I hope you won't hold it against me."

"Don't be bloody daft," someone said.

"Lets have some tea," Corporal Dawson said, proceeding to set up a small, self-contained burner.

"It's ironic, isn't it? I probably know more about venomous snakes than anyone in Rhodesia except for the curator of the Snake Park in Salisbury, and I'm at a loss as to what to do."

"Would you like some whiskey?" Jock asked, unscrewing a small flask.

"There's an idea," Richard said, reaching for the flask.

"That's absolutely forbidden in treating snake bite," Austin said, "but what the hell."

Richards took a long swallow. They could tell by they way he was writhing that he was in deep pain, but he didn't complain. Austin gave him some morphine, but it didn't seem to help much and Richards soon started having convulsions, losing and then regaining consciousness. When awake, he tried to describe what was happening inside him, then he started to talk about culling elephants, what a shame that was because, despite what cattlemen thought, they didn't carry rindpest. "I've killed elephants traversing the corridor from Zambia," he said, "and snakes that were after pygmy goose eggs. They were so thick around the henhouse, Annette was afraid to go out there. In the morning, after a rain, the clover lays like a blanket on the veld and Annette wants to walk barefoot on the grass, but she's afraid of snakes. I tell her they're more afraid of you, but she doesn't believe me and when she combs out her hair in the morning sun, there's. . . ."

He passed out then, but a few minutes later he came back.

He was fighting against worsening pain; his lips were cracked and now he was babbling in African tongues. Austin heard him call out a name that sounded like Ndatembwa and there were other names and his wife's name before he lost all consciousness. He died half an hour before the transport arrived.

This was in 1979, and a great deal more is known about snake bite and how to treat it. Given current knowledge, Austin might have been able to save his friend's life. The immediate injection of everyone's antivenin, ten additional doses, might have done the trick. However, the curator at the Snake Park told him later that even a single bite of a Gaboon Viper would require "heroic efforts" to countermand. Where the victim was bitten twice, the venom injected was enough to kill ten men.

The saddest part of the story was that Nhongo had called the meeting off when he heard that Ncobe's vehicle had been found. Ncobe had crossed the border into Mozambique the previous night.

Richards had died in vain.

15

One hope was left the protectors of white rule in Rhodesia: get the Fat Man!

What had once been strongholds were now sieves. Terrorists broached borders by day and night to raid farms and plant mines; bandits claiming to be freedom fighters pillaged country stores and terrorized African shopkeepers, then ran off to buy beer with their booty and curse capitalism.

The government responded in curious fashion by imprisoning the innocent to protect them. Villagers were resettled in new townships, guarded enclaves far from ancestral lands where facilities were inadequate and customs ignored. Resentments flared, breeding terror that the townships had been designed to prevent.

In London, war by other means was being waged by slippery negotiators. In Salisbury, a moderate African acceptable to the ruling class was elected to lead a coalition government, but Bishop Muzorewa was not acceptable to ZIPRA or ZANLA or the OAU. Negotiators curled up to Nkomo, slithered over to Mugabe, whispered sweet nothings in Smith's ear. Everyone smiled for the camera during photo ops.

To Austin, bandits were preferable to politicians and considerably more honorable. Bandits did not pretend they were raping you for your own good. "Rhodesia's only hope," Austin told anyone willing to listen, "is to blow away Nkomo and Mugabe."

"While negotiations are in progress? World reaction would be immediate and dreadful," Hickman said.

"While you're singing that old song, our enemies are rehearsing new dance steps." Austin appealed to Ted Sutton-Price: "We are losing the war because our hands are tied. I saw it happen in Vietnam. For God's sake don't let it happen here!"

"What are you proposing?"

"That we take out Nkomo and Mugabe."

"It's simply not done," Flowers said.

"The CIA does it with equanimity," Ted rejoined.

"I'd rather we use the Selous Scouts," Walls laughed and looked around to see who else appreciated his wit.

"It's a last resort," Ian said, "but I'm not convinced all other options have been explored." He was back from London where negotiations were stalemated. Things might have stayed stalemated in Salisbury as well had not the Fat Man himself brought convincing arguments to the discussion. Another Viscount was shot from the skies by ZIPRA terrorists armed with Russian ground to air missiles, and Nkomo took credit for the attack and hinted there was more to come. When Special Branch informed Ian of military strategies developed by the Soviets for imminent implementation by ZIPRA, Ian threw up his hands. He asked Austin to draft preliminary plans to assassinate Nkomo at his Lusaka residence.

The Russian strategy was revealed to Special Branch courtesy of the logistics officer captured during the training camp raids in Zambia. With very little encouragement—no skinned baboons or venomous snakes—he told his interrogators that Nkomo's KGB advisors had developed plans to launch a full-scale conventional war against Rhodesia. The attack would be backed by tanks and armored personnel carriers that the Soviets had recently shipped into Zambia. Rhodesian intelligence confirmed that conventional warfare was probable within six months and Rhodesia would not be able to repel an invasion. Evidence obtained in the Mkushi raid revealed that ZIPRA had over 21,000 trained terrorists in Zambia and an additional 4,500 trained tank and armored vehicle operators. When Ian asked General Walls point blank, the harried General confessed that Rhodesia could not withstand, much less defeat, a massed armored attack.

"We ran 'sand table exercises' on this scenario with the Armoured Car Regiment," Walls told Ian's advisors and ComOps staff at a meeting in the Milton Building, "and the most optimistic appraisals give us one week before Salisbury is captured. This time frame is predicated on our belief that ZIPRA will *not* receive air support from the Zambian Air Force. With air support, we have less than a week." Ian asked the head of the Selous Scouts for a report. Lt. Colonel O'Brian stood up, blew his nose, cleared his throat and said that his operatives in Zambia knew the location of Nkomo's personal residence in Lusaka. They had taken numerous photos of the structure and the surrounding compound. "One of our men is a farm implement salesman specializing in heavy equipment. His reports confirm an influx of heavy military equipment into Zambia. Something is brewing there," O'Brian concluded, "and unless we do something to cool the Fat Man's enthusiasm, we're going to get scalded." Clearing his throat once again, O'Brian sat down.

Dieter reported that the BBC had recently aired a personal interview with Nkomo in which the Fat Man talked about his day-to-day life. "Ve haf acquired a copy of zis tape from friends in England, and ve haf studied architectural drawings from the period of confederation. Both are wery interesting."

Nkomo's house was the former residence of the Governor of Northern Rhodesia, and Intelligence had blueprints of the place as it existed twenty years earlier.

"There have been no major renovations to the structure that we are aware of," Flowers informed them.

Overall planning for the raid was awarded to the SAS with Austin in the limited role of special advisor to the Prime Minister. It would be Joe's responsibility to review the plans for ComOps, but, as he told Captain O'Rourke, the Irishman who would be leading the SAS forces, "I'm personally involved in the success of this mission, and I've a personal score to settle with the Fat Man."

" 'ow's that, Colonel?"

"I spent a miserable week baby-sitting the bastard in Geneva. I could have taken him out right there and then and made it look like a ZANLA hit. Instead, I all but tucked him in and kissed him good night. I figure his ass belongs to me."

"My brother-in-law went down with the second Viscount. I've a claim to a piece of his bloody arse meself."

"Fortunately," Austin laughed, "there's enough for everyone."

When Austin repeated the joke to Brigit, she said, "I wish there was more of you for me. I have a feeling I'm not going to be seeing much of you for a few months."

"A few weeks is more like it. You can have Oso back if you're lonely. He misses you; he's been off his feed since he left your place."

"I'll give you some of my bratwurst to feed him. He loves it."

"Have you heard from your friend, the breather?"

She shook her head. "I think he got tired of me. You men are so fickle."

"How about if I come over tonight and whisper dirty things in your ear?"

She giggled. "I might like that."

"Oh, wait, I can't. I promised Captain O'Rourke I'd go over some maps with him."

"Call me when you get home then, all right?"

"I promise," Austin said and promptly forgot when Sutton-Price walked into ComOps waving some papers and looking for him. Austin was having coffee with Captain O'Rourke and going over the plan he'd developed for storming Nkomo's Bastille in Lusaka. O'Rourke had worked up ballpark estimates on the manpower and equipment that would be required to implement the plan and Austin had sent the roughs to Sutton-Price.

Ted had the prelims in one hand, a tout sheet in the other. "Congratulations are in order. Ian likes your numbers."

"They're just rough figures. They need study and confirmation."

"Yes. We've all got a lot of work to do and very little time to do it in. Four hours sleep, that's all I permit myself." Ted tossed the tout sheet on the table, saw his mistake and quickly replaced it with the proposal. "Connect the dots for us, would you? The fine print, timeline, contingencies—the bottom line, as you chaps put it."

"I'll have it for you in a week," Austin said, giving the thumbs-up sign to Captain O'Rourke who had excused himself but couldn't help watching from across the room.

"Not to rush you," Ted said, "but Ian would like to have it Friday. Things are getting a bit dodgy."

They made it in time, but Austin had to cancel another date with Brigit. She hung up on him when he wouldn't tell her why. "I can't discuss it with you," he said. "I can't think about—"

"Then think about this!" She interrupted, slamming the receiver into its cradle.

He had no time to think about anything but the hundred and twenty miles from Lake Kariba to Nkomo's doorstep, so Austin did not call back. His mind replayed the assault on Pungwe.

It had worked there, but Hickman thought it was a fluke that wouldn't fool anyone a second time. Hickman had been wrong so often that Austin was convinced it was worth trying again. The SAS had several surplus Sabre Land Rovers which O'Rourke ordered painted dark green with yellow blotches. At a distance they could pass for Zambian Army vehicles. Close up, anyone could see that the youngest of these puppies was at least ten years old and more than a little clapped out. Still, the Territorials were able to sweeten seven of them so that, like old whores in a dim light, by the time you could tell they weren't spanking new you'd lost your trousers.

It would take sixteen men to assassinate Nkomo and anyone foolhardy enough to get in the way, but the possibility of interference from the Zambian Army, the distance that had to be covered, and the availability of seven cherried-out vehicles permitted forty-two men to take part in the raid, almost enough men, Austin felt, to wipe out ZIPRA and all the acronyms in Africa.

"Better safe than regretful," Austin said. "It's 200 kilometers from the border crossing to Nkomo's front door, and anything can happen."

O'Rourke rubbed his hands together. "Right you are. It's not a bloody picnic we're going on," he said, sounding as if it were just that. "We're going to blow up a bleeding building in the bloody capitol of a hostile nation."

"When we get back," Austin said, "I'm going to teach you a litany of swear words. Obscenities by the score, profanities by the bushel basketful, and not a drop of blood in any one of them."

"A Yank teach a Dubliner to swear?" O'Rourke lifted an eyebrow. "For cataloguing body parts and bodily functions, no one can beat the Irish. For insults and taunts, aspersions and blasphemy, innuendo and diminuendo, we've no equal. And there's not a word in any book says it all so roundly as 'bloody'. 'Shit' is sweeter, 'fuck' is drier, 'Goddamn' misses the wound by a mile—"

"We've got work to do!" Austin interrupted him. "I haven't got all bloody day!"

"Apology accepted," O'Rourke said mildly. "As I was saying, we need the added men should we run into trouble going into the country and to compensate for losses to the hit team. But our primary concern is having enough men—and fire power, to get us out of the bloody country afterwards."

"There's an even better reason for the extra men," Austin mused, "but Ian won't authorize it."

"What's that?"

"With the extra men we could clean the nest of advisors. That's where the Fat Man gets his venom, you know."

O'Rourke looked puzzled. "Can't say I do."

"Getting rid of Nkomo will slow things down, but getting rid of his Russian advisors would completely disrupt ZIPRA's war efforts, no matter who succeeds the Fat Man."

"What did Ian say?"

"Flowers convinced him that the international repercussions would be intolerable. That's a crock, and Flowers knows it. Nothing is intolerable when a nation's existence is at stake. Besides, the Russian Ambassador to Zambia is a high-ranking KGB officer, and Nkomo's advisors report directly to him. What would be the political repercussions of that disclosure? Would it be worth making a stink about a Russian advisory team? I don't think so."

"They don't pay me to think," O'Rourke said.

"You can read a map, can't you? Take a look at this." Austin unrolled a street map of Lusaka and pointed to a spot less than half a mile from Nkomo's residence. "This is the exact location of the compound used by the Russians. Is this a piece of cake?"

"We could blow it up easy as look at it."

"That's what I told Ian."

"What'd he say?"

"He wouldn't countermand Flowers. Ken is Sandhurst and Cambridge. I can't buck the old boy network. The British wage war according to outmoded codes of behavior. No, it's not just the British. They aren't much different from West Pointers. I don't know what it is. The Communists are willing to do whatever it takes to win; why aren't we?"

"Perhaps because we're not ideologues like the Reds; perhaps because winning isn't everything."

"Well, let me tell you something, Captain. Winning may not be everything, but losing is nothing at all."

"Surely you don't think we're trying to lose? Something else is eating at you, Colonel. What is it?"

Austin smiled sheepishly. "That's very perceptive of you, Captain. Yeah, there's something else all right. From the day I came to Rhodesia, it seems like, I've been haranguing Ian Smith to let me kill Nkomo. When he finally approves the plan, he won't even let me go along."

"You're much too valuable, Colonel. Why, if you were captured—"

"I know, I know. Ian said the same thing, but I'd give my left nut to be with you when you see the sweat on the Fat Man's face."

'Operation Bastille' demanded absolute secrecy. At first, only the seven drivers were briefed. Since Austin had coordinated the plans for the operation, his presence was required during the briefings to answer questions and provide contingencies for ComOps in real time.

One matter of concern to the politicians at ComOps was the reaction of the Zambian Army. Nkomo's residence was within two kilometers of a major Zambian Army compound. Another concern was the proximity of the residence of the President of Zambia, Kenneth Kaunda. "His bleedin' house is lit'rally a mortar shot away from Nkomo's," O'Rourke warned, "and it's guarded by British-trained personnel."

"We lucked out there," Austin said. A chorus of cat-calls from the drivers greeted his remark. He pretended they were flowers, doffing his beret and bowing in acknowledgement.

"One bright spot," O'Rourke said when the men had quieted down, "is that the President's corps of bodyguards is under the command of an ex-British officer whose chief duty is keeping Kaunda healthy. The bloody man's a professional; he'll stay away from our bleeding party."

"Or lose his bloody 'ead in the bargain!" someone shouted.

The briefing was unlike any Austin had ever sat in on. The relationship between officers and enlisted personnel in most Special Forces units is unlike that in 'straight leg' or regular outfits; however, even for a Special Forces unit, the reaction was a little unique. After listening patiently to the entire plan, a sergeant who'd been hand-picked to drive one of the Sabres, stood up and queried Captain O'Rourke. "Are you fucking mad?" he demanded.

There were only two ways O'Rourke could respond: he could laugh or he could yell. O'Rourke burst out laughing. "That's exactly what ComOps said when Colonel Austin came up with the bloody idea in the first place." Austin rose to acknowledge the whooping ribaldry with another elegant bow. "And," O'Rourke added, "I've got to admit, that's what I thought when I first heard about the plan. But the more I thought about it, the more sense it made."

"I was at Pungwe, mates," said a soldier Austin instantly recognized, "and if Colonel Austin said he had a plan to storm the gates of Hell, I'd volunteer to lead the charge."

For this display of enthusiasm, Sergeant Major Halverson was heartily booed. Then someone else stood up to ask, "Has anyone considered how funny it would be to catch the Fat Man in his teddy bear pajamas?" An argument ensued as to Nkomo's nightwear, with suggestions ranging from grotesque hairsuits to slinky nighties.

By the time someone stood up to say, "We're going to make history, gents," everyone in the room was excited by the possibilities and, to a man, were eager to have a go at it.

The rest of the men selected to accompany Captain O'Rourke were only told to get their kit together for an outing to Lake Kariba. On the way out, the convoy stopped in a small town for tea and pee. A curious resident asked a trooper where they where headed, and the soldier jovially responded, "We're off to Lusaka." Although it was treated as a joke by all concerned, Captain O'Rourke decided to tell his men the nature of their mission as soon as they reached the base camp at Kariba. Upon their arrival, he restricted everyone to camp for security reasons and called a meeting. If he was afraid the men would respond to the news with misgivings, his fears were unfounded. No one complained about being restricted to camp, and everyone wanted to take a shot at the Fat Man. Not a man present was without family or friends who'd died on one of the Viscounts. The opportunity for revenge was too good to pass up.

At the base camp, they built a full-scale mock up of Nkomo's compound. The fences and walls surrounding the Fat Man's home were outlined in the dirt, and a movie-set likeness of the house was constructed. While they waited for the Selous Scouts operative to radio from Lusaka that their bird was in its nest, the SAS troopers rehearsed every move the actual assault team would make during the raid.

Nkomo was in and out of the country. He traveled to London to take part in the endless rounds of negotiations, and to other African countries in search of aid. Even when he was in Lusaka, he frequently spent the night at homes he visited. His security was good, and the farm implement salesman working for the Selous Scouts was unable to predict his movements.

Finally, the words they'd all been waiting for. "Bastille, Go!" radioed the agent in Lusaka, followed by a bit of unauthorized encouragement. "And good shooting, fellows!"

Austin was in Salisbury when the call came in. He would have time to catch a few hours sleep before Greg drove him out to the airport. Although he would not be entering Zambia with O'Rourke and the SAS, he would be aloft in the Dakota to provide fallback command, if necessary. He was undressing when the phone rang. It was Brigit. "I saw you this afternoon," she said. "I didn't know you were back in town."

"I just got in yesterday."

"Is your mission over?"

"Not exactly. Soon."

There were long pauses in their conversation, and he had to press the receiver hard against his temple to hear what she was saying. "I know...your work. I understand...."

Suddenly he heard Greg shout. "I'll call you later!" He hung up the phone and raced downstairs, gun in hand. The night was overcast; there was a hint of smoke from a woodfire in the air. "Oso!" Where was his dog? "Greg!" He moved quickly from one protected position to another: house to tree to garage. A burst of fire from the garage flattened him against the outside wall. There was an answering burst, a scream that ended in a bloody gurgle, then Greg's calm voice.

"You can come in now, Joe." Austin pushed the door open with his foot, breathed deeply, ducked inside. A penlight on the concrete floor faintly illuminated a dead but still twitching man bent over the bonnet of the BMW like an engrossed mechanic. "I think he's alone," Greg said, flipping the switch. Frozen in sudden light, caught in the act of ingesting its victim, the vehicle winked a broken headlight at them.

A sudden movement behind the car alerted Austin. "Look out!" Diving to his right, he double tapped the .45 and caught a familiar terrorist in the act of firing. The impact hurled the terr against the gardening tools hung on the wall, impaling him on a rake. He was wearing a tattered police coat and he died cursing. "Watch it, Greg. There might be more of them. You cover the grounds to the left. I'll meet you at the gate. Can you handle a gun in that?"

Greg was still wearing a sling from their last brush with assassination. "Ask the mechanic," he said. They separated and scoured the grounds but found nothing. "If there was anyone else," Greg said, "he be long gone."

They went back to the garage. Fuel was leaking from the BMW and spreading the blood flowing from the impaled policeman and the mechanic dangling from the BMW's maw. "We just had the damned thing repaired, too," Austin said.

"Think of it this way, if the bomb they were planting went off, there'd be nothing left to repair. Nothing left of us, either," Greg replied.

"How'd they get in?" Austin wanted to know. "Where's Oso?"

"Outside my door. I think he's dead." They left the carnivorous scene and ran over to the cottage apartment. There was muffled laughter followed by applause from Greg's television. Lights interplayed with shadows on the lawn where Oso lay dead in a pool of vomit. "He made it all the way over here to warn me," Greg said. "You can see where he dragged himself through the grass. I heard him whine when I went out for a stretch."

"It's a wonder you can hear anything over that damn telly. Call Special Branch. Find out what killed him, then bury him with honors. Find out if my floppy is who I think he is. I'm going to bed. Wake me at 0400. And find us another car. I need to be at ComOps at dawn." Austin started inside, then stopped. "Next time, don't say you're alone until the meat wagon leaves."

"I guess I owe you one, Joe."

"Three," Austin laughed, "but who's counting?"

16

They crossed Lake Kariba the following afternoon in a ferry. The 'Sea Lion' carried the seven vehicles and the 42-man raiding party across without mishap. A small force was deployed on the Zambian side of the lake to defend the debarkation/embarkation site. Almost half the route was over dirt roads, and the Sabres were able to traverse most of the rough track that led to the main highway without using headlights.

The landing site had been determined by reconnaissance prior to the landing, but there had been no rehearsal of this phase of the operation for reasons of security. Nevertheless, everything went according to schedule. The attack on the residence was to take place at 0300 hours, and the time to get from the debarkation point to downtown Lusaka had been worked out to the minute. Everything but the unpredictable was accounted for. The unpredictable happened.

Control of the operation, and any coordination that might be required between the attacking unit and the Air Force was to be handled by Austin aboard a command Dakota that flew back and forth on the Rhodesian side of the lake. Strict radio silence was obeyed, but in an emergency the command ship could enter direct radio contact with the attacking force, the Air Force and Com-Ops. Austin boarded the plane that afternoon after receiving confirmation that the terrorist he'd killed was indeed Ncobe. Why had the renegade risked coming back? Was it a personal vendetta? Oso had died from eating a poisoned sausage. Why had he taken it from a stranger? Every question led to more questions. He paced into the tail section of the Dakota. The plane refueled at Kariba airport at 2200 hours. No one had yet broken radio silence.

The attack force was running late. During the trip to Lusaka, one of the Land Rovers was accidentally rolled when a trooper sitting beside the driver somehow got his rifle caught in the steering wheel. There were no serious injuries and the vehicle was no worse for being rolled, but it took half an hour to get the vehicle back on its wheels and repacked. Fortunately, the machine guns had not been mounted. Each vehicle carried one 12.7mm and one 14.5mm machine gun taken from the enemy in previous encounters. All small arms were also courtesy of retired terrorists. The only weapons not of communist manufacture were the personal sidearms carried by individual troopers.

One of the stumbling blocks to getting ComOps approval of the mission was the need to cross a major highway bridge. This was the only significant river crossing between the take-off point and the city of Lusaka. Intelligence reports indicated that the bridge would be carefully guarded. Conventional wisdom also dictated that the structure would be heavily protected, which was one reason for taking more vehicles and men than were actually required to do the job. The entire operation depended upon the ability to take and hold this bridge without alerting the Zambian military in Lusaka.

The convoy moved slowly up a sweeping surfaced grade, then stopped. Captain O'Rourke climbed out of the lead vehicle and ascended an outcrop to look at the stone pillars and steel girders of the bridge 500 meters away. The night was clear, but he could see no movement through his night-vision binoculars, not even a sentry station. Perhaps the bridge was defended only on the Lusaka side. He climbed down and sent Sergeant Major Halverson down the column to check that all machine guns were mounted and loaded. Each gun carried 1500 rounds, with a mix of one tracer for every three rounds instead of one every four rounds, so the men could see where they were shooting. If a single guard escaped to radio Lusaka of the impending attack, a deadly welcoming party would be waiting for them. O'Rourke could only hope that the few vehicles they had passed accepted them as a Zambian Army unit.

Sergeant Major Halverson told every man to take the safety catch off his rifle and put the selector on full auto. Halverson's .22 pistol was equipped with a silencer, which O'Rourke hoped would be the only gun necessary. Halverson spoke the local dialect and was dressed as a Zambian Army Captain. Wearing 'Black is Beautiful' make up, he would try to bluff the convoy through. If that didn't work, he would signal O'Rourke to deploy the troops and then use his silenced pistol to best effect. If all else failed, a fusillade would wipe out the sentries.

With the entire operation on the line, everyone was tighter than a new pair of shoes. The column passed the pillars and hummed over the bridge. Nothing! Not even a barricade. They approached the far side—still nothing—not a living soul! The bridge was clear. Captain O'Rourke noticed he was holding his breath and let it out. Breathing deeply, he ordered one Sabre to remain, securing the bridge for the return trip. Then he led the rest of the convoy onto the main road. This was one fire-fight he was happy to have avoided.

As they entered the capitol city of the hostile country, a handsome roadsign greeted them. "Welcome to Lusaka!"

The city, center of the command structure of the Zambian Defense Forces, headquarters of ZIPRA and home of the Fat Man, was lit up like Picadilly Circus! Six Rhodesian Land Rovers, bristling with heavy machine guns, blushed beneath the lights. In each vehicle, six white soldiers wearing 'Black is Beautiful' makeup tried to be natural while armed to the teeth. *No one here but us tourists, baas.*

Four Sabres were to attack the Nkomo residence. The other two were to cover the retreat of the attacking force after the assassination. The covering vehicles took their positions, and the remaining four headed for Josh Nkomo's date with death.

Nkomo's compound was triangular in shape, and each leg was approximately 100 meters long. Two side of the triangle faced main streets: Presidents Lane and Nyerere Road. The compound was enclosed by a two-meter high security fence on two sides and a two-meter high brick wall on the side facing Presidents Lane. Inside the compound were Nkomo's official residence, the servants' quarters and a large house where Nkomo's personal guards lived. Intelligence indicated that the normal contingent when Nkomo was at home was twelve armed, uniformed guards plus six personal bodyguards in addition to unarmed staff and servants.

A sentry station blocked the gates that faced Nyerere Road. Where the security fence was chain link, burlap was interwoven to prevent people from seeing into the compound. Plans called for two of the Sabres to crash the main gates, blocking access and egress. Their orders were to kill everyone in sight. Constant fire from four heavy machine guns, RPG-7 rockets and small arms would neutralize any opposition.

Captain O'Rourke and his team in the third vehicle moved into position between the two gates to provide covering fire up and down Nyerere Road, if necessary, and to assist the hit-team should they encounter unexpected opposition.

The fourth Sabre carried the assassination team. It pulled up behind the security wall facing Presidents Lane. This wall came to within ten meters of the corner of Nkomo's residence.

After the compound had been shocked by the firepower from the other vehicles, the hit-team would blow a hole through the wall with a specially-made, shaped charge and the team would dash in and pluck the Fat Man from his boudoir. Like so many well-wrought plans of imperfect minds, things went to hell immediately.

The Sabre no one was supposed to notice, the one carrying the hit-team, came under fire before it reached its position, before the other Sabres had fired a shot, as if it had been expected. A trooper was wounded in that first burst of fire.

Hearing the fire, one of the Land Rovers out front hit a gate and burst through. The troops immediately started shooting, directing heavy machine-gun fire into Nkomo's residence and into the guards at the rear of the house who were engaging the hit-team. Meanwhile, the second Land Rover had hit its assigned gate at an angle, and the gate refused to give way. The chain held, and the lock wasn't even scratched. Sergeant Major Halverson commanding the Sabre rolled out with a knock knock charge while his men answered fire from sentries who'd taken cover behind some vehicles parked in front of the guard house. There was also fire from the guard house itself. The fence wasn't bullet-proof, but the burlap woven into it prevented the troopers from seeing their targets, so fire was wild as Halverson reached the gate. He pulled the pin on the knock knock, set it alongside the gate and made a mad dash back to the Sabre.

The bomb exploded, the gate opened, the Land Rover pulled into the breach and let loose with its machine guns and RPG-7 rockets. The return fire from the guards, the intense fire from four heavy machine guns and the noise of the explosions from the RPG-7's was so loud that no one even heard the shaped charge explode in the back of the residence, but a hole had at last been blown through the back wall.

The assault team knew the house by heart. Not a single command had to be given as each member went about his business quickly and methodically. The original plan called for throwing a bunker bomb through Nkomo's bedroom window as a house-warming gift prior to the team's entry, but there were grenade screens on the windows, the only windows in the house that were protected in this way.

The hit-team broke in through the servants' entrance and started to clean house, room by room. Nkomo's bedroom was the fourth room to be cleaned, but the Fat Man wasn't there! They made their way through the house, clearing the way with bunker bombs. Dust and plaster and remnants of furniture got in the way. By the time they were finished, every member of the attacking force had been hit by masonry and scarred by flying glass.

The only room left was across the hall from Nkomo's bedroom. They kicked in the door, but before a trooper could pull the pin on his grenade, a burst of fire from inside the room spun him around. The team leader dove for the grenade and tossed it into the room. Someone else threw a bunker bomb inside, and, on the heels of the two explosions, the team leader rushed into the room, spitting fire and killing two brave bodyguards.

No Nkomo! The firefight took less than fifteen minutes from the time the opening rounds were fired by the security guards within the compound until the signal to pull back was issued by Captain O'Rourke. Instead of the normal contingent of guards, more than thirty bodies littered the grounds, not counting the wounded and those hiding inside the guard house and servants' quarters. SAS casualties were three wounded, and they all made it back to Rhodesia, though not without a final scare.

It was obvious that the attack had been expected, and this was later confirmed. But why had there been no interference from the President's palace, which was only five hundred meters away, or from Zambia's Army or Police? Had Nkomo gotten word with enough time to make good his escape but not enough time to alert Kaunda's forces? The Fat Man later claimed he had escaped by climbing through the bathroom window, but Nkomo weighed over 300 hundred pounds and it would stretch more than the frame of the bathroom window to accept his story.

Meanwhile, the SAS had to get out of Dodge in three vehicles, for the Land Rover that had come under attack when Halverson blew open the gate with the knock knock wouldn't start and had to be destroyed. They picked up the two rearguard Sabres at the edge of town and redistributed the load so that the wounded were more comfortable. They left quickly, encountering not one road block, not one impediment. The exit from Lusaka was as silent as the entrance.

O'Rourke broke radio silence to notify the Land Rover at the bridge they were *en route*, but there was no attendant response that the message had been received. On board the Dakota, Austin tersely signalled that he'd intercepted the message and ordered O'Rourke to report when he reached the bridge. Had the Zambians overrun the Sabre guarding the bridge? Were they lying in wait for the rest of the force? What had happened at the compound? Austin could tell from the way O'Rourke affirmed receiving his signal that things had not gone according to plan, but he did not know what had gone wrong until the Dakota landed at the Kariba airport at daybreak and he was besieged by a pack of reporters.

The problem at the bridge was insignificant by comparison. The Sabre holding the bridge was the same vehicle that had been rolled the previous evening. Its radio had been damaged in the accident, but no one knew it had happened since radio silence was in effect at the time. The Sabre was waiting, the men blissfully ignorant of O'Rourke's attempts to reach them. The rapid return over the dirt track was uneventful, and the force was ferried into Rhodesia at 0900. They would have been greeted by waiting reporters had not an irate Joe Austin cordoned off the debarkation site.

Austin had been playing cat and mouse with the press for hours. He refused to answer their questions, feigning ignorance of any attack. They refused to say where they got their information. "Information about what?" Kitty asked.

"This attack that you allege took place last night."

"Who took part in that attack?" Kitty asked.

"What attack?" Austin countered.

"Are you aware that Nkomo escaped?"

"What makes you think anyone was trying to get him?" He sorely wanted to arrest the lot of them, but he needed authorization from Salisbury and he couldn't get hold of Ian Smith. He was sure Ken Flowers was responsible for the leak, but he had no proof. "Try Salisbury again," he instructed the air traffic controller. "See if you can reach General Walls."

After Captain O'Rourke secured the gates of the base camp, restricting everyone to camp until further notice, he flew back to Salisbury with Austin for a debriefing at ComOps. Security had been broken, that was even obvious to General Hickman, but there were other things to consider. How should the government respond to the outcry from the press? Had the mission succeeded, no response would have been necessary, success being its own reward, but to condemnation coupled with failure an official explanation was required.

The United Nations was calling it an "unprovoked attack against a nation at peace." The British Government infuriated the Rhodesians by congratulating Nkomo on his "fortuitous escape" and condemning "the barbaric attack."

"The very same British Government," Austin added, "that failed to condemn the shooting-down of two unarmed passenger planes, at Nkomo's direct command."

"Thank you for your views, Colonel Austin," said a chilly Sutton-Price. "If we have further need of you, we'll let you know."

Austin was just as glad to get out of the meeting as the Rhodesians were to be rid of him and his opinions. It was a clear day with a high, blue sky. Austin walked over to Special Branch and dropped in on Superintendent Fitzgerald. "Nice day for a boat ride."

"If I never set foot in a boat again, that's all right with me. How are you, Colonel? What can I do for you?"

"I've been better," Austin admitted, "and you *can* do something for me."

"So long as it's on *terra firma*, I'm at your command."

"I want you to trace all international calls emanating from the Milton Building from 0900 yesterday to 0300 this morning."

"That's less than 24 hours; shouldn't be much of a problem. What're you looking for?"

"A cup of coffee would be nice," Austin said rubbing his forehead. "It's been a long day."

"Sure thing. How do you take it?"

"Black and bitter as my soul." He drank the cup, then another, while Fitzgerald got the phone company to copy the previous day's records.

"Well bugger me!" Fitzgerald said, looking up from the computer printouts he was reading. "Someone in ComOps phoned Lusaka six hours before the hit. If you ask my opinion, there's a traitor in ComOps. You know who he is?"

"I've a strong suspicion," Austin said as he rose to leave, "and it's time to confront the bastard!" The sky was darkening, and the last of the roguish sanction-busters, pert secretaries and stern ministers were exiting the Milton building when he walked in. The security guards he had installed waved as he walked down the corridor.

He had to give Flowers credit for one thing: he didn't flinch when a gun was pointed at him. "It's silly to take matters into your own hands, Joe," Flowers said, lighting a cigarette. "Sit down and let's talk things over."

"You talk; I'll listen."

"The war's over, Joe."

"And what side were you on?"

"The right side."

"How long have you been working for the Fat Man?"

"I don't know what you're talking about."

"I bet you do. A call was made from your phone to Nkomo's residence six hours before this morning's raid. As a result, the Fat Man slipped away. He had enough time to increase his guard, resulting in three serious injuries to our forces, but not enough time to alert the Zambian Army."

"*Our* forces? Joe, you've been here too long. It's time you went home to your own country. And let me give you some advice. Bet your money on pistol shooting, not detective work, unless you're like Ted and have money to burn. All my calls go through the switchboard. Anyone in the building could have placed that call. Now, you put your gun away, and I'll forget this little *contretemps* ever took place. You have my word of honour."

"Honor! What do you know about honor?" He lowered his gun. "I'm not going to shoot you, Ken, but I'm not finished with you, either. You see, Ken, you made one mistake. You boasted about what you'd done."

"Mistake?" His hands trembled. "What mistake? Who has implicated me?" Visibly upset, Flowers picked up his cigarette and put it into his mouth the wrong way, burning his tongue. He flung the cigarette to the rug and scraped his tongue with the thumb and index finger. "What are you talking about?" I don't know what you're talking about."

"No?" Let me give *you* some advice, Ken. Refuse the

polygraph test. You're a dead give-away." He left the head of intelligence kicking at sparks that threatened to ignite the rug and went looking for Kitty Canty.

He found her holding court in the bar at Samantha's Disco. He bought some flowers, had the doorman deliver them anonymously and counted on her coming outside to satisfy her vanity, if not her curiosity. The doorman opened the door of the Mercedes Greg had requisitioned, and Austin reached from the darkness to take hold of her hand and then pulled her fiercely inside as Greg burned rubber driving off. "What's the meaning of this?!" she shrieked, kicking and clawing in the back seat. "Let me go! I'll have you thrown in jail! I'll—"

Austin grabbed both her wrists in one hand and slapped her hard with the other. "You'll shut up and do exactly what I tell you to do," he said viciously.

"I will not!" You can't order me around like a Kaffir, you son of a bitch! Who the hell do you think—" His hand went around her throat and he squeezed until her eyes started to bulge before he released her. Her blouse was torn and she was gasping when he threw her back against the upholstery. She crouched there, staring hatefully at him. They were outside the city limits and on the road to Harare township. There were no houses, and no lights to diminish the grandeur of the starlit sky. Greg pulled off the road and dimmed the headlights. Austin got out, then reached in and dragged the reporter outside and threw her against the side of the car.

"You've one chance in three to make it out of this alive," he said, "so listen carefully and do exactly what I tell you. Do you understand?"

"You won't get away with this," she whispered. Her eyes were still full of hate, but her voice quavered.

He slapped her again and tore off her blouse. Sobbing, she clutched herself as his words bit into her. "Do you know what I do for a living? I kill people. Do you see him?" He pointed at Greg. "He has been wanting to tear your face off ever since he saw you with your hand in that

Kaffir's trousers. Your only hope is to talk fast and say nothing but the truth. Now do you understand?"

"Yes." The hatred was gone from her eyes. All that remained was terror.

"Who told you we were going to attack Nkomo?"

She was frightened but a trace of defiance returned to her voice. "This morning you said there was no attack."

He slapped her again. "Flowers leaked it to you, didn't he?" Another slap. "He called you last night, didn't he?"

"Flowers? Ken Flowers?" She was open now, but instead of the emotionless outpouring he expected, she giggled.

"Don't play innocent with me, bitch!"

"It wasn't Ken," she laughed. "No, it wasn't Ken Flowers."

"What in hell are you laughing about?" He shook her and, when that didn't stop her, he slapped her again.

"I mean, ha-ha, maybe Ken spooked Nkomo but, hee-hee, he wasn't the one who called me, oh no, hah-ha."

She was hysterical, sobbing and laughing so hard she couldn't hold herself up. She had to grab the sideview mirror for support. He waited for her to stop, then asked, "If it wasn't Flowers, who was it?"

Her laughter narrowed to a sneer. "It was the same person who tried to stall the attack by killing you. Twice she tried to kill you, but you have more luck than Nkomo." As the realization flooded his face, she laughed hysterically. "You never knew! To the end you never even suspected!"

Without a word, he threw her back into the car and got in beside her. She had urinated in her clothes and the acrid stench almost made him gag. He rolled down the window and Greg started the engine and pulled back on the roadway.

Austin ran it down in his mind looking for flaws. "I was talking to her on the phone when Ncobe and the mechanic slipped into the compound."

"She wanted to be close to the action. It made her hot. She gave Ncobe some bratwurst for your dog. Did she tell you that?"

There was no breather! The realization sickened him. She just wanted Oso out of the way. When that didn't work, she trained him to her goddamned sausages. Kitty was telling the truth! Brigit had set him up from day one. "She knew Ncobe?"

"Knew him?" She started to say something then thought better of it. "Yes, she knew him. In a way, I introduced them. He came to me after his brother killed Samantha Blake. He didn't know what to do. He thought I could help him get to America. Bloody fool!"

"How did you know Brigit would, would help him?" He was shaking.

"I didn't, but I had a feeling she might be working for the Russians and I threw Ncobe her way to see if she'd pick up on him. She did."

"Brigit was working for the Russians?"

"East Germans, actually."

He was back in control and trying to fit it all together. "But Ncobe was Mashona."

"The Russians were already in Nkomo's pockets. They were looking for someone to penetrate ZANLA. The Chinese have them locked out. Ncobe would do anything Brigit asked. Bloody fool."

"And Flowers, is he working for the East Germans, too?"

"No MI-6, I think."

"Jesus! Who else? Neukirk? Hickman?"

"I don't know. I don't think so."

Harare township was darkened by curfew, but here and there clumps of people had gathered together to drink and party. Near one such gathering, Austin told Greg to slow down. Then he opened the door and pushed Kitty outside. As they drove away, they heard a man shout, "Hey, somebody throwed away a white woman down there."

They drove to Brigit's apartment, but she was gone. Austin woke the landlady, a slovenly middle-aged woman who smelled of whiskey. "She moved out, she did."

"When?"

"Early this morning. She got a phone call late last night; it woke me up and once I wake up I can't go back to sleep until I've had a glass of hot milk with a little brandy. I heard her packing. Then this morning she gave me the key and went off in a taxi."

"Did she say where she was going?"

"No, but she said she wouldn't be back. It looked like she was leaving the country. So many young people are these days. The boys go because they're afraid to fight. The girls leave because there aren't any boys."

"Can we see her room?"

"You're with the police; you don't have to ask. What did she do? It's always the pretty ones. They're wild, never satisfied." The landlady shuffled up the marble stairs, talking incessantly. "I run a nice place. Ask anyone. I only take government workers, no students and no riffraff."

"We were told," Greg said, "that she had a Kaffir living with her."

This caught her short and she turned in midstairs to deny the accusation. "Not in my place, she didn't. I don't allow that sort of thing. I would call the police first thing."

"It's not against the law like it is in South Africa," Austin said.

"Well, it should be. We're at war, aren't we?"

"Yes, ma'am."

There were two apartments upstairs to match the two below. The landlady unlocked the door to Brigit's three-room flat and let them in. "I haven't had a chance to get the cleaning girl in as yet. Independent as they are, they come when it suits them. And they'd steal from you as quick as spit in your face. I'd clean house myself if my varicose veins would let me. Look at this mess."

Books and magazines were scattered on the floor. Brigit had gone without taking her kitchenware or her bedding. The flywhisk he'd given her was lying on the floor. There was no sign that Ncobe had stayed there, but Austin hadn't the heart to search closely.

The phonebook was open to the airlines section, and flight schedules were scribbled on a sheet of paper beside the phone. Greg made some calls and was able to confirm that Brigit Wolfe left the country on South African Airways flight 85 to Frankfurt.

And that was the last anyone saw of her.

The time had come to burn their bridges. They were not the only ones with matches in their hands either. The failure to assassinate Nkomo, along with the knowledge that ZIPRA was preparing for an all-out conventional war against Rhodesia, forced the hard-liners to forget about world opinion and think about covering their butts. Unfettered, Nkomo would be in Salisbury in a fortnight, but ZIPRA would find it very difficult to move armored vehicles into Rhodesia if there were no bridges to cross and no railroad lines to carry tanks to the border.

For the last time, the SAS was assigned to destroy targets inside Zambia. Once the destruction started, it would have to be done quickly and efficiently, for Zambia's ability to feed her people would be threatened by the destruction of her economic lifeline. This time, Kaunda would react with all the rage of a wounded lion.

Three bridges were absolutely essential to Nkomo's predicted attack. These bridges were on the main road between Lusaka and Kafue, the nearest rail and road junction to the Rhodesian border. Intelligence indicated that the main thrust of Nkomo's attack would be through Chirundu, Rhodesia's closest town to the Zambian border. Chirundu was only thirty kilometers from one of the three bridges.

The raid used four of the Bell helicopters Austin had purchased in London. Each of three helicopters carried a demolition team and explosives to blow up one bridge. The fourth helicopter supported a stick of SAS troopers who landed two kilometers northwest of the furthest bridge and blocked all attempts to interfere with the destruction of the bridges. It took only twenty minutes to destroy the bridges, and there were no casualties. However, it turned out that Nkomo didn't need to attack. While the raids were underway, the Lancaster House Accords were adopted and Rhodesia was given away.

The sibilant serpents of diplomacy whisked Mugabe into the presidency, but as he prepared to enter Salisbury one hundred loyal Rhodesians under the command of Colonel Austin waited for word from General Walls to blow away the pretender to power, along with his sycophants and bodyguards. When the call came, Austin couldn't believe his ears.

"It's been called off. Dismiss your men," the General said.

"You're going to let Mugabe take it?" Austin was incredulous. "Not you, General Walls."

"It's over, Colonel."

"It's *never* over."

"Dismiss your men or face arrest and certain execution. It's over."

And it was. Power passed to Mugabe and Rhodesia became Zimbabwe. What was done came undone; what was unfinished remained unfinished. Some Rhodesians cut their losses and went to work for Mugabe. Among them were Ken Flowers and General Walls. Some, like Ian Smith, retired to their farms and left the work to those who had the stomach for it. For two Americans, it was get out while there was still time to get.

Greg drove Austin to Beitbridge where they were

whisked through customs. During his entire stay in Rhodesia, through all his comings and goings, no entry into Rhodesia had been stamped in Austin's American passport. "Stamp it," he told the immigration officer. "I want proof somewhere that Rhodesia once existed." Then he got back into the battered BMW, a parting gift from Ian Smith, and Greg drove him across the bridge into South Africa.

EPILOGUE

Rhodesia's European population dropped at an alarming rate. When the war started in earnest in 1975, approximately 250,000 Europeans lived within her borders; by they end of 1979, there were 170,000. When Mugabe took office in April of 1980, there were fewer than 160,000 Europeans residing in Rhodesia. More than 80,000 had 'taken the gap,' and the greatest percentage of these were young men between 17 and 35 years of age. They left to escape the constant call-ups, to further their education or career, or because they were afraid. Older Rhodesians with fewer options stayed behind and kept their fingers crossed.

Casualties on both sides were heavy. According to the *Rhodesian Herald,* **"White Rhodesian casualties have been calculated as being proportionately ten times more than those suffered by the Americans in Viet Nam and half of Britain's losses during the Second World War."**

By the end of the war, the morale of the Territorial Troops was at an all-time low as a result of call-ups that forced them to spend 26 days in, 26 days out, with worsening prospects.

The business picture was even gloomier. The Reserve Bank increased restrictions on foreign currency to the point where many small businesses could not get the foreign exchange they needed to operate. Rhodesians traveling abroad could exchange no more than $500 (Rhodesian), regardless of the journey or the length of time they would be away.

The war was costing Rhodesia over R$800,000 ($1,200,000 in U.S. currency) per day in cash, not in credit or weapons given by sponsor nations. The Soviet Union gave Nkomo over $1,000,000,000 U.S. in cash and aid, and the Chinese probably lavished as much on Mugabe.

On September 10, 1979, while the war still raged, the 'All Parties Conference' convened to determine Rhodesia's future. With one eye on elections and the other on the battlefield, Nkomo and Mugabe jockeyed for position. Mugabe had many thousand more ZANLA personnel within Rhodesia than Nkomo had ZIPRA forces, but Nkomo had more heavy artillery and tribal distinctions that he felt gave him the edge.

The Matabele had always been more aggressive than the Mashona, but Mugabe had trained his people well, and his ZANLA forces had withstood the brunt of the war with the Europeans, suffering far heavier casualties than ZIPRA.

ZIPRA was poised to strike, and there is no reason to believe that Nkomo was not planning to take over Mugabe's government by force at some point, but Mugabe got there first. Mugabe not only had the votes, he had a better military strategy. If Nkomo failed to deploy his conventional army because he thought he could beat Mugabe in a beauty contest, he was mistaken. When the votes were counted, Mugabe had won. There was a brief honeymoon, but that ended before Mugabe carried Nkomo across the threshold.

Mugabe's military strategy revolved around a personal brigade ostensibly trained as palace guards in Umtali by the North Koreans. Answerable only to Mugabe, the brigade was as strong as any single military unit in Zimbabwe and circumvented the Lancaster House Accords mandating that the country's military establishment maintain professional standards and basic autonomy.

After subjecting Nkomo to public ridicule, Mugabe sent the North Korean Brigade to Matabeleland where its members found pretexts for killing Nkomo supporters. When Nkomo responded with military units of his own, Mugabe sent the full weight of his private army against Nkomo's forces. Battles raged within the city limits of Bulawayo, the second largest city in Zimbabwe and the base of operations for ZIPRA. Nkomo was forced to flee the country and send his forces back into the bush so that Mugabe would not destroy them. During the first six months of 1980, many European farms in Matabeleland were raided, probably by the North Korean Brigade posing as ZIPRA units in order to destroy Nkomo's credibility. This allowed Mugabe to solidify his rule and strengthen his government to the extent where he could invite Nkomo to return to Zimbabwe and serve in a minor advisory capacity.

WEAPONS APPENDIX

Although this is a work of fiction, it is based on real incidents in a real war. Military strategists, insurgency and counter-insurgency analysts, and casual readers interested in the methodology of non-conventional warfare might therefore find the following listings of weapons useful.

It might surprise the casual reader to learn that terrorists (or freedom fighters, depending on one's point of view) are often equipped with superior, more modern weapons than the government forces they are fighting. This was certainly true in Rhodesia, where government troops were also frequently outnumbered by as many as forty to one.

Lacking the manpower resources and technology, the RDF's success in battle after battle against ZIPRA and ZANLA must be attributed to the following:
1. Superior individual troop training.
2. More involved and direct command structure.
3. Generally shorter and more accessible supply routes.
4. The use of air power.
5. Most importantly, the ability to pick the time and place to initiate contact—in other words, mobility.

The following charts give a side-by-side comparison of the arsenals of the Rhodesian Defense Forces and the terrorist organizations, along with the arsenals of the countries that supported these organizations (commonly referred to as the "frontline states"). The defense forces of both Zambia and Mozambique were directly involved in the fighting between the RDF and terrorist insurgents.

The constant threat of air intervention in the war was something that had to be considered whenever cross-border incursions were planned. Both Zambia and Mozambique had far larger and more modern Air Forces during the last two years of the war. Direct intervention would have witnessed results as basic as in a rock fight. Even had Rhodesia won the air battle, it would have immediately lost the war.

Raids into Mozambique almost always involved contact with FRELIMO, and the threat of armored intervention by tanks was a likelihood that had to be considered in all RDF plans.

Rhodesian intelligence had access to ZIPRA's long-term military plans. Developed by the Russians, these plans called for short-term conventional warfare against the RDF. Upon conclusion of this phase of the war, ZIPRA would besiege Mugabe's forces, and ZANLA would find itself unable to offer a defense against a massive conventional army. Nkomo's army was to be supported by Russian-trained and Russian-advised armored contingents of a least divisional strength.

Rhodesia's military units, particularly the Special Forces, could not have carried on the war without resupply from captured arsenals. The Selous Scouts were entirely equipped with such weapons; their roll mandated the use of enemy materials of war. It was a simple matter to resupply with captured equipment, especially ammunition, when on cross border raids. Weapons of choice, were frequently the enemy's own weapons of war.

The RPG-7 rocket-propelled grenade was only available to the enemy, but were rapidly adopted and used by the RDF. Their land-mines were far superior to the RDF's World War II types, and there can be little argument that the AK-47 is one of the finest killing machines ever invented. Captured terrorist weapons were initially very good barter items with the South African Defense Forces. However, when the SADF became embroiled in their own war, they were able to capture the same or similar weapons and no longer had to trade for them.

Cost, of course, is a another compelling argument for the use of captured equipment. Rhodesia's lack of foreign exchange was a controlling factor in the planing of military operations. For example, the ammunition for the 30mm cannon used in the Hawker Hunter jet, cost $12.00 (Rhodesian currency) per round, which translated to $18.00 U.S. per round of ammunition. The Hunter aircraft carried four Aden 30mm cannons, each cannon firing 1,200 to 1,400 rounds per minute (rpm). The actual cost of this ammunition became a critical factor in military planning. Here was a unique situation for Rhodesia, a war material readily available but very expensive.

As an interesting aside, it might be noted that the pilots' skill was such that single round kills on non-armored vehicles were documented. One Hunter pilot from Texas—where else?— boasted of his shooting prowess, resulting in a rather sizeable bet concerning his ability. The intrepid young man bet that he could hit a garbage can from his Hunter with one round. The can was placed in the middle of a clearing at the range outside Que-Que. The pilot took off from Thornhill, and his deed was as good as his word. The can was bronzed, and kept on display in the Officers Mess.

The following tables are not exhaustive, for many sub-types of weapons were used in the Rhodesian War. However, they do show the dominant types and will give the reader an overview of the weapons used.

Rhodesian Defense Force	Terrorists & Supporting Countries

Small Arms — Handguns

Name:	Star Spain	Scorpion Czechoslovakia
Caliber:	9mm Parabellum	.32ACP
Function:	Recoil Semi Auto	Blowback Semi & Full Auto
Rate of Fire:		750 rpm
Overall Length:	8''	11''
Barrel Length:	5''	4.5'' w/o silencer
Feeding Method:	9 round magazine	10/20 round magazines
Weight:	2.2 pounds	3.2 pds loaded
Cartridge Velocity:	1300 fps	1040 fps
Name:	Browning Hi-Power	Tokarev Model 1933 Russia
Caliber:	9mm Parabellum	7.62 mm
Function:	Recoil Semi Auto	Recoil Semi Auto
Rate of Fire:		
Overall Length:	8''	7.7''
Barrel Length:	5''	4.6''
Feeding Method:	13 round mag.	8 round mag.
Weight:	2 pounds	1.9 pounds
Cartridge Velocity:	1300 fps	1378 fps

Rhodesian Defense Force	Terrorists & Supporting Countries

Small Arms — Handguns

Name:	Enfield Revolver
Caliber:	.38 S&W
Function:	Revolver
Rate of Fire:	
Overall Length:	10″
Barrel Length:	5″ 2″ available
Feeding Method:	Cylinder 6 rounds
Weight:	1.5 pounds
Cartridge Velocity:	600 fps

| | |
| Rhodesian Defense Force | Terrorists & Supporting Countries |

Small Arms — Shotguns

Name:	Greener Great Britain None
Caliber:	12 bore
Function:	Single Shot
Rate of Fire:	
Overall Length:	43''
Barrel Length:	28''
Feeding Method:	single shot
Weight:	6 pounds
Cartridge Velocity:	varied, used different loads, bird shot, buck shot and slugs Note: Issued only to Guard Force.

Name:	Browning Belgium
Caliber:	12 bore
Function:	Recoil Semi Auto
Rate of Fire:	
Overall Length:	48''
Barrel Length:	28''
Feeding Method:	5 rounds - internal magazine
Weight:	7.5 pounds
Cartridge Velocity:	See Greener

| Rhodesian Defense Force | Terrorists & Supporting Countries |

Small Arms — Submachine Guns

Name:	Uzi Israel	PPSH Model 1941 Russia
Caliber:	9mm Parabellum	7.62mm
Function:	Blowback full auto	Blowback semi & full auto
Rate of Fire:	650 rpm	700/900 rpm
Overall Length:	25''	33''
Barrel Length:	10''	11''
Feeding Method:	30/40 round magazine	35/71 round mag/drum
Weight:	9 pounds loaded	9.5 pounds loaded
Cartridge Velocity:	1400 fps	1650 fps

Name:	PPS Model 1943 Russia
Caliber:	7.62 mm
Function:	Blowback full auto
Rate of Fire:	650 rpm
Overall Length:	33''
Barrel Length:	9''
Feeding Method:	35 round magazine
Weight:	8 pounds loaded
Cartridge Velocity:	1600 fps

Rhodesian Defense Force	Terrorists & Supporting Countries

Small Arms — Rifles

Name:	Lee Enfield No. 4 GB	SKS Carbine Russia
Caliber:	.303	7.62X39
Function:	Bolt action	Gas semi auto
Rate of Fire:		
Overall Length:	44.5"	40.1"
Barrel Length:	25.2"	28.7"
Feeding Method:	10 round magazine	10 round magazine
Weight:	9 pounds	8.8 pounds
Cartridge Velocity:	2400 fps	2410 fps

Note: These two weapons were used only by reserve or 2nd echelon troops.

Name:	FN (FAL) (R-1) RSA	AK-47 Russia
Caliber:	7.62X51 NATO	7.62X39
Function:	Gas semi/full auto	Gas semi/full auto
Rate of Fire:	659 rpm	600 rpm
Overall Length:	40"	34.25"
Barrel Length:	21"	16.75"
Feeding Method:	20 round magazine	30/40 round magazines
Weight:	10 pounds loaded	10.5 pounds loaded
Cartridge Velocity:	2650 fps	2370 fps

Rhodesian Defense Force	Terrorists & Supporting Countries

Small Arms — Rifles

Name:	G-3 Spain	AKM Russia
Caliber:	7.62X51 NATO	7.62X39
Function:	Delayed blowback semi/full auto	Gas semi/full auto
Rate of Fire:	600 rpm	600 rpm
Overall Length:	40"	34.25"
Barrel Length:	18"	16.4"
Feeding Method:	20 round magazine	30/40 round magazines
Cartridge Velocity:	2500 fps	2370 fps

Name:	M-16A1 USA
Caliber:	5.56mm .223
Function:	Gas semi/full auto
Rate of Fire:	700 rpm
Overall Length:	39"
Barrel Length:	20"
Feeding Method:	20/30 round magazines
Cartridge Velocity:	3250 fps

Note: Received in limited numbers towards the end of the war. Used by Special Forces only.

	Rhodesian Defense Force	Terrorists & Supporting Countries

Small Arms — Sniper Rifles

Name:	Lee Enfield Mk4 (T) GB	Mosin-Nagant Russia
Caliber:	.303	7.62X54R
Function:	Bolt action	Bolt action
Rate of Fire:		
Overall Length:	44.5"	48.5"
Barrel Length:	25.2"	28.7"
Feeding Method:	10 round Magazine	5 round internal mag
Weight:	9.5 pounds w/scope	11.3 pounds w/scope
Cartridge Velocity:	2400 fps	2660 fps
Name:	Brno Czechoslovakia	Dragunov (SUD) Russia
Caliber:	7.62X51 NATO	7.62X54R
Function:	Bolt action	Gas semiauto
Rate of Fire:		
Overall Length:	42"	48.25"
Barrel Length:	24"	24"
Feeding Method:	5 round internal mag	10 round magazine
Weight:	8.5 pounds w/scope	9.5 pounds w/scope
Cartridge Velocity:	2540 fps	2660 fps

Note: These were commercial rifles modified to military specifications for accuracy.

Rhodesian Defense Force	Terrorists & Supporting Countries

Small Arms — Light Machine Guns

	Rhodesian Defense Force	Terrorists & Supporting Countries
Name:	Bren Great Britian	RPD Degtyarev Russia
Caliber:	7.62X51 NATO	7.62X39
Function:	Gas semi/full auto	Gas full auto
Rate of Fire:	400/500 rpm	700 rpm
Overall Length:	43"	41"
Barrel Length:	23"	20.5"
Feeding Method:	30 round magazine	100 round drum
Weight:	22.5 pounds	16.5 pounds
Cartridge Velocity:	2650 fps	2410 fps
	Note: These were originally .303 guns modified in the RSA	
Name:	MAG Belgium	RPK Russia
Caliber:	7.62X51 NATO	7.62X39
Function:	Gas full auto	Gas full auto
Rate of Fire:	700/800 rpm	600 rpm
Overall Length:	49.5"	41"
Barrel Length:	21.5"	23"
Feeding Method:	Varies, non-disintegrating metal belt	75 round drum 30/40 round magazines
Weight:	24 pounds	11 pounds
Cartridge Velocity:	2650 fps	2410 fps
	Note: Basic LMG in RDF usually 1 LMG per 4 man stick.	Note: The RPK may be finest LMG in use today.

Rhodesian Defense Force	Terrorists & Supporting Countries

Small Arms — Light Machine Guns

Name:	Browning M1919A6 USA	DP Degtyaryova Russia
Caliber:	7.62X51 NATO	7.62X54R
Function:	Recoil full auto	Gas full auto
Rate of Fire:	500/600 rpm	500/600 rpm
Overall Length:	53"	51"
Barrel Length:	24"	24"
Feeding Method:	Varies, disintegrating metal link belt	47 rounds flat pan type drum
Weight:	32.5 pds gun only	21 pounds
Cartridge Velocity:	2650 fps	2660 fps
	Note: Converted from 30/06 caliber weapons used primarily as a vehicle mounted weapon.	Note: Seen early in war, replaced by RPD and RPK.

Rhodesian Defense Force	Terrorists & Supporting Countries

Small Arms — Light Machine Guns

Name:	Browning M2 Aircraft USA
Caliber:	.303
Function:	Recoil full auto
Rate of Fire:	1100 rpm
Overall Length:	40''
Barrel Length:	24''
Feeding Method:	Varies, disintegrating metal link belt.
Weight:	23 pounds gun only
Cartridge Velocity:	2400 fps

Note: Due to the inadequate supply of LMGs these aircraft types were used, both a single and double gun mounts. The rate of fire was a real problem and malfunctions were common.

Rhodesian Defense Force	Terrorists & Supporting Countries

Small Arms — Heavy Machine Guns

Name:	Browning M2 HB USA	DShK Degtyarev Russia
Caliber:	.50	12.7mm
Function:	Recoil Semi/full auto	Gas full auto
Rate of Fire:	450/550 rpm	600 rpm
Overall Length:	65"	62.5"
Barrel Length:	45"	42"
Feeding Method:	Varies, disintegrating metal link belt	50 round metal link belts
Weight:	84 pounds gun only	79 pounds gun only
Cartridge Velocity:	2850 fps	2750 fps

Note: Used on vehicles only, very few in RDF.

Note: Used to defend training camps, very seldom brought into Rhodesia.

Name:		KPV Russia
Caliber:		14.5 mm
Function:		Gas-assisted recoil full auto
Rate of Fire:		600 rpm
Overall Length:		79"
Barrel Length:		53"
Feeding Method:		Varies, Metallic link belt
Weight:		108 pounds gun only
Cartridge Velocity:		3280 fps

Note: This is the most powerful machine gun in world. Found in Training camps only. The RDF used many of these guns after capture from the terrorists.

Rhodesian Defense Force	Terrorists & Supporting Countries

Small Arms — Heavy Machine Guns

Name:	ZU-23mm Cannon Russia
Caliber:	23mm
Function:	Gas full auto
Rate of Fire:	1000 rpm
Overall Length:	15 feet
Barrel Length:	79''
Feeding Method:	50 round boxed metal belted
Cartridge Velocity:	3000 fps

Note: This is really a cannon, and not a HMG but is listed hereon as encountered in raids in Mozambique and Zambia, where it was used as both in air and ground combat.

Rhodesian Defense Force	Terrorists & Supporting Countries

Rockets

Name:	Super Bazooka USA Spain	RPG-2	China
Caliber Rocket:	89mm	80mm	
Length Launcher:	1549mm	1194mm	
Weight Launcher:	5.5 kg	2.83 kg	
Weight Rocket:	4.4 kg	1.8 kg	
Effective Range:	110 meters	150 meters	
Maximum Range:	1200 meters	900 meters	
Purpose:	Anti armour Anti personnel Note: Seldom used except on cross border raids, where bunkers and fortified positions were encountered.	Anti armour Anti personnel Note: The RPG-2 was encountered early in the war. The RPG-7 a more effective device, was more predominate.	

	Rhodesian Defense Force	Terrorists & Supporting Countries

Rockets

Name:	RPG-7 (Rocket propelled Russia Grenade)
Caliber Rocket:	85 mm
Length Launcher:	950 mm
Weight Launcher:	7.9 kg
Weight Rocket:	2.25 kg
Effective Range:	300 meters
Maximum Range:	950 meters
Purpose:	Anti armour Anti personnel Note: One of the terrorist's most effective weapons. Used to terrify locals and very effective in ambushes. Also used to great effect in farm raids.

	Rhodesian Defense Force	Terrorists & Supporting Countries

Artillery

Name:	25 Pounder	Great Britain	None
Caliber:	88mm		
Function:	single shot		
Rate of Fire:	5 rpm		
Overall Length:	26 feet		
Weight:	4000 pounds incl firing platform		
Range:	13,250 yards		
Crew:	6 men		
Ammo Type:	High explosive armour piercing smoke.		

Name:	Pack Howitzer M56 GB
Caliber:	105mm
Function:	single shot
Rate of Fire:	4 rpm
Weight:	2800 pounds
Range:	10,700 yards
Crew:	5 men
Ammo Type:	High explosive

Note: These weapons were issued to Territorial troops only.

	Rhodesian Defense Force	Terrorists & Supporting Countries

Armoured Vehicles

Name:	Eland Armoured Car RSA	None
Weapons:	90mm Cannon	
	2x7.62X51 machine guns	
	2x40mm smoke dischargers	
Weight:	11,000 pounds fully combat loaded	
Speed:	60mph on paved surface	
Gradient:	60x	
Engine:	1x90hp, 4 cylinder gas	
Crew:	3, Commander, gunner, driver	
Armour:	8 to 12mm	

Note: The 90mm gun fires high explosive (HE) high explosive anti-tank (HEAT) rounds. Both of these are fin stabilized, even though the tube is rifled, with a very slow twist. There was a 200 meter safety range built into the fuses on these rounds, making their use at short range impossible. This is why the "Beehive" round was developed. The RDF never had the HE round and depended upon the HEAT round as a general purpose round. The HEAT round had a muzzle velocity of 2900 fps and an effective range of 1600/2000 yards. This was the most accurate cannon in the RDF arsenal. It should be understood that the terrorists RPG-2 and RPG-7 rockets could destroy the Eland easily, as could their 12.7mm and 14.5mm machine guns.

| Rhodesian Defense Force | Terrorists & Supporting Countries |
|---|---|//

Tanks

Name:	None	T-34/85 Russia
Weapons:	1x85mm cannon
	2x7.62X39 machine guns
	1x12.7mm machine gun
Weight:	35 tons
Speed:	30mph on level ground
Range:	200 miles with external fuel tanks
Gradient:	60°
Engine:	500hp 12 cylinder diesel
Crew:	5 - Commander, gunner, loader, driver, bow gunner. Note: The Rhodesian terrorists did not have tanks. But the FRELIMO in Mozambique did and they attempted to use them against the RDF on cross border raids.

Rhodesian Defense Force	Terrorists & Supporting Countries

Tanks

Name:	T-54 Russia
Weapons:	1x100mm cannon
	1x7.62X39 machine gun
	1x12.7mm machine gun
Weight:	40 tons
Speed:	29mph on level ground
Range:	264 miles w/external fuel tanks
Gradient:	60°
Engine:	529hp, 12 cylinder diesel
Crew:	4 - Commander, gunner, loader, driver

Note: This tank was in use by FRELIMO in Mozambique. The Russians had stock piled this model tank in large quantities in Zambia, for issue to ZIPRA when their troops had been trained to operate them. This was to begin a conventional type war against the Rhodesian people.

Rhodesian Defense Force	Terrorists & Supporting Countries

Helicopters

	Rhodesian Defense Force	Terrorists & Supporting Countries
Name:	Alouette III France	None
Normal Weight:	4,189 pounds	
Maximum Speed:	120 mph	
Service Ceiling:	10,670 feet	
Range:	300 miles	
Engine:	550hp turbine	
Crew:	Varied with mission; Pilot and co-pilot with four troopers in the "G" Car configuration. Pilot and co-pilot with gunner firing a Hispano 20mm cannon in the "K" Car configuration. Note: Without the Alouette it is safe to say that Rhodesia could not have waged the war as successfully as she did.	
Name:	Bell 205 (UH-1D) USA	None
Normal Weight:	8,801 pounds	
Maximum Speed:	111 mph	
Service Ceiling:	21,980 feet	
Range:	325 miles	
Engine:	1,100hp turboshaft	
Crew:	2 Pilot and co-pilot, The Huey could carry 11 fully equipped troops. Note: Without this helicopter the raids that were carried out towards the end of the war, in neighboring countries would not have taken place.	

	Rhodesian Defense Force	Terrorists & Supporting Countries

Aircraft

	Rhodesian Defense Force	Terrorists & Supporting Countries
Name:	Hawker Hunter GB	Mikoyan MIG-17 Russia
Type:	Fighter/ground attack	Fighter/ground attack
Maximum Weight:	25,000 pounds	14,000 pounds
Maximum Speed:	700 mph	690 mph
Service Ceiling:	55,000 feet	54,450 feet
Engine:	1x10,159lb thrust turbojet Rolls-Royce	1x5,950lb thrust turbojet Kilimov
Crew:	Pilot	Pilot
Maximum Combat Radius:	700 miles	720 miles
Armourment:	4x30mm Aden cannon plus air to air missiles and external ordnance	1x37mm cannon 2x23mm cannon Atoll air to air missiles and external ordnance.

Note: The Rhodesian terrorists did not have aircraft. However, the "frontline" countries did, and there was a constant threat of their use.

	Rhodesian Defense Force	Terrorists & Supporting Countries

Aircraft

Name:	DeHavilland GB Vampire	Mikoyan MIG-21 Russia
Type:	Fighter/ground attack	Fighter/ground attack
Maximum Weight:	13,160 pounds	17,100 pounds
Maximum Speed:	525 mph	1,317 mph
Service Ceiling:	40,000 feet	59,450 feet
Engine:	1x3,450lb thrust turbojet, Goblin	1x9,920lb thrust turbojet, Tumansky
Crew:	Pilot	Pilot
Maximum Combat Radius:	625 miles	750 miles
Armourment:	4x20mm Hispano cannon, plus external ordnance	2x23mm cannon, Atoll air to air missiles plus external ordnance

Note: This was the first operational jet made in England. The Vampire was put into service immediately after the 2nd World War. This aircraft at one time was used by more countries than any other jet fighter. However, Rhodesia's were very old and tired, and they were used only in dire emergencies.

Note: See 'note' on MIG-17. The FRELIMO had an estimated 47 MIG 21 aircraft and Zambia had at least 48 MIG-21s and 24 MIG-17 fighters. The Rhodesian Air Force had 26 Hunter aircraft and 12 Vampires. These totals are misleading as there were never anywhere this many available, due to the lack of spares.

Rhodesian Defense Force	Terrorists & Supporting Countries

Aircraft

Name:	Canberra Mk8 GB
Type:	Bomber/reconnaissance
Maximum Weight:	51,000 pounds
Maximum Speed:	550 mph
Service Ceiling:	48,000 feet
Engines:	2x7,500lb thrust turbojet Rolls-Royce
Crew:	3 - Pilot, co-pilot bomb aimer
Maximum Combat Radius:	800 miles

Note: The Rhodesian Air Force Canberra's were in very poor condition, and spares almost impossible to come by. The RDF derated the performance of these aircraft considerably. Particularly as relates to top speed. In 1976, Rhodesia had only 10 of these aircraft, but several were used as spares.

Aircraft

Name:	Cessna 337 (Lynx) USA
Type:	Observation/ ground attack
Maximum Weight:	4,630 pounds
Maximum Speed:	192 mph
Service Ceiling:	19,320 feet
Engines:	2x210hp piston 6 cylinder Continental
Crew:	3 - Pilot, co-pilot observer
Maximum Combat Radius:	985 miles

Note: This aircraft was very unpopular with the Rhodesian pilots. At the altitudes and weights they were operated at in Rhodesia, the plane would not fly on one engine.

	Rhodesian Defense Force	Terrorists & Supporting Countries

Aircraft

Name:	Dakota (C-47)	USA
Type:	Transport	
Maximum Weight:	26,000 pounds	
Maximum Speed:	185 mph	
Service Ceiling:	24,000 feet	
Engines:	2x1,200hp piston gas, Wright	
Crew:	3 - Pilot, co-pilot crew chief - 28 fully equipped paratroopers	
Maximum Range:	1,500 miles	

Note: This aircraft, as in many other parts of the world, was the work horse of the Rhodesian Armed Forces.